MAGIC MAN

A GOOD GUYS NOVEL

JAMIE SCHLOSSER

DEDICATION

To Gus,
No matter what, I promise to always love you on
accident and on purpose.

Casey

I've been putting my son first for so long that I've forgotten how to be me. Each monotonous day bleeds into the next, and I feel like I'm struggling to keep my head above water.

But a kiss at the top of a Ferris wheel with a man I barely know changes that.

Jay reminds me that I used to be bold. Vivacious. Funny.

Strong.

Now if only I could convince him his past mistakes don't define the man he is today.

Jay

I can perform over a dozen illusions with a simple sleight of hand, but I can't make the felony on my record disappear.

The last thing I should be doing is hanging around a young single mom and her kid.

But Casey doesn't know that I've been watching her. That I want her for myself. That I'm addicted to her dimples, her tenacity, her fierce love for her child.

If I was a better man, I'd leave her alone, but she pulls off the biggest magic trick of all time: making me believe I'm a good guy.

PROLOGUE

Jay

The first time I met Casey Maxwell, I told her two lies and a truth. After all, deception was one of my best talents.

Knocking on the screen door of her doublewide trailer, I stepped back on the rotted wooden porch. I studied the faded yellow siding while mentally rehearsing the answers to the questions she would ask.

She'd be curious about the stranger on her doorstep with a mysterious wad of cash, and I had the lies locked and loaded on the tip of my tongue.

Seconds ticked by, and I knocked again.

I knew she was home.

I knew a lot of things about her I shouldn't.

Like the fact that she'd turned sixteen two months ago, her favorite color was blue, and she worked at the diner down the road. She rode her blue bike everywhere because she couldn't afford a car. She got straight A's in school, and she lived in this piece of shit trailer with her mom. Her dad had been out of the picture since before she was born.

And, if she hadn't gotten knocked up by an abusive psycho, she would've been going into her junior year at Brenton High School at the end of the summer.

I heard the rattling of locks before the door opened a little. One apprehensive blue eye peered at me through the crack.

"Can I help you?"

"So," I started, my tone jovial as I raked a hand through my hair. "Last night was a shit show, huh?"

A quizzical quirk of her eyebrow was the only agreement I got, and I could read the sarcastic comment running through her mind.

Ya think?

My assessment of the events that led me here were accurate—an illegal fighting match at an abandoned farmhouse, bloodshed, and the biggest drug bust this small corner of the world had seen in decades.

And Casey was at the center of it all.

Although my memories from the past twenty-four hours were hazy, I remembered seeing her last night. Out of place, too young to be there, heavy makeup meant to make her look older.

After her boyfriend got knocked out, she'd fallen to her knees next to him and quietly admitted she was having his baby.

"Jaxon didn't even tell me where he was taking me last night." Casey's jaw worked with annoyance. "I'm not a fan of violence."

Well, she was dating the wrong guy then.

She probably didn't even know what a bad guy Jaxon Meyers was.

But I did.

Casey wasn't the first vulnerable girl he'd pursued. At least that fucker got the ass whooping he deserved, courtesy of my buddy, Jimmy.

Jimmy had been blood-thirsty on behalf of his girlfriend, Mackenna. She'd been a victim of Jaxon's abuse years ago. The bastard almost killed her. In the couple months since Jaxon got released from prison, he'd been harassing Mackenna with threatening letters.

And apparently also getting a sixteen-year-old girl pregnant. Busy guy.

"Hi, I'm Jay." I offered Casey my right hand.

Without opening the door further, her skeptical gaze landed on it, then flitted back up to my face. No handshake then.

She was afraid of me. Good girl.

I dropped my arm. "I'm a friend of Jaxon's."

That was the first lie. The words felt wrong coming out, but I needed Casey to trust me enough to accept the gift I wanted to give her.

"What does he want?" Her voice was hard. "I'm not bailing him out. Even if I had the money, I wouldn't do it. If I'd known he was dealing drugs, I wouldn't have been dating him. I'm not that kind of girl, so if he gets out you can tell him to stay away from me. I already told him it's over."

Okay, so maybe being friendly with her ex wasn't the right angle to play. Unfortunately, it was the only angle I had.

"No bail for him," I reassured her. "Thanks to the meth the cops found in his pocket, I don't think Jaxon will be seeing life outside bars for a long time."

A relieved sigh left her and some of the worry vanished from the one eye I could see. She opened the door wider, and then I had a full view of her heart-shaped face.

That trust I was seeking? I could sense Casey's defenses coming down a little.

But I wasn't innocent either—not when it came to drugs. I'd been selling and using for years, and it was only a matter of time until I got caught.

After the fight was over, all hell had broken loose when we'd heard the sirens approaching. High on painkillers and panic, I'd tried to outrun the police.

I just wasn't fast enough.

My biggest regret was almost taking Jimmy down with me. Instead of pulling my car over and keeping my cool like any sane person would've done, I drove into a ditch then took off on foot into a cornfield, leaving Jimmy behind to deal with the consequences.

While searching my car, the cops found my stash and took Jimmy in for questioning. It was probably a good thing he was oblivious about my 'pharmaceutical occupation.' He gave his full cooperation and walked out of the station a free man.

I wasn't so lucky.

There was a warrant out for my arrest, and it was the final nail in the coffin of my downward spiral.

After this last good deed, I was going to turn myself in.

I'd been on the wrong path since I was too young to know better, directed there by the one person I should've been able to look up to. I was my father's son. He'd made sure of it, and now I was going to suffer the same fate as him—a dark, lonely cell.

In an attempt to redeem myself, I'd promised Mackenna I'd find some things out about Casey, because when she'd heard about the baby situation, she was concerned.

Hence, the reason why I was at Casey's house.

I told myself it wasn't because I wanted to personally check on her. It wasn't because I wanted to catch one last glimpse of her before I went away for a long, long time.

Because no matter how pretty she was, I wasn't a pervert. I didn't fuck around with girls who were four years younger than me.

I only had one thing to offer her.

Extending my arm, I held my palm out, facing up. "Here, Jaxon wanted you to have this."

Lie number two.

Casey stared at my empty hand, then glanced from side to side like she was questioning her own sanity. "Um, there's nothing in your hand."

"Oh, silly me. I forgot to do this…"

Closing my fist, I turned it over. I tapped the back of it with my fingers, then opened it again. Seeming to appear out of nowhere was an envelope. The white rolled-up paper uncurled, and Casey's eyes widened in wonder.

It was a magic trick I'd perfected. An illusion. An entertaining sleight of hand.

Snatching it quickly, she made sure our hands didn't touch. When she looked inside, she frowned, then speared me with a glare.

"This is four hundred dollars. Jaxon didn't win the fight." She tossed it back to me. "If it's his drug money, I don't want it."

I just shrugged because she wasn't entirely wrong—it was drug money, only it wasn't Jaxon's. It was mine.

I held it out to her again. "Please? For the baby."

"Shh!" Quickly glancing behind her, she clamored out onto the porch and slammed the door behind her.

Stepping close, Casey ran a hand through her dark strands.

The space suddenly felt much smaller with her out here. I could smell the fruity scent of her hair in the breeze.

Needing distance, I stumbled back ungracefully, leaning my ass against the unstable railing.

Casey crossed her arms over her light-blue tank top and she quietly muttered, "My mom doesn't know yet, okay? She might kick me out when I tell her."

Shit.

It'd been a long time since I'd cared about anyone but myself, but for some reason, the thought of this girl alone and scared made me feel weird.

"All the more reason for you to take this." I shook the envelope.

Indecision warred in her mind as she toyed with her necklace. A small prism hung from a silver chain, and she ran it back and forth as she considered my offer.

I studied her face for signs of recent crying, but there were no splotches on her cheeks. Her eyes weren't red or puffy, and I respected the determination shining in her crystal-clear blues.

Without the makeup, everything about Casey screamed of youth.

Innocence that had been stolen too soon.

Her rosy cheeks were slightly rounded, and her body was thin. Her hips lacked curves, and her denim shorts hung loosely on her slender frame. Her lips weren't overly full, but the shape was attractive. The corners naturally turned up, like she wore a constant smirk. The arm that was lodged under her breasts pushed them up, creating cleavage that was extremely distracting.

I smiled a little when I looked down at her knobby knees.

She was totally rocking that awkward stage between childhood and maturity, and hints of the woman she'd grow into peeked through.

Someday, she was going to be a knockout.

And I shouldn't have been thinking of her that way.

Averting my stare, I waved the envelope again and the tense muscles between my shoulder blades relaxed when she reluctantly took it.

My mission was complete.

"You have red hair," she blurted out, then blushed the prettiest shade of pink. "I just didn't notice it last night because it was dark, but in the sunlight, it's really obvious." Flapping a hand toward my head, she looked down at her bare feet and rubbed her toes together. "Sorry. You know what color your hair is. I just don't know any ginger guys."

Throwing my head back, I laughed. She wasn't saying it like it was a bad thing. Just a light-hearted observation.

Trapping her bottom lip between her teeth, Casey tried to contain a grin while lifting her shoulders in an awkward shrug. When her smile won out, dimples appeared in both cheeks.

Aw, fuck, she was cute.

Gazing at her, I imagined the what-ifs.

What life could've been like in an alternate universe where I wasn't a fuckup. A place where I took the straight and narrow, did well in school, went to college. Got some job with a suit and tie. Another world where Casey wasn't too young for me, and I wasn't too messed up to be good for someone like her.

One last glance at her knobby knees put me back in my place, and the tremble in my fingers reminded me of the hellish drug withdrawal I was about to experience.

"Well, good luck with everything." I nodded my head toward the trailer, hoping her mom would be supportive. Then I added, "Keep your chin up and your standards high. You hear me?"

The amused twist of her lips sobered as she hugged her middle. "I hear you."

"Promise," I demanded.

"I promise."

When I turned away, I trailed my hand over the rough wood of the railing as I soaked up the last remnants of my freedom.

Wind rustled the tall maple trees surrounding the trailer park. The sky was a perfect cloudless blue. The summer breeze smelled like fresh-cut grass and cornfields.

I'd miss all this.

Just as I made it off the bottom step to the cracked con-crete, Casey asked, "Will I see you around?"

I hadn't expected that question, or the hopeful expression on her face when I glanced over my shoulder.

I gave her a sad smile. "No."

And that was the truth.

CHAPTER 1

Casey
Two Years Later

A loud cry woke me with a start.

Just like every other night for the past fifteen months.

My body shook from the shock of being yanked from deep sleep so fast. No matter how many times this happened, I couldn't seem to get used to it.

I stared up at the water-stained ceiling, blinking to get my bearings. Light from the streetlamp outside cast a glow over the room, and the sound of crickets came in through the open window with the summer breeze.

Another impatient shriek made me wince as I glanced at the clock on the nightstand. My kid had an internal clock like nothing I'd ever seen.

Every night at one a.m., it was party time to Gus.

Sighing, I dragged myself out of bed and walked the few steps to the crib in the corner of the small bedroom. Gus was standing behind the bars with a big pout and tears in his eyes.

"I don't know why you always look at me like I've betrayed you," I told him. "We've had the same routine your whole life."

Around nine o'clock, he'd fall asleep in my arms while I watched the local news. Then I'd gently set him down on his bed, hoping he'd make it through the night. Praying for a full eight hours of sleep.

Looked like tonight wasn't my lucky night.

I picked him up, kissed his cheek, and settled down onto the twin-sized mattress with him. Tucking the covers around us, I lay on my back while cradling his body between mine and the wood panel wall.

Gus was a cuddler, so he didn't mind the close proximity. Which was a good thing. The bed I'd had since I was a kid might not have been big enough for the both of us, but an upgrade wasn't in the budget.

"Nyuk." The request was mumbled around the thumb in his mouth.

"You want milk, buddy?"

He nodded. "Nyuk. Nyuk."

"All right, bubsy bubster."

I had a lot of nicknames for my little dude. Buddy. Bud. Bubbie goo. Mister buddy goo goobie goo man. Sometimes I got a little obnoxious with it—I even had made-up theme songs just for him.

But the name I used most was Gus. Short for August.

When I'd scoured the internet for baby names, nothing could grab me. Then I saw the name August. It seemed fitting that he was named after my favorite month of the year. It was the same month I found out I was going to be a mom. The same month I learned a little person would join me on this crazy journey called life.

Back then, I'd been blissfully unaware of how hard motherhood was.

I'd never known an infant could cry as much as my son did. From day one, I'd affectionately called him Grumpy Gus, because he was the grouchiest baby in the history of ever.

My foggy, sleep-deprived recollections from those first few

months included a lot of screaming on his part and quite a few frustrated tears from me.

Although his disposition had improved and I'd dropped the 'Grumpy' title, the name Gus just stuck. It stuck so hard that I rarely called him by his actual name. He knew if I broke out 'August Michael' he was in big trouble.

"Someday, right?" I asked him, swinging my legs off the bed and hoisting him up on my hip. "That's what they tell me. Someday you'll sleep."

I shuffled out to the kitchen in the dark.

Even though I couldn't see, my footsteps were sure and steady because I'd memorized every square foot of this one-bedroom trailer. The brown carpet was worn down, and wood paneling covered every inch of the walls. The appliances were yellow and probably a few decades old.

It was far from fancy, but it was mine.

Light from the refrigerator briefly illuminated the kitchen before I grabbed the already-filled bottle and made my way to the loveseat in the living room. I turned on the TV and handed the milk to Gus.

He pushed it back and gave me a stubborn glare.

"You're old enough to feed it to yourself," I insisted quietly. "You're a big boy."

He disagreed. Whining, he attempted to wrap my hand around it with his chubby fingers.

Sighing, I popped it into his mouth because I didn't have the energy to fight about it. Pick your battles and all that.

He happily went to town on the milk while toying with the collar of my T-shirt. He rubbed it between his fingers, occasionally clenching the bunched fabric in his fist. It was something he'd done since birth. Didn't even matter what shirt I was wearing. As long as it was on my body, it was like his own personal security blanket.

As an infomercial played on the TV, I tried to keep my eyes open. They were selling a jewelry box. The spokesperson opened the top drawer for display, and the sparkles got Gus's attention.

I moved the bottle with the turn of his head so he could watch, too.

He pushed the nipple out of his mouth long enough to say, "Dewey."

"Yeah. That's a lot of jewelry."

He loved shiny things. Rings. Necklaces. Anything that glittered had his heart.

Gus pointed at the show and made a few grunting noises as the woman revealed a secret compartment in the back of the box.

"I agree with you. It's really nice."

More grunting.

"Maybe I could get you something like that for Christmas. The kid version, of course. I know it's four months away, and that's like a thousand years in baby time, but it's something to look forward to."

While most toddlers wanted cars or dolls, Gus just wanted all the rings. He had a bucket-full of costume jewelry under his crib. Every time we went to the supermarket, I tried to scrounge for a couple quarters to get him one from the cheap toy dispensers on the way out.

Gus stopped tugging on my T-shirt and moved his fingers to my necklace.

The small teardrop-shaped prism was meant to be hung in a window, not worn, but I never took it off. The silver chain had broken long ago—a casualty of Gus's tugging habits—and I'd replaced it with a black nylon string that was durable enough to withstand even the hardest of yanks.

The prism had been a birthday present from my mom when I turned twelve, and there was sentimental value in it.

I thought back to that day. My mom and I had gone to an arts festival—one of our rare mom-daughter outings—and she'd gotten it for me. Sometimes it made me sad that I didn't have more memories like that.

I looked down.

The bottle was empty and Gus's grip on my necklace had loosened.

Sleepy hazel eyes blinked up at me with adoration and love. They began to close, and I couldn't help smiling.

Drawing in a breath, I softly sang one of his songs.

"Who is the sleepiest boy? It's Gus. It's Gus. And who is the handsomest boy? It's Gus. It's Gus. And who is the funniest boy? It's Gus..."

And he was officially out. Victory.

I stared at him for a few minutes, taking in his squishy cheeks and button nose. His blond hair was getting a little too long. Wispy bangs nearly hung over his eyebrows and he was rocking a mini mullet in the back.

He was a beautiful boy. I didn't have to be his mother to see that, but the resemblance to his father was unnerving at times.

Why couldn't his eyes have been blue like mine? I hated myself for thinking it, but sometimes I wondered what else he inherited from that man. The man who'd taken advantage of me when I was young and vulnerable.

Jaxon had lured me into his life with promises of safety and love he couldn't deliver. I'd been so naïve, believing his intentions were good.

So what if he'd just gotten out of prison? He told me he'd been wrongly accused. It was all a misunderstanding. He was innocent.

Yeah, right.

That summer, the women around the trailer park—both

young and old—were falling all over themselves for the broody convict who'd moved into the vacant doublewide at the back of Brenton Estates.

I'd thought I was lucky because he set his sights on me, but now I realized I was an easy target for a predator.

With an absent father and an emotionally unavailable mother, I was so desperate for attention that I let Jaxon into my life with blinders on. He didn't even have to take me on dates to impress me. Showing up on my doorstep with a daisy he'd picked from my own garden was enough to make me swoon.

And when he convinced me I was ready for sex, I believed that, too. Just a month later, I found out I was pregnant, and he said he would take care of us.

It was all lies.

I wasn't ready for any of it, and his idea of taking care of us was dealing drugs.

A few short weeks after my life had been altered forever, Jaxon ended up back in jail and I was left alone.

Sixteen and pregnant.

Just like my mom at that age.

I was a walking cliché. A statistic. As the result of a teen-age pregnancy, I was 22% more likely to become a teen mom myself. Or something like that.

Weren't most statistics made up anyway? I sure hoped so, because the numbers weren't on Gus's side. The son of a young unwed mother and an incarcerated father didn't set him up with the best chances for success.

It didn't matter. I was determined to break the cycle. I re-fused to let my mistakes become my son's disadvantage.

Sometimes the pressure to be the best mom in the world was intense. I knew I was too hard on myself. I didn't allow myself to take breaks, to have hobbies, or to practice self-care.

I was overcompensating, trying to be a hundred times better than my mom was to me. Trying to be so awesome that Gus wouldn't even realize he was missing a father.

Most days, I felt like I was failing, but that didn't stop me from getting up the next morning with renewed motivation.

We lived well below the poverty line, but we had everything we needed. A home. Food. Clothing.

And love.

Gus would never have to question my love for him.

He was everything to me. Any personal goals or dreams I used to have disappeared the moment he was born. My new mission was to ensure he had the best life possible.

And I would sure as hell guarantee he didn't end up like his father.

CHAPTER 2

Jay

Most people would assume the first thing I did when I got out of prison was go find a woman.

And they were right, just not in the way they thought.

One girl in particular had been on my mind almost every hour I lived in that cell. No matter how much I tried not to, I spent way too much time worrying about Casey Maxwell.

At night when I closed my eyes, I pictured her innocent face and thought about what she looked like as her stomach grew with her baby. Was it a boy or a girl?

I'd often wondered if she was okay and if she got to finish high school.

As soon as I'd stepped on free ground, my mind went to her, and I had to know how she was doing.

After I'd settled in at my mom's house in my hometown of Daywood for a temporary stay, I drove the twenty-minute trip to Brenton.

I'd pulled up to the apartments across the street from the trailer park and watched the little yellow house for hours.

Around four in the afternoon, Casey rode past my car on her bike in a blur of creamy skin and dark hair. She'd parked in front of a different trailer than the one I'd been watching. The light-blue trailer was one of the smallest in the lot, but it was nice. Taken care of.

I'd held my breath as she walked to a beige trailer four spots away. An older woman answered the door with a baby on her hip.

Casey's son. One of the cutest kids I'd ever seen.

With her ponytail swinging in the breeze, Casey had planted at least a dozen kisses on his cheeks as they walked back to their tiny home and disappeared inside.

I'd gotten the answers I was looking for.

I'd told myself that was enough. I could move on.

But that was a lie.

Because Casey wasn't a girl anymore. She'd turned into a gorgeous young woman and a great mom. And mother-fuck-ing-dammit, I was attracted to her.

Drawn to her.

What started as innocent curiosity had turned into an un-controllable obsession.

I had no business hanging around an eighteen-year-old girl who was just trying to provide a good life for her kid.

Didn't stop me from doing it, though.

Now—three months later—I sat on my second-story bal-cony in that same apartment complex across the street from the trailer park.

After saving up enough money for a rental deposit on my own place, I'd moved to the Brenton apartments because they were the cheapest in the area.

Another lie.

Yeah, they were affordable because this small town was shit. But the truth was, I wanted to be near Casey.

The extra creepy part was that I hadn't talked to her. Hadn't gone near them. I just lurked in my apartment and watched.

What I was doing was intrusive and stalkerish, but I was beyond caring.

Being prone to addiction, I'd always needed something to focus on. When I was eleven, it was car keys. I used to collect them, memorizing which shape went with each make and model.

Then I got into magic. I used to spend hours every day practicing tricks with any object I could get my hands on—keys, cards, coins.

In my teenage years, it was drugs.

And in prison, it was working out. I spent my energy on health and fitness, because it was a lot better pretending I lived in a gym than a jail.

Now, it was Casey.

On nights like tonight when I couldn't sleep, I could always count on her son waking up. I had a straight view into their living room from the chair on my balcony.

Sometimes when the wind blew this way, I could hear Casey singing to Gus. Her sweet voice carried through the windows she always kept open when it was cool enough to turn off the AC.

The silly, upbeat tune made its way to my ears and I smiled.

Insomnia was a bitch, but at least I had entertainment.

Gazing lovingly at her sleeping son, Casey stayed on the couch for a few minutes before yawning. Then she carried him back to their room.

I had no idea how she found the energy to do this by herself day in and day out. It was obvious she loved him more than anything, but she looked so tired.

I wished there was something I could do to help. Simply standing by and watching her struggle was a special kind of hell for me.

But what did I have to offer?

Nothing. Absolutely nothing, except for a bad past and a dead-end future.

Before I went away, I had no idea how it was going to affect me long-term. The time I spent in that place changed me. I used to be a rebel, laughing in the face of consequence.

Not now.

There was nothing funny about the ruin I brought upon myself and countless others.

As I headed back into my lonely apartment, an idea came to me, and I paused after shutting the sliding glass door. Maybe there was something I could do for Casey after all.

Grinning, I formed the perfect plan as I fell to my king-sized mattress, ready to chase elusive sleep once again.

CHAPTER 3

Casey

Morning came quickly, and the normal events followed.

I took a quick two-minute shower while Gus screamed outside the glass door, his face beet-red while angry tears streaked his cheeks.

I'd stopped trying to convince him he was fine standing there without me—he never listened anyway. To be honest, I was surprised no one had called Child Protective Services on me yet. Anyone who heard it would probably think I was starting off every day with beating my child.

"You're okay," I said, stepping onto the pink bathmat as I wrapped a towel around my body.

I squeezed the excess wetness from my strands into the pedestal sink.

Ruffling Gus's hair, I set him on the small sink ledge while I got out my blow dryer. He held onto me, grasping the side of the towel like his life depended on it. Stuffing his thumb in his mouth, he tucked his face against my chest while I turned the dryer on high.

He started crying again because he hated the noise.

My dark brown strands whipped around from the force of the hot air, and I realized I was in desperate need of a trim. It was almost down to my waist.

"We both need haircuts, huh?" I said over the dryer, trying to distract him with conversation.

It didn't work.

"You were completely bald when you were born, so you never needed one until now. Maybe Doreen can help us out."

The mention of his babysitter's name made his wailing pause for a brief second before he resumed letting me know how he really felt.

Doreen McMillin lived in the trailer four doors down, and she had some serious life skills. Cutting hair. Growing a garden. Fixing appliances. Caring for kids.

If it was a useful talent, she could do it.

Guess that's what happened when you depended on yourself your whole life.

I aspired to be like her one day. She'd been a resident of Brenton Estates trailer park for decades, and she did me a huge favor by watching Gus while I worked. No other daycare in town would ever let me get away with paying only five dollars a day. Plus, if anything ever happened and I needed to come get him, my job wasn't far away.

After getting dressed in my usual jeans and black Gloria's Diner polo shirt, I put Gus in his favorite green dinosaur tank top and blue shorts. Then we headed to the kitchen for a quick breakfast.

Frowning, I dug around in the small cabinet I used as the pantry. I'd need to go grocery shopping soon. I was out of coffee. Good thing I worked at a restaurant where I could get it for free.

We had one strawberry Pop-Tart left, so I broke it in half and gave the bigger piece to Gus.

He only had six teeth at the moment—four on top and two on the bottom—but he could use those chompers like nobody's business.

He was nibbling on his breakfast as I carried him out the door. Trying not to tip over from being overloaded with his weight, a diaper bag, and my purse, I ambled down the porch stairs.

The sun was up, shooting bright rays over the tall cornstalks behind the rows of trailers. It'd rained overnight, and the air was warm and muggy as we walked to Doreen's.

"Ammaw," Gus said, pointing at my mom's place.

"Yeah, maybe we'll see Grandma this weekend," I told him, hoping it was true.

I invited her over often, which spurred the same conversation every time. She'd ask me why we never came over to her house, and I'd tell her—for the thousandth time—that until she stopped smoking, we couldn't.

Gus had asthma and smoke caused him problems. She'd even witnessed one of his attacks before, which was scary as fuck every time, but it wasn't enough for her to kick the habit.

Anger and resentment bubbled to the surface, because my mom had chosen an addiction over me. Over us.

When I'd told her I was pregnant, I'd expected her to freak out, just like her mom had done to her. Much to my surprise, she didn't. She just sat back on her floral sofa, lit up a cigarette, and asked me when I was due.

Hope and happiness had overwhelmed me when she'd started talking about digging out my old baby clothes and fixing up a corner of my bedroom to be a nursery. For a little while, I wasn't alone in my excitement over the life growing inside of me.

But a couple weeks later when morning sickness hit, just a whiff of cigarette smoke was enough to send me into a violent puking fit.

After several days of not being able to keep any food down, I asked her to quit. Not just because it was making me sick but also because it was bad for the baby. Seeming open to the suggestion, she'd nodded, tossing the pack down on the kitchen table.

But when it was clear she had no intention of following through, I quickly formed a new plan.

Emancipation.

I didn't want to disown my mother, but I needed to have the legal means to survive on my own. Thanks to some money I'd had stashed away, I was able to move into my own trailer.

My thoughts were interrupted by the familiar sound of chugging and a loud whistle in the distance. A mile away, train tracks lined the south side of Brenton, separating us from Elmer, a town we shared a high school with. Most of its residents ranged from middle class to downright wealthy.

Brenton, Illinois, was literally on the wrong side of the tracks.

It was the mystical land of single moms, trailer parks, and poverty.

I didn't hate it, though. I definitely didn't want to be here forever, but it was the only home I'd ever known.

Doreen's screen door opened with a loud creak, and her head popped out. She wasn't much older than fifty, but life had worn her down. Her long wheat-colored hair was streaked with white and her skin was like weathered leather.

"Hi, Doreen." I waved, and Gus followed suit.

"Hiya." Her brown eyes turned to Gus. "How's my favorite man today?"

He smiled around his thumb, shyly leaning his head on my shoulder as we shuffled inside. Doreen's trailer was a lot like mine. Small, with a lot of wood paneling.

"I have news," she announced as I dropped the diaper bag on the kitchen table. "Shelby had her baby last night."

Doreen's daughter was one of Brenton's success stories. Meaning, she got the hell out of here. Shelby had gotten a degree in social work, and she'd married a doctor. She was proof that growing up in this town didn't destine someone to a life of failure.

"That's great." I smiled. "Congratulations on being a grandma. I thought she wasn't due for another three weeks, though."

Doreen shrugged. "She wasn't, but fate had other plans. The baby—a girl—she's doing just fine and they're letting her out of the hospital tomorrow." Her proud grin faltered a little. "I hate to leave you high and dry, but I'm traveling there tonight. I need to go up to visit her for a week. No matter how old a woman gets, she still needs her momma in times like these."

"Yeah, I know." My throat got tight.

Doreen was right, but the comment was a painful reminder of what I didn't have.

My mom had talked a good game when Gus was born— she had big plans for things like sleepovers, trips to the zoo, and coming over to help me with never-ending laundry.

I'd given up on hoping any of that would actually happen.

Maybe it was for the best.

It wasn't that my mom wasn't capable of taking care of a kid—obviously I'd turned out just fine, and she'd watched Gus for the occasional hour or two. But the sad truth was that I didn't trust her with my child for an entire day.

Which left me with a problem. I didn't have a backup babysitter. The week I'd requested off from Gloria's didn't match up with when I needed it.

"I'm really sorry to leave on such short notice," Doreen apologized again, wringing her hands.

"Don't worry about us." Lifting Gus, I set him into the highchair. Cheerios were already spread out for him, and he started munching on the cereal. "We'll figure something out. I'll see if Gloria will let me switch my vacation dates."

And if she didn't… well, I'd have to use some sick days. Unpaid.

My wallet wouldn't be happy about that, but thanks to my small savings, we'd be okay. If I knew one thing, it was how to stretch a dollar.

"You're a tough girl, Casey. What you're doing isn't easy, but I'm proud of you."

My spirits lifted at the praise. Doreen never tried to spout optimistic bullshit at me, and I appreciated it.

If one more person reminded me that *they're only little once*. If one more neighbor said the phrase *the days are long, but the years are short*. If anyone else told me I'd *miss this*.

I would scream.

They all meant well, but their words didn't add extra hours to my day, make money appear in my bank account, or put food on my table.

They were right—someday I'd look back and yearn for these times. But right now, I was simply too busy being buried alive to see the light at the end of the tunnel.

One glance at Doreen's clock told me I had ten minutes to get to work. "I gotta go. I'll be back at four."

"Mama!" Gus's voice cracked as he started to wail. "Mamaaa."

His little hands reached for me, and my heart constricted.

We'd done this every day for over a year now. You'd think he'd be used to me dropping him off. You'd think I'd become immune to his tears.

But leaving him still devastated him and crushed me every time.

"It'll be okay, bud. I'll be back soon."

After delivering a kiss to his tear-streaked cheek, I tried to tune out his crying as I jogged back to my house and mounted my bicycle. The paint was rusted to hell, but it was my main source of transportation. I owned a car now, too, but I drove it sparingly because the old Ford Focus needed to last as long as possible.

My legs pumped the pedals a few times, but as I passed by my car, a glimpse of white on my windshield caught my attention.

Kicking back to slam on the brakes, I skidded to a stop in the gravel.

The sight of an envelope tucked under my wipers made my heart pick up with a happy patter. It reminded me of the last time I received one of those.

From a super-hot guy.

Jay Langston.

I only talked to him once, but I remembered his boyish smile, manly scruff, sky-blue eyes, and reddish-brown hair.

He'd been a beacon of hope in my darkest time. He was smooth, confident, and mysterious. He gave me money I desperately needed, and he made me smile when all I wanted to do was cry.

In my mind, I'd come to think of him as my magic man. It was a silly, school-girl-crush thing to do. I'd built him up as some sort of knight in shining armor.

Only, he wasn't.

News travels fast in a small town, and the day after I met him, I found out he went to jail on drug charges.

It was a damn shame.

Knocking down my kickstand with my toe, I paced over to my car and picked up the envelope, excited about what I might find inside.

CHAPTER 4

Jay

Taking a sip of hot coffee, I savored the caramel macchiato creamer while I stared at Brenton Estates.

Ah, this was good shit. We didn't get stuff like this in prison, and sometimes it was the little things you missed the most.

Like watching the sunrise.

Around five a.m. I let insomnia win. It was just as well. I had a surprise to carry out, and it gave me the opportunity to see the sky lighten. Kicking my feet up on my balcony, I'd gazed at the wispy clouds on the horizon as they lit up with pink and orange.

Daylight was in full swing now, and I anxiously tapped my fingers on the plastic armrests as I waited for Casey to appear.

I perked up when I caught sight of her.

Every morning when she worked, she and her son would come out. They'd walk four doors down, and the little guy would scream bloody murder when she dropped him off. She'd try to keep that fake smile plastered on for him until the door shut, but her façade crumbled as she left him behind.

Then she'd hop on her bike and ride the half-mile trip to Gloria's Diner.

I gulped the rest of my coffee as the scene unfolded exactly how it did every Monday, Tuesday, Wednesday, and Friday.

Only this time was slightly different.

When Casey got to her car, she noticed the envelope on her windshield. Glancing around, she picked it up and looked inside to find twenty yellow tickets along with a note inviting her to the carnival in Daywood tonight. Anonymously, of course.

Nervousness caused my stomach to flip, and I shook my head at how ridiculous I was being.

It wasn't like I was asking her on a date or anything. I probably wouldn't even have time to see her.

I just wanted her to have a good time, and a few free tickets was one of the shitty benefits of my job.

Getting hired with felon status was hard. The only place I'd been able to find decent pay was the traveling carnival. Every weekend took us to a different small town around central Illinois.

I performed in the magic show and helped run some of the rides. There wasn't much prestige in being a carnie, but it was better than nothing. Plus, it was temporary.

The Daywood gig was our second to last job for the summer.

I was hoping Casey would show up.

Judging by the grin on her face as she peddled down the street, I was pretty sure she would.

CHAPTER 5

Casey

When someone gives you free carnival tickets, you don't ask questions—you just go. Okay, maybe a normal person would've been more cautious, but I was just so grateful for a night of fun.

I was more excited than Gus as we approached the dazzling lights of all the rides and games.

Squeals of glee echoed through the warm evening air. Whimsical music from the carousel floated our way. The smell of fried food made my mouth water.

I let out a happy sigh.

"Bubs, look at that! I love the baseball game." Someone threw a wicked pitch and knocked down half the pins. "I was really good at softball. I played for my high school team."

Blinking, Gus gave me an unimpressed look.

"Seriously. I was kind of a big deal. I probably would've made varsity if…" I snapped my mouth shut. *If I'd been able to go to school.* That was the complete sentence, but I never wanted to make Gus feel like he made me miss out. "So, what do you want to do first? The slides? We could go down together."

Continuing to suck his thumb, he didn't answer as he twisted the collar of my shirt around his other hand. Screaming from one of the rides made him wince, and he hid his face against my neck.

Dang. This was so not his jam.

I hadn't considered the fact that this entire place was over-stimulation to the max. He wasn't a fan of rides—he didn't even like the swings at the park.

New plan. We could play some games.

We passed a ring-toss booth that had baby lop bunnies as prizes, and I promptly pivoted in the other direction.

That was a big hell no. If Gus spotted rabbits, he'd never let me see the rest of the carnival and our tickets would be gone in minutes. Ring toss wasn't a talent I possessed and if by some stroke of luck I actually won, what then?

We'd have to take the bunny, that's what.

Like I said—hell no.

I saw a kid's game where they got to pick up floating rubber duckies out of a baby pool. That was more our speed.

Within three minutes, half our tickets were gone, and Gus had a little stuffed frog and a plastic butterfly ring to show for it.

Just as we started to walk away, he tugged on my hand. "Dewey."

"Yeah, you did get jewelry. Good job."

The pulling became more insistent and I looked down. "I can't carry you the whole time. Can you just walk with me for a while?"

Shaking his head, he pointed to something behind us, and I followed his line of sight.

Ohh.

Rings. Expensive-looking ones.

Twenty feet away, there was a balloon dart game and a clear display box full of shiny objects on the counter. While most of the games had a seemingly endless supply of stuffed animals mounted, this one had large inflatable diamonds hanging from the ceiling.

"Dewey!" Gus began bravely marching away, determined. He turned back, raising his eyebrows at me. "Mama? Dewey."

"Okay, okay." I followed him, grabbing his hand as we approached the booth.

When we got closer, the carnival worker shouted his spiel. "You could be your little boy's hero tonight! Win him a prize of his choice. It's just five tickets for three darts."

"I haven't played darts in years, but I used to be pretty good," I boasted to the skinny bearded man. "How many balloons do I have to pop?"

"Three."

Simple enough. I could do this.

I didn't want to risk missing one, so I placed all ten tickets in front of him, going all-in. He replaced them with six darts.

Moving Gus to stand on my left side, I took hold of his fingers and hooked them into the pocket of my white denim shorts. "Just hold onto me."

He did as I said, and I rolled the dart between my fingers as I positioned it over my shoulder. My arm whipped forward, and the first balloon popped.

Giddy, I bounced in my tennis shoes as I picked up another.

This one didn't hit the mark. Landing between a pink and a green balloon, it was about two feet away from where I'd meant for it to go.

I frowned but picked up the third. Another miss.

The fourth. *Pop.*

I had two tries left, and I needed to get one more to win.

The next one hit a yellow balloon but bounced right off.

What the…?

I blew out a breath and picked up the only dart I had left. Last chance.

Pop.

Yes!

"I did it." My feet hopped with a happy dance when I announced my victory to Gus. A huge smile stretched across my face as I picked him up, propping him on my side. We moved closer to the rings. "Which one do you want?"

"Whoa, now." The carnival worker produced a small metal bucket from somewhere behind the counter. "These are what you get to choose from."

I shook my head at the cheap whistles. That wasn't what we came to this game for. It wasn't what Gus wanted, and he'd hate how loud they were.

I pointed at the display. "Why not these?"

"Those are on the top tier of prizes. You gotta pop fifteen balloons to get one of them."

Fifteen?

"Then why are these the only thing on display?" I asked through gritted teeth, not even hiding the fact that I was pissed.

He just shrugged, like he didn't care that our night was about to be ruined.

I couldn't play again. The six dollars in my pocket from today's tips was meant for food, not games, and it wouldn't have been enough anyway.

"Look—whistles." Trying to sound cheerful, I redirected Gus's attention to the bucket.

He was not okay with this.

Reaching for the rings, he began babbling nonsensical protests. I could tell the situation was going to escalate quickly, so I grabbed a blue whistle and hightailed it back to my car before too many people could witness the epic meltdown heading my way.

As I powerwalked through the grass in the parking area, Gus screamed while trying to escape my arms. My ears rang from the shrill sounds, and embarrassment heated my cheeks when I saw a group of people gaping at the spectacle.

Fighting my own distress, I sat Gus on the hood of my car.

"I know." I took a deep breath to control my reeling emotions. "I know you wanted the ring, and I wanted to get it for you."

Looking down at his lap, he cried louder, and the sad sound pierced my heart.

"I tried. I really did. I'm sorry." My voice cracked, and sudden tears blurred my vision.

It was a silly thing to cry over. He'd probably forget all about it by tomorrow.

But for me, it wasn't just about the prize. It was about feeling inadequate.

Constantly falling short.

My own tears spilled over, running down my face. "I'm so sorry, bud."

Sorry you got stuck with me as a mom. Sorry I can't give you more. Sorry my best isn't good enough.

Suddenly stopping the fit, Gus touched my wet cheek with his fingers. Confused, he clumsily dabbed at my skin and looked at the droplets on his fingertips.

Then the most unexpected thing happened.

Gus hugged me. He wrapped his little arms around my middle and squeezed.

I wanted to laugh and sob at the same time. It was his first show of compassion. The first time he'd ever put his own feelings aside for mine.

That alone was worth the disappointment from five minutes ago.

I rarely let him see me cry. In fact, I didn't cry often. When you're in survival mode, there's no time for breakdowns.

"Thank you." I hugged him back, cradling the back of his head while sifting through his soft mini mullet.

It wasn't his job to comfort me, but I was glad he did. Life might've been hard, but we were in it together.

"We're a team, right, bubba?" Sniffling, I kissed the top of his head and wiped my face. "We don't have to leave yet. Are you hungry? There are snacks."

Food was one incentive I could always count on with him. He'd never been a picky eater and the word snack got his attention. Maybe I could convince him to share a funnel cake with me.

Popping his thumb into his mouth, he wiggled to the ground and slipped his fingers around mine.

I blew out a sigh.

Crisis averted, all because my child felt sorry for me.

Well. I'd take it.

Hand in hand, we walked back to the carnival.

CHAPTER 6

Jay

She came.

Casey and Gus actually showed up. Unfortunately, they didn't appear to be having the best time.

I saw her get cheated at Turner's booth. He was a sleaze and I knew the game was rigged.

Asshole.

When Casey carried her crying son away, I thought they left for good. But then I saw a flash of long dark hair go by my tent. Blue shirt. Knobby knees.

I really liked that her knees hadn't changed. Maybe the feature wasn't a childhood characteristic—it was just the way her legs were shaped. Either way, it was fucking cute.

I also liked how her shorts cupped her ass. She was wearing makeup tonight. Some mascara, blush, and lip gloss. She always looked pretty, but under the twinkling lights of the Ferris wheel, she was stunning.

I smiled as Casey and Gus got in line to buy an elephant ear.

Focus.

Looking out at my audience, I tried to keep myself from getting distracted. Magic shows took a certain amount of concentration and skill. If I wasn't careful, I could mess up. And quite frankly, that would be embarrassing.

"Pick a card, please." Spreading the red deck like a fan, I held it out to a blond woman in the front row.

Giggling, she grabbed one from the middle. Even with her pre-teen kids on either side of her, she wasn't covert about sending me some serious fuck-me eyes.

It was always like this. Every single show, I could count on at least one woman trying to slip her number into my pocket or my deck of cards.

Like any great illusionist, they saw what I wanted them to see—a young, buff, charismatic guy. They saw my top hat and my red-and-black blazer. My tattoos were covered, and nothing about me screamed danger.

The blonde bit her lip as she waited for my next instructions, and some of her pink lipstick ended up on her teeth.

"Memorize the card and put it back anywhere you like," I directed.

The woman did as I said, and she tried to make our fingers brush when she chose to insert it on the far left. I backed away before any physical contact could happen, and with a quick sleight of hand, her card was up my sleeve.

I didn't have anything against older women. It wasn't her age, her appearance, or her desperation that put me off.

I simply wasn't interested in anyone other than Casey.

Sometime in these past few months, my irrational obsession with her had turned into something more. Something deeper.

Seeing her—and Gus—was the best part of my day.

They were ordering their food now. Casey was speaking into the window of the large food van while Gus clung to her leg.

"Charlene," I addressed my assistant. "Please put this deck somewhere for safe keeping."

Accepting it from me, the middle-aged woman made a show of trying to figure out where to stash it.

She was good at this—the performing aspect of the job. She loved the giant flaming-red wig, the bright lipstick, and the fake eyelashes. Over the summer, we'd gotten to know each other, and she was like a second mom to me now.

She enjoyed making people laugh, and she did just that when she gave an exaggerated glance toward her cleavage and shoved the deck into her pink flapper-style dress.

Snorts and laughs rang out under the red canopy, rippling through the small crowd sitting in the folding chairs.

Just like we'd rehearsed, I sighed deeply and deadpanned, "Really, Charlie?"

"Really. You're gonna have to come get it." She did a shoulder shimmy.

I smirked. "I have a better idea."

Letting my hand hover over my suit pocket, I produced the card, making it seem like it'd been there all along. I showed the two of spades to the audience. "Ma'am, was this your card?"

"Yes." The blonde gaped, impressed.

Everyone clapped, and my gaze was once again drawn to Casey in the distance. Through the open flap of the tent, I could see her paying. Gus was still clinging to her shorts.

But what I saw next had my heart in my throat.

Suddenly, Gus let go. His attention was on the balloon dart game again. Much to my horror, he started walking away from Casey, and she didn't notice because she was digging around in her purse for money.

My eyes bounced back and forth between them—Gus getting farther away while Casey handed over some dollar bills and took the large plate of fried food.

Come on, I silently urged, wanting her to look down. Trying to mentally convince Gus to go back to his mom.

One of those things happened; Casey glanced to where

Gus had previously been, and the color drained from her face when she realized he wasn't there. Even from twenty yards away, I could see the terror play out on her beautiful face.

Frantic, she turned in a circle, searching the area with panicked eyes.

Welp. Show's over.

"You've been a wonderful audience." I backed up to the tall, thin 'time machine' behind me. The gold-plated box had a false back, and we used it to end the show with a disappearing act. "But I have to say goodbye. I'm late for a date in ancient Egypt."

Confused about why I was cutting out early, Charlene's crow's feet deepened when she narrowed her eyes.

"Farewell!" With a final wave, I shut the door, knowing I had approximately eight seconds before Charlene opened it to prove I was gone.

I quickly shed my top hat and blazer, leaving them on the floor in a heap. Then I exited the back of the tent and sprinted to where Gus had been just moments before.

At first, I didn't see him. He was so little, and there were a lot of people milling about.

Scary how fast someone could lose sight of something so important.

In my peripheral vision, I saw the funnel cake drop from Casey's hand, falling to the ground in an explosion of white powdered sugar.

"Gus!" Her heart-wrenching scream cut through the air, slicing through my chest like the sharpest knife. "Gus? Where are you? August Michael!"

Good thing I knew where the little dude was headed.

I took a shortcut between the lemon shake-up stand and the corndog vendor, coming out on the other side near the game.

All the while, I could hear Casey pleading with random strangers.

"Have you seen my son? Please! I can't find my son. He—he's only fifteen months old. He's wearing a green tank top, navy shorts, and black sandals. Gus!"

I spotted him. He was just ten feet from his destination.

Carefully, I approached him. I didn't want to scare the little guy. A weird man picking him up would probably freak him out.

I kneeled down in front of him, and he looked at me with startled hazel eyes.

We stared at each other for a second, and everything around me faded away as he curiously tilted his head. Like he was saying hello.

I never thought I'd get to be this close to him, and the moment felt important.

"Hi, Gus," I said reverently, swallowing hard. "I'm Jay. I think your mom's looking for you."

Saying 'mom' snapped him out of his trance, and fear was evident on his face when he realized they'd been separated.

Whipping his head from right to left, he searched the sea of unfamiliar people.

His bottom lip quivered.

Oh, fuck.

That was heartbreaking.

"Come with me." I kept my voice soft, extending my hands toward him. "We'll find her."

Surprisingly, he came willingly. Before he had a chance to completely lose his shit, I sprinted away, following Casey's panicked voice.

A crowd had formed around her. Several other moms were there with their children, looking like they were ready to spread out on a search.

"Here!" I shouted, nudging a couple bystanders out of the way with my shoulders. "He's here."

Rotating in my direction, Casey's gaze homed in on Gus.

"Oh my God." She ran to us and snatched him from my arms. "Oh, I thought I lost you." She squeezed him tight. "Where did you go?"

I knew he was too young to tell her, so I answered for him.

"I saw him go that way." I motioned behind me. "He was trying to get to one of the games."

"Oh." Sounding out of breath, she looked in the direction I pointed. "He was probably trying to go after the rings. He really wanted one. Don't do that to Momma again," she scolded, holding Gus far enough away to look him in the eyes. "You scared me."'

Affected by her anger, Gus's lip wobbled again.

All of the sudden, Casey flung herself at me, wrapping her free arm around my waist. A tearful, whimpering Gus was smushed between us as she mumbled out, "Thank you. Thank you. Thank you."

Her gratitude, along with the group hug, was unexpected. I hadn't been embraced by anyone except my mom and sister for years. Human contact was something I'd learned to live without.

My skin tingled in all the places she touched me, and I didn't know what to do with my hands.

"No big deal," I told her, hesitantly returning the gesture by rubbing her shoulder. Heat from her body seeped into my palm. "Anyone would've helped. I just happened to get to him first."

"And it's you." Casey glanced up, hero-worship and relief shimmering in her blue orbs. "You're here."

Shit. She recognized me. Girl had a good memory. We'd only had one conversation that lasted a few minutes, and that was years ago.

Suddenly, a new look of fear passed over Casey's face as she clutched her chest. Her knees went weak, and I tightened my hold on her to keep her upright.

"I—I'm having trouble—breathing. Dizzy. My—chest hurts." Her face paled as she wheezed, "Help."

Panic attack. I'd had a few of those in my life. I used to rely on illegal substances as a cure, but that wasn't an option in jail. I'd been forced to learn some self-regulation techniques.

Casey needed a quiet place to calm down.

"Can you walk?" I asked her.

Nodding, she leaned on me while taking a few small steps. People were still hanging around, watching with wide eyes and open mouths.

"Everyone's—looking—at me." Embarrassed, she turned her head to hide her face against my chest.

Air whooshed in and out of her lungs as she breathed too quickly, and her warm breath fanned through the fabric of my shirt.

Screw this. She was going to hyperventilate.

Scooping her and Gus up, I carried both of them away from the onlookers. I weaved between the games on the outskirts of the carnival and made it to the RV we used for breaks.

Charlene was inside. She'd already changed into jeans and a white T-shirt. Her wig was off, revealing her natural short blond curls.

She was sitting in front of her portable lighted mirror, peeling off her fake eyelashes when she drawled, "Well, well. Look who's back from ancient Egypt. Next time you decide to take off five minutes early, take me with you, huh?"

"I need the RV for a while," I huffed out, winded from hauling the extra weight.

Charlene's expression turned to one of shock when she glanced my way and saw two people in my arms.

"Do I need to call an ambulance?" she asked, standing.

"No," Casey hissed, wrenching her head from side to side. "I don't want to put him through that." She caressed Gus's head, who was clinging to us both like a baby koala.

"She couldn't find her son for a second and I think she's having a panic attack," I explained to Charlene. "Cover the slides for me. Please?"

Now that the magic show was over, I was switching roles. It was my duty to man the slides for the last hour. A jack of all trades, right here. I could go from performing professional tricks to taking tickets and handing out burlap sacks for the ride down.

Nodding, Charlene gave Casey a look of sympathy before leaving us alone.

Sitting sideways on the padded bench seat, I propped my feet up. I placed Casey between my legs, cradling her body there. Gus straddled her lap, cautiously looking around at the unfamiliar surroundings.

At least he wasn't crying anymore.

"Lean your head back on my shoulder," I told Casey.

She obeyed, and her voice came out strained when she said, "Sorry. I'm sorry."

I wasn't sure if she was talking to Gus or me, but she didn't owe anyone an apology. "These things happen. Everything's okay. Just breathe. Has this ever happened to you before?"

"No, we rarely leave the house. I've never lost him, I swear. I watch him like a hawk."

"Not that." God, did she really think I was criticizing her parenting at a time like this? "I meant the panic attack."

"Twice," she answered. "But this is the worst one I've ever had. It feels like a heart attack. What if it is? I can't die. Gus can't be without me. I'm all he has. If anything happens to me…"

"You know it's not a heart attack. Don't even think that, because it's not going to help." Laying my hand on her upper chest, my fingers covered her prism when I said, "Feel me here. Feel your chest rise and fall against my palm. Concentrate on that and picture a good place. Somewhere peaceful, where you feel like your problems don't exist. Close your eyes and go there."

"I don't know any place like that."

"Then you can have mine. It's a meadow. There are wild-flowers as far as the eye can see. Butterflies love wildflowers and there are thousands of them flying around. It smells like summertime. You know that smell after it rains and the sun dries up the water?"

"Uh huh." The trembling in Casey's body lessened.

"It smells like that. Like flowers, dirt, and sunshine."

"Sounds nice. Where is this place?"

"Over in Daywood, behind the old house I lived in when I was a kid. We had a metal swing set out there. It was old and rusty and probably a safety hazard." I chuckled. "But I loved sitting in my backyard and looking out at that meadow."

Without turning to look at me, Casey hesitantly said, "You're a friend of Jaxon's, right?"

"No, I'm not."

"You just said that because you wanted me to take the money?"

"Yes."

"I knew that. You're a bad liar, you know?"

"Is that so?" I asked, amused. "I happen to be a very good liar if I want to be."

She made an unimpressed noise. "Not exactly something to brag about."

My lips quirked up at her chastising tone.

"I know." We sat silently for a few moments before I asked, "Are you okay?"

She didn't respond right away, but when she did, her answer came out broken. "I'm drowning."

"It's just a panic attack, and you're already getting better," I reassured her. "Just breathe."

"I don't mean this. It's not just tonight. It's everything. I'm drowning in failure. No matter how hard I try to find my way up, I can't. I work at a shitty diner for shitty tips. I live in a shitty trailer and I drive a shitty car." A sound of distress escaped. "And I just said 'shitty' in front of my son four times—no, I guess that makes it five times now."

"You're being way too hard on yourself. And look—he didn't hear you anyway."

Dipping her chin, Casey glanced at Gus. He was asleep, his face squished against her shoulder.

"He was a really difficult newborn," she went on, quiet. "He still cries a lot. He's very opinionated and stubborn. Don't get me wrong—I love him more than anything, but I'm burnt out."

Before I could think better of it, I blurted, "Why don't you take him to your mom's? Doesn't she want to help?"

She stiffened. "How do you know my mom isn't very involved?"

Shit. I'd just given away my biggest secret. For a second, I thought about making up a smooth lie, but I didn't want to do that. Besides, she'd probably see right through it anyway.

Sighing, I admitted, "I live in the apartment complex across the street from you. My balcony faces the trailer park." I omitted the part about how I might've chosen that unit on purpose. "I'm good at… observing."

"You've been watching us?"

"Yeah."

"You gave me the carnival tickets." It was a conclusion, not a question.

"Yes."

And this was the part where she'd realize I was a total creep. Maybe she'd call me a pervert or a peeping Tom. Tell me to stay away.

Surprisingly, she didn't. Instead, her muscles started to relax against my chest, like she was completely at ease with a guy who'd basically just confessed to stalking her.

"I really appreciate the tickets. I don't know how many times I can say thank you to one person in a day, but seriously—"

"You're welcome," I cut her off, uncomfortable with the praise.

Nothing I'd done was over the top or special. Obviously, common decency from men wasn't something Casey received often.

"Last year, Gus got pneumonia," Casey started. "He was really sick, and he had to be hospitalized for a few days."

"I bet that was scary."

"It was. Ever since then, his lungs haven't been the same. He has asthma, and my mom smokes like a chimney. Gus can't be around it. That's why she's not in the picture more."

That explained a lot. "Sorry. That sucks."

"You don't smoke, do you?" Her head turned slightly, until she could see my face out of the corner of her eye.

"Do I look like I smoke? On second thought, don't answer that." My image didn't project goody two shoes. "More importantly, do I smell like it?"

"No. Actually, you smell really good." She sniffed. "It's citrusy. I like it."

I thought I caught a blush on Casey's cheek before she looked straight ahead again.

"I used to smoke," I told her. "Kicked that habit a long time ago, though. Addictive substances and I don't get along. It's best if I just don't go there."

Not only did I avoid drugs and cigarettes, alcohol was out, too. Even considering it was risky. I had to keep myself in line. One misstep, and I could end up spiraling back down.

"Do you know what my situation says about his future?" Casey's tone was defeated as she ran a loving hand down Gus's back. "He's likely to end up in prison just like his father. What if he's doomed from the start?"

Like father, like son, a voice taunted in my mind.

Did I know what she was talking about? Hell, yeah. I lived it. I was that boy.

My gut twisted at the thought of the vicious cycle getting ahold of the baby in her arms.

"That won't happen to him." My voice was firm. "Because you'll keep your standards high when it comes to men," I said, repeating the same advice I'd given her two years ago. "Someday, a great guy is gonna come along. He'll be the love of your life and the father your son needs. He'll love you and he'll love your son like he's his own. Don't ever settle for less."

The mental image of her with that guy—someone who wasn't me—made my blood boil.

But as much as I wished I could be, I wasn't the right man for Casey. My life was a sinking ship, I refused to drag her down.

Casey's breathing had returned to normal now, and I relinquished my hold on her.

"Better?" I asked, scooting away.

"Yeah." She swiveled toward me.

Gus was completely limp in her arms, and he let out the cutest little baby snore.

Since the seat wasn't very wide, we were still just inches apart from each other.

I gripped her chin with my thumb and forefinger. "Keep your chin up and your standards high, you hear me?"

"I hear you," she whispered.

"Promise."

"I promise."

"Wanna go have some fun?" Enough of this abysmal shit. "The carnival isn't over yet. I can show you around."

That pulled a smile from her, and her dimples came out to play. "I thought you have to work."

"Charlene will cover for me. She owes me anyway."

The dimples faded as her grin melted away. Lifting Gus slightly, she repositioned him so his cheek was resting higher on her shoulder. "That's really nice of you, but he's getting so big now. I can't carry him around for a long time like I used to."

"I could carry him," I offered before I could think better of it. What the hell was I doing? "I mean, that is, if you trust me?"

Say no. You should say no.

Her smile returned, and I knew I was fucked.

"Yeah, I trust you."

CHAPTER 7

Casey

I snuck a covert peek at Jay. We were walking side by side in the humid night air, and he hoisted Gus up so a good portion of the weight was supported by his shoulder.

Compared to Jay, Gus looked tiny, but I knew after a while Jay's muscles would start to burn. It'd only been five minutes, but sweet relief already flowed through my aching arms and back.

An amused smile tugged at my lips while I watched Jay internally debate where to put his hands. He had one arm hooked across my son's chunky thighs to keep him anchored, but his palm hovered over Gus's spine, switching back and forth between lower or higher.

Ending his indecision, I gently grasped his wrist and pressed his open hand in between Gus's shoulder blades.

"You're doing great," I praised.

"Thanks. I don't—I've never held a little kid before."

He gave me a sheepish grin, and it was seriously adorable to witness such a vulnerable, uncertain moment from him. He always seemed so hard. Tough. That was true two years ago, and even more so now.

Tattoos peeked out of his black tank top. Designs were inked on his chest over his heart, and something was scrolled on the inner part of his left bicep. I couldn't read the words because they were in a different language.

The reddish stubble on his face matched the slightly messy hair on his head. He had a piercing in each ear. Nothing flashy. Just two black matte studs.

And his muscles. My God.

Shoulders and pecs bulged as he supported Gus, and I didn't miss the appraising looks he got from women passing by.

I couldn't blame them.

Seeing a man hold my sleeping child was weird. A good weird. The heartwarming sight caused a fluttery sensation in my stomach.

Or maybe that was just hunger.

I pressed a hand to my growling abdomen, hoping Jay couldn't hear it.

Charlene waved at us as we strolled by the slides.

"What does she owe you for?" I asked, not caring that I was being nosy.

Jay was a mystery, and this was probably the only time I'd ever have a chance to talk to him. I wanted to find out as much as possible. Plus, my opportunities for adult conversation were extremely rare. I didn't need rides or games. Just walking around and talking was enough fun for me.

"Hmm?" He looked confused by my question.

"The woman who's covering for you. You said she owes you."

"Oh. Charlene. Yeah, it wasn't a big deal. I just helped get her son into rehab a couple months ago."

My feet stopped moving. "That actually is a really big deal."

He shook his head. "Nah."

"Do you always downplay the good stuff you do?"

He pinned me in place with his sky-blue eyes, all light-heartedness gone. "I don't want you to have any misconceptions about who I am. I'm not a good man, Casey."

"Says who?"

"Says my criminal record. Says the dozens of dealers I sold drugs to. Says the thousands who are now addicted, passed out in a gutter somewhere because of me. Addiction ruins futures. Ends marriages. It even kills people. For all I know, Charlene's son was a casualty in the domino effect of my actions. I was just making it right. Fixing something I probably broke in the first place."

Speechless. I didn't have a response for that.

I'd never heard anyone own up to so many mistakes, and it was startling. Most people would make up a million excuses before taking responsibility for their actions.

And, at this point, most girls would've been grabbing their baby and running in the opposite direction.

But there was something about Jay that made me feel safe. There was so much kindness in his eyes, and when he looked at me… it was like he saw me as an individual, not just a woman who was an extension of her kid. Like I was important. Valued.

"How did you convince him to get sober?" I asked, continuing the conversation.

"I took him to visit the prison I'd just gotten out of. Showed him what his future looked like if he didn't clean up his act. Did you know I'm a felon?" Jay's tone was challenging.

Hard. Tough. Just like him.

Slowly, I nodded. "Small towns don't keep secrets."

His eyebrows furrowed, and for a second it looked like he was preparing to give me another lecture about how bad he was.

But we got interrupted.

"Casey Maxwell, is that you?"

Groan.

I recognized that voice, and she knew damn well that it was me.

I pasted on a smile as I turned toward my former best friend. "Hi, Erin."

Erin and I went way back. Like, all the way back to pre-school. Our friendship had always been complicated—there was a competitive edge to our camaraderie. I used to think it was because we sort of looked alike and strived to be like each other.

Imitation is the sincerest form of flattery, right? Spelling bees. Tests. Boys. Everything was a contest with her, and she usually won because she was born into better circumstances.

She was from Elmer. I used to love having sleepovers at her house because it was always a luxurious experience. Her home was basically a mansion by a pond, and she always had the best toys.

And yeah, there were times when I was jealous. How could I not be, when she had everything I ever wanted?

When I got pregnant and dropped out of high school, she seemed to relish in the victory instead of being supportive. To this day, she still came into the diner every few months, and she never failed to remind me of my situation. Or hers.

Juggling her footlong corndog, the brunette leaned in for a quick hug. "I thought I wouldn't get to see you again before we leave for college." She motioned behind her to her boy-friend. "Brian and I are headed off to Cornell soon."

"Yeah, I remember you saying that." About a dozen times.

Brian was the quiet, nerdy type, so thankfully all I got from him was an awkward wave.

"We're both studying vet med," Erin went on, taking a bite of her food. The next words came out garbled as she chewed. "Oh, the campus is just beautiful. You should come visit sometime."

"Thanks." I trapped my tongue between my teeth.

The invitation was just another jab. I wouldn't be going anywhere, and she knew it.

Erin's eyes swung to Jay and Gus.

"Little guy is all tuckered out, huh? Is this—" Shifting closer to me, she took another bite of her dinner and whispered, "Is this the dad? I thought he was in the slammer."

"This is my *friend*, Jay," I explained, mentally calling on all the strength of the good Lord to stop myself from slapping a ho.

I felt a muscled arm bump against my shoulder as Jay leaned close to Erin like he was about to divulge a secret.

"Uh, just a word of warning," he said quietly. "The meat for the corndogs is imported from overseas—Asia, I think. Rumor has it, those they're made from actual dogs. You know, to keep the budget down."

Erin paled and her chewing slowed. "Are you serious?"

Jay gave her a nod. "I heard they use Great Danes. They're big—almost like small horses. More bang for their buck."

Spitting the mangled food back into the paper container, she made some retching sounds. "Oh my God. That's disgusting."

Unfazed, Jay shrugged. "You never know what you're getting at a carnival. Also, the Ferris wheel is the most romantic ride we have, but old Lewis…" He tipped his chin toward the elderly man taking tickets at the entrance of the ride fifty feet away. "He's blind in one eye. Considering he's the one who put the damn thing together, I'd be careful." Then he directed his attention to Brian. "And every game here is rigged. Doesn't matter how accurate your aim is or how strong you are. You're just wasting your money."

"That's it. We're leaving." With a huff, Erin pulled Brian away. She dumped her corndog in the trash before stomping toward the parking lot.

I gaped at Jay.

I was trying really hard to contain my smile when I said, "You just ruined their night."

He grinned wide. "I know."

The smile I was trying to hold back made a grand appearance, stretching over my face. Because Jay put Erin in her place. No one had ever done that before.

"You deal with assholes like that a lot?" he asked, falling back into step like he hadn't just done something huge.

"Not really," I answered, forcing my small legs to keep up with his long, confident strides. "Erin is a rare breed, and thankfully, I don't see her often. I don't get out much, and Gloria's isn't exactly a hotspot for teenagers. We get a rotation of the same usual customers, but most of them are older. When someone I know from school does come in, they're usually polite. I think they're too scared I'll spit in their food if they're rude."

"Would you?"

"Would I what?"

"Spit in their food."

I wrinkled my nose. "No."

He gave me a half-smile. "You're sweet."

"Because I follow basic sanitary laws? I think that's just called being a decent employee."

Jay shrugged. "Guess I'm not as good as you because I just ruined corndogs for that girl forever, and I'm not even sorry."

"Is it true?" I asked. If so, I planned to avoid fair food for the rest of my life.

"No." He chuckled. "It's just a run-of-the-mill hotdog."

"And Lewis?"

"Well, he is blind in one eye, but he's a military veteran. Meticulous as fuck. Anything he puts together would probably outlast a tornado."

"And the last one? About the games?"

Jay grimaced. "Unfortunately, there's truth to that one. The games here are hard to win for a reason."

I nodded, thinking of the way we got tricked earlier. Circling around to the place where I lost Gus, I saw my discarded funnel cake on the ground. It'd been trampled on and smashed to pieces. My stomach gave another displeased rumble at the loss.

"You really chapped Erin's ass," I said to Jay, ignoring my hunger. "It's funny what you said about the dogs, because she has a Great Dane. That animal is like her baby."

"I know. Goes by the name of Sally."

My footsteps faltered, because I was confused. "You know Erin?"

Shaking his head, Jay readjusted Gus. "Nope. Never met her before."

"Then how did you…?" I cocked my head to the side.

"Her keychain."

"Her keychain," I deadpanned, coming to a complete stop again.

"You can tell a lot about a person by looking at their keychain," Jay explained, facing me. "Keys, membership tags, pictures. One glance and I know Erin loves her dog enough to carry around a name-plated picture of it. She drives a Prius. She goes to the Daywood Body Works gym, she swims at the Champaign public pool, and she goes to Starbucks too often."

My jaw dropped.

Sly. Smart. Unbelievably Perceptive.

Who the hell was this guy? Criminal record or not, he was too good to be working at a place like this.

"Let me see yours." He held out his hand, keeping his forearm firmly anchored to Gus's back.

Narrowing my eyes, I handed my keys over. Not like there were many to give.

He studied the two on the ring—one to my house and one to my car—and the double-sided picture of Gus and me from last Christmas.

"You drive a 2004 Ford Focus. You're a home-body," he murmured, rubbing a thumb over the photo. "And you love your son more than anything."

Taking them back, I dropped the key ring into my purse. "But you already knew those things about me, didn't you?"

He just smirked. I took that as a yes.

"Also, you really want a funnel cake," he added with a grin.

The mention of food made my stomach growl again, and I gave an embarrassed shrug. "No, it's okay."

I'd grabbed a burger and fries from Gloria's for Gus and me to split for dinner, but that was hours ago.

"You want it. The greasy goodness. The sugar," Jay taunted.

My mouth watered. "I don't have any cash left."

"Good thing I'm paying, then. I'm also going to win one of those rings." He jerked his head toward the balloon game and sauntered away.

I had no choice but to follow. "I don't want to waste your money. You already said yourself that they're rigged."

Amused, he flashed his white teeth. It wasn't an innocent smile. It was ornery and naughty. Full of mischief.

And really freaking sexy.

"Fortunately for you two, I know the tricks." He winked. "Food first. Then we'll get that prize."

CHAPTER 8

Jay

Very few people could finish an entire carnival-sized elephant ear all by themselves. But, yet again, Casey managed to surprise me. She'd been polite enough to offer to share, but I had a feeling she didn't get many things to herself.

So I declined.

And holy shit.

The girl could pack away some food.

While I straddled the picnic table bench with Gus in my arms, Casey went at the dessert like she was out to win a competition. There was no rhyme or reason to her methods. She tackled it in the middle and worked her way out, sometimes hopping around to the edge pieces.

White powder covered her hands, her mouth, and the front of her shirt. She'd even gotten a couple smudges on her nose and forehead.

It was adorable.

Gus's dead weight was starting to take a toll on my biceps. No matter how many hours I spent working out, time in the gym didn't compare to carrying around a twenty-pound body for this long.

How the hell did Casey do this?

She was a tiny thing, but she was in shape. Obviously, her muscle tone was from hard work; riding her bike instead of using her car, being on her feet all day at the diner, and carrying her kid around for hours.

When she began scraping up the remnants of sugar and licking it off her fingers, I laughed.

Looking over at me, she blushed. "Funnel cakes are my favorite."

She uncapped the bottle of water and downed half of it in a few gulps. Some dribbled down her chin.

Chuckling, I extended some napkins her way. "You're a beast. It's impressive."

She giggled, and the sound made my stomach flip. It was the first time I'd ever heard her laugh—really laugh. Not the forced kind when she was putting on a brave face.

I liked it a lot.

After wiping her hands and mouth, she brushed off the front of her shirt. "Better?"

"Actually…" Grabbing another napkin, I dabbed it against the cold bottle of water, collecting some of the condensation to dampen it. I held Gus securely to me as I scooted forward. "You have some right here."

I swiped her nose, then her forehead.

All clean.

But just because I liked touching her, I continued to blot at her face in quick, exaggerated motions.

Casey laughed again. "Oh, come on. Now you're just being dramatic. It can't be that bad."

"You're one of the messiest eaters I've ever seen," I teased, pretending she had sugar in her hair. I even wiped her ear.

That giggle again.

My heart soared.

And because I was a greedy bastard, I moved my focus down to the corner of her lips. There wasn't anything on that part of her face, but damn if I'd miss an opportunity to touch her there. Just once.

I rubbed the rough material slowly from one side to the other before caressing her cheek with my thumb.

"Done," I said huskily, letting the pad of my finger travel over her bottom lip.

A gasp left her pretty mouth. We locked eyes, and I kept my hand on her face.

Heat and desire reflected back at me in her darkened pupils. The look she gave me wasn't just fleeting sexual attraction. There was a deep well of need inside her. I recognized it because the same need resided inside of me.

The need for physical contact.

The need for an emotional connection.

The need to be loved.

And I felt like I was literally holding a dream come true in my hand.

With just one look, Casey made me feel like I wasn't just an ex-junkie. A loser. Undeserving and worthless.

Her tongue slipped out—just for a second—as she wet her lips. Whether it was intentional or not, she licked me, and I almost jumped out of my seat from shock.

My hand fell to my lap, and my thickening cock strained painfully against the zipper of my black slacks.

I'd spent the past three months wondering what it would be like to touch Casey, and now I knew.

It was like a hit of the finest drug. Intoxicating. Thrilling. Addicting.

Gus chose that moment to sigh deeply, reminding me of where we were.

"Place is gonna close up in about twenty minutes," I said regretfully, swaying back. "I've probably hogged this little guy for too long."

I lifted Gus, unplastering his sweaty body from my chest as I prepared to hand him back to his mom.

"Oh." She frowned as she scooped him into her arms. "Right. I guess we should get going."

"Here." I wrapped one last small remaining chunk of the dessert in a napkin and slipped it into her purse on the table. "For Gus."

"Thanks. He'll really like that." Her words were sincere, but she avoided my gaze.

The moment was broken, and it was for the best. Obviously, I had no self-control around this girl.

I stood before extending my hand to help her up. "You can't leave quite yet—not until I win that ring."

∼

"Hey, Turner." I slapped five dollars onto the counter.

"Dang it, Jay. I've got customers," he complained. "You're gonna clog up my line."

"Seriously?" I glanced over my shoulder at the vacant grass behind us. "I don't see a line."

"One round," he grumbled. "That's it."

Turner dropped three darts in front of me. One was perfect—straight, with three full feathers on the end to ensure good aim. I tested the weight of it in my palm, satisfied with how heavy it was.

But the other two... the feathers had been shaved down, and they were lighter. Probably hollow on the inside.

I pushed them back to Turner. "How you gonna do me like that, man?"

"What?" He played clueless.

"These crappy-ass darts couldn't hit a haystack. Give me the real ones."

Turner cursed, and Casey made a noise of disbelief next to me.

When I turned toward her, she was glaring at the deceptive pieces. She shot a mother-like stink-eye at Turner. It was so full of venom, even I felt ashamed. But this wasn't my booth and I had no say over how Turner ran his game.

Still, I wanted to make it up to her.

Time for Turner to learn a lesson.

As soon as I received the real darts, I paused and glanced at the beautiful girl on my left to do a short introduction. "Casey this is Turner. Turner, this is Casey and Gus. They're my special guests here tonight."

Then I threw the darts in rapid-fire fashion, hitting three balloons in quick succession.

Pop, pop, pop.

Still muttering, Turner produced the cheap prize bucket.

I shook my head and tossed another five dollars his way.

He swore again but gave me the same three darts.

Pop, pop, pop.

I could practically feel Casey's excitement. I stole a glance. She was biting her lip and bouncing Gus as her gaze hopped between Turner and me.

He picked up a bigger bucket—the 'tier two' prize. It was full of little stuffed animals. A variety of dogs, cats, and rabbits. Most kids probably would've been thrilled to have one, but it wasn't good enough for my new friends.

"This what you want, Casey?" I smirked, pointing at the prizes.

She shook her head, just like I knew she would.

I pushed the container away and handed over more money. "No, thanks. Again."

Three more balloons gone.

With a pleading glance, Turner showed us a teddy bear the size of a basketball.

I smiled slowly. "No."

"Fuck, man." Fidgeting, he was clearly agitated as he doled out another round. "I said once, Jay."

"Watch your language around the kid, Turner."

"How many times are we doing this?"

Pop, pop, pop.

"Until I get one of these." I stabbed a finger at the rings.

"Fine," he huffed. "Gimme five more."

It was the last of my cash, but having an empty wallet was totally worth it to see Casey's massive smile as she watched me kick ass. My aim was on point, hitting every intended target.

All the commotion must've drawn some attention, because when I glanced over my shoulder, a crowd had gathered, and a line was forming behind us.

So many hopeful, ambitious faces. The risk takers who saw someone do the impossible. The gamblers who thought they had a shot at achieving the same result.

Most of them would be leaving with an empty wallet just like me, only they probably wouldn't make it to the grand prize.

Turner didn't look so unhappy anymore. In fact, his tone was downright cheerful as swept his arm toward the clear display case.

"These are real sterling silver and cubic zirconia, ma'am," he said to Casey, projecting his voice so people could hear his sales pitch. "Which one would you like?"

Casey didn't need time to choose. She tapped the plastic case near the top row. "The pink one. Gus's favorite color is pink."

His keys jingled as he unlocked the back, reached in, and plucked up the ring. The jewel was about the size of a fingernail, and it sparkled under the lights when he handed it to her.

When Casey faced me, her face was bright with happiness.

"Don't thank me," I said, chucking her under the chin. Pressing a hand to her lower back, I led her out of the way so the next customer could have their turn.

"But—"

"I just made things right. On behalf of all carnies everywhere, you have my sincerest apologies for getting scammed."

"Okay," she conceded, stuffing the ring into the pocket of her shorts. "You just have no idea how happy this will make him." She patted Gus on the back. "I wish you could see his face when I give it to him."

I wished that, too.

But winning a prize didn't change reality—this was probably the first and last time I'd get to hang out with them. Because they were better off without me.

How many good deeds would I have to do before I felt like I'd made up for my past? I didn't know the answer, but at least I was one step closer to redemption.

CHAPTER 9

Casey

"**W**ant me to walk you to your car?" Jay asked.

"Sure." It wasn't necessary. I'd been walking myself to my car for years, but I wanted a little more time with him.

As we weaved back through the carnival, rides started shutting down and the food vendors were closing up. Little by little, the life drained from the fair. People filtered out, and I was sad it was over.

The evening might've gotten off to a rough start, but I hadn't had this much fun in a long time.

I had to keep reminding myself this wasn't a date, but it was difficult to remember when Jay was walking so close to me. When I could smell his citrusy scent. When his elbow kept bumping mine.

We were passing the Ferris wheel when he stopped. Charlene was sitting in the chair behind the chain that had a 'Closed' sign on it. She looked up from her phone and waved.

"Where's Lewis?" Jay glanced around.

Charlene rolled her eyes. "Beer tent. He asked me to take over for the last ten minutes so he could go booze it up."

"Who took the slides?"

"Slides were dead." Her gaze went to me. "You two wanna ride?"

"Oh." I looked down at Gus. "I'd love to, but he's zonked out. I don't think he'd enjoy it much."

Charlene chuckled.

"I meant you two." Gesturing between Jay and me, she opened her arms. "I'll hold the baby while you're up there."

Involuntarily, I tightened my arms around Gus. Random people didn't get to hold my kid. Jay was a rare exception. He wasn't a complete stranger, and despite his warnings about his character, he'd helped me on numerous occasions.

I didn't know Charlene at all.

Her eyes softened with understanding, and she slowly lowered her hands.

"I've been where you are now. Motherhood is no joke. Twenty years ago, I was young and raising my son alone. When you're in the thick of it, it feels like you'll never get out. Every tiny mistake feels massive." A bittersweet smile appeared on her face. "But eventually, they grow up, and they want to be away from you. Then they'll make their own mistakes. You never stop loving them, though."

"Yeah," I agreed, wondering what mistakes lay ahead for Gus.

"Sometimes you gotta take a few minutes to enjoy yourself, and that often means putting your trust in people who haven't earned it yet. It's scary, I know. But your sanity is important, too. Not just for you, but for him. What I'm trying to say is, he's safe with me. If you want five minutes on this thing, you got it." She flicked a finger at Jay. "You don't even have to go up with this knucklehead."

Jay barked out a laugh. "Ouch. I thought we were friends."

Nodding, she got up and approached us.

"Better than friends." Her face became serious as she pulled a silver chain over her head. In her palm, she cradled a plastic coin and showed it to Jay. "You saved my Dusty. He had this made for me. It represents one month of sobriety." She moved her hand toward me. "You can hang onto this for me while I hold your son. For collateral. It's the most precious thing I own."

"She's really good with kids," Jay supplied quietly. "She's a preschool teacher in the off-season."

That was actually really reassuring, and I let myself consider Charlene's offer.

Longing tugged at me as I looked up at the Ferris wheel. The pink lights along the spindles were so beautiful against the cloudless night sky. Twinkling stars shone above us in the end-less darkness, and I wanted to be closer to them.

I wanted just one ride. Just a few minutes to be me.

Some of my stress was self-inflicted—I was aware of that. I put so much pressure on myself because I had a hard time depending on other people.

"I'll sit right here with him," Charlene went on. "You'll be able to see us the whole time. If he wakes up, I'll bring you down."

I found myself bobbing my head as I stepped closer to her.

"This is Gus," I said quietly.

He let out a sigh when I placed him in her outstretched arms, but he didn't wake. Charlene cradled him perfectly across her middle, and she released her grasp on the necklace as it transferred to my fingers.

The round plastic piece felt so light in my hand. Cheaply made. Probably not meant to be durable, but it was beyond valuable.

And she was trusting me with it, just like I was putting my faith in her.

As I stuffed the coin into my pocket, Charlene slowly sank into the folding chair next to the control panel.

Tipping her head toward the metal stairs, she said, "Jay can help you get secured. Just wave at me when you're done."

"Okay." Apprehension and excitement warred within me as my tennis shoes made heavy clanking sounds on the structure.

I climbed into the car, which started rocking under my shifting weight. I let out a nervous giggle and looked up at Jay as I sat.

Now that my view wasn't blocked by Gus, I was able to see his entire upper body.

His very muscled, very chiseled body.

He shoved his hands into his pockets, and his arms tensed, causing his triceps to pop. Although his stance was somewhat casual, there was a keyed-up aura about him.

Wound tight.

With every breath he took, the inhale and exhale had a rippling effect on his abs. The black tank top was thin, and I could see the outline of his nipples through the material.

I thought about what it would be like to touch him. All the lines and indents. Nooks and crannies to be explored by my fingertips. Or my tongue.

A ball of heat formed in my lower belly, and I suddenly found it difficult to breathe. This time, when I struggled for air, it wasn't a panic attack.

My body came alive.

My nipples puckered in my bra, and my clit started pulsing. Squeezing my thighs together, I tried to quell the ache in my center, but the pressure only made it worse. I could feel dampness on my panties, and I was a little bit humiliated that this was happening in public.

Arousal was somewhat unfamiliar to me.

I was never given the chance to want a man—really want a man—with no coercion. Never allowed to travel the natural progression from innocence to being ready for sex.

Boy, was I ready now.

Swallowing hard, my gaze drifted up to Jay's eyes, hoping like hell he couldn't see the effect he had on me.

And his face. That was a work of art in and of itself. His features were an alluring combination of hard and soft. The line of his jaw was sharp, and his full lips looked like pillows. His nose was cute. Straight, a little bit wider than average, and the tip was rounded. It paired well with his prominent cheekbones.

Some serious sparks had gone off between us at the picnic table, and my stomach flipped at the thought of sitting so close to him again.

"Aren't you gonna get in?" I asked, scooting over.

He lifted his shoulders in a tight shrug, causing more rippling of muscles. "Figured you might like to have some time to yourself."

Suddenly shy, I glanced down at my lap. "Does anyone actually want to ride the Ferris wheel alone?"

A few seconds ticked by. "Not usually. Everyone I've seen going solo looks… sad."

"Do you think I'm sad?" I couldn't stop the words from coming out of my mouth, and I immediately regretted it. I didn't want to know the answer.

"Yeah," Jay replied.

I released a breath. He might as well have punched me in the stomach. It would've been less painful.

The truth hurts.

I was a mess. If he'd been watching us for any amount of time, that much would've been obvious.

But then he continued, "I also think you're beautiful. And strong, motivated, smart. I could think of a dozen other awesome adjectives. You're amazing, Casey. Don't ever forget that."

My mind was stuck on the word beautiful.

Beautiful. Beautiful. Beautiful.

That was just about the last word I would've used to describe myself.

I used to think I was pretty.

Not anymore.

I was too run down. I always had dark circles under my eyes. I rarely had time for makeup, all my clothes were old, and I was paranoid that I had the greasy-diner odor permanently embedded in my skin.

But somehow, hearing the compliment from Jay's lips made it somewhat believable.

Before I could form a response, he was getting in the car with me. The space was small—designed for two people sitting closely together—so our thighs were touching when he lowered the metal bar across our laps.

He gave a thumbs-up to Charlene, who looked pleased as punch to be rocking my son.

Then we were moving.

The wind ruffled my hair as we went backward and up. Up and up. The world slowly came into view as we peaked. My head went from one side to the other as I tried to take in all the sights, but then we were going down again.

When we made it up high a second time, I craned my neck, surveying everything below us.

Jay chuckled as we dipped. "You like it up there."

"Yeah, don't you? It's the best part." I looked to him and he nodded.

On the next way around, he signaled Charlene as we flew past her. "Hey, can you stop us at the top?"

The ride began to slow. We rotated for a full circle before we started moving at a snail's pace. Slowly, we inched up to the pinnacle of the Ferris wheel.

When we came to a halt, a feeling of peace fell over me.

Sometimes I felt like I just needed time to stop for a minute. A pause button for life. Just a few moments to sit back and find my bearings.

This was the closest I'd come to that since I was sixteen.

Up here, my problems seemed smaller. My blessings, bigger.

Grasping the bar, I leaned forward and looked at the tiny people in the distance.

There were so many lights.

Charlene and Gus below.

The twinkling stars above.

Jay didn't say anything as I gazed out at everything around us, but I could feel his eyes on me. When I'd looked my fill and relaxed, he finally spoke.

"So tell me more about you."

"Not much to tell."

"I don't believe that. Fill me in on the last two years. I bet yours is more exciting than mine."

I shrugged as I tried to think of where to start. It wasn't all that thrilling, but I had to admit it was better than being in prison.

"During the pregnancy, I kept working and I got my GED. Gus and I got our own place. That's about it. Pretty boring, huh?"

"Not boring at all. In fact, it's really impressive." When his response earned a skeptical glance from me, he continued, "I'm serious. You gotta get it out of your head that you're a failure. You're not doing anything wrong."

"You don't know me," I replied weakly. "You have no idea how often I disappoint myself."

"You're your own worst critic. No one is harder on you than you. Are you doing your best?"

Unsure of how to answer, I shook my head. "I don't know. I guess. I mean, I *try*."

"Are you doing your best?" He emphasized every word, saying them slowly, his voice firm.

Was I? Was there anything I could be doing better? I thought about the sleepless nights and the days I busted my ass serving food and coffee. How we always had enough to eat. All the doctor appointments when Gus got sick. His closet full of clothes and his basket of rings.

And I knew the answer. "Yes, I'm doing my best."

Jay grinned. "Damn right you are."

I smiled, and it was strange to feel good about myself. High self-esteem was a foreign concept to me, but as I hovered a hundred feet off the ground, I felt proud.

Still, Jay didn't seem to understand how much I'd changed over the years, and not for the better.

"Once upon a time I was different," I said, gazing up at the sky. "I wasn't afraid of everything. I was funny. My friends always said I was the smart one." I scoffed. "Back when I had friends, anyway. I guess they changed their minds about that when I got pregnant. But you know what? I don't regret it. I could never regret Gus."

A small smile tugged at Jay's lips. "Good. I'm glad there's a Gus, too."

My heart gave a happy thump at the sincerity in his statement. "I guess sometimes I just miss who I used to be. I used to watch TV shows that weren't cartoons. I used to do my makeup and paint my nails. I used to love to read and draw and listen to music and dance. I haven't gotten to do those things in a long time. I didn't even get to go to prom."

"Well, we have that in common. Not the painting the nails part," he added jokingly. "But I'm not who I used to be either. Although, in my case, that's a good thing. And I didn't go to my prom because I got too fucked up. Passed out before I could even get my tux on."

"I bet your date was pissed."

Wincing, he scratched his jaw. "I let a lot of people down back then. Friends, girlfriends, family. I didn't care about anyone but myself when I was high."

"But you're different now," I surmised. "You're better."

"I like to think so. And you're better, too, even if you don't realize it. All that stuff you told me is great, but I'm not interested in who you used to be. I'm interested in who you are now."

"You're interested in me?" I held my breath while I waited for his answer.

"More than I have any right to be," he replied, his intense stare boring into mine. His lips curled up when he reached forward to touch my necklace. "You still have this thing."

His knuckles brushed my skin as he rolled it between his fingers.

I shivered.

"I never take it off." Unintentionally, I swayed forward a fraction, putting our faces less than a foot apart. "The chain broke a long time ago, but the string holds up pretty well."

"It reminds me of you," he said, still studying the glass.

"What do you mean?"

"A teardrop represents sadness." Holding it a few inches away from my skin, he angled the prism so it caught the light. Dozens of colorful reflections danced on his neck and face. "But this shines rainbows on everything around it. It's selfless. Self-sacrificing. Heartbreakingly beautiful."

There was that word again.

"You keep calling me beautiful." My voice came out quiet, but inside, my heart was thundering.

Jay's eyes bounced up to mine. "That's because I mean it." His gaze dropped to my lips. "You ever been kissed on a Ferris wheel?"

"No."

"Let's fix that."

And then he was closing the distance.

It was like my life was in slow motion when his lips softly met mine. I jolted inside, as if electricity flowed between us.

His hand came up to cup my cheek, and our mouths fused in a sensual closed-mouth kiss. I could say with complete certainty that Jay's lips were as soft as they looked.

I thought that was it. A quick pity kiss for the sad single mother.

I was wrong.

Because what started out somewhat chaste turned hot. Fast.

Jay's palm slipped to the back of my neck to hold me in place while his tongue swiped over the seam of my lips. I made a satisfied noise as I opened for him.

Delving into my mouth, his tongue was smooth as it expertly massaged mine.

I didn't know it was possible to kiss someone like you had all the time in the world, but the pace was unbelievably slow.

I also didn't realize kissing could be a full-body experience, but I felt every lick and nibble from head to toe.

I was dizzy. My chest felt full, but my throbbing core was painfully empty. My fingertips and toes tingled.

As our tongues pushed against each other, I held in a moan. Jay pulled back, sucking at my top lip before going back for more.

We moved together in perfect rhythm, our mouths melding as the kiss deepened.

Needing something to hold onto, I brought my hand up to grasp his wrist, and that was when I realized I was shaking. I was so turned on, so overwhelmed with sensation, so overcome with excitement, my body was buzzing.

My trembling fingers squeezed his muscled forearm, and I pressed closer. My right breast grazed his chest, and a *zing* went through my hardened nipple all the way down to my clit.

Hooking his thumb under my jaw, Jay tilted my head as he slanted his mouth over mine from a different angle.

So good.

He devoured me. Consumed me.

When he kissed me like this, he didn't have to say I was beautiful, because I felt it.

My quivering hand slid up Jay's arm. The tips of my fingers bumped over his bulky shoulders as my palm glided to his firm chest.

I'd just sucked on Jay's plump lower lip when he abruptly pulled back. Our mouths separated with an audible smooch as he scooted away from me.

Well, as far as he could get without diving over the edge.

Eyes wide with shock, he swiped a thumb over his lips, looking at me like he couldn't believe what just happened.

Was he wiping my kiss off? Oh, God. Was I a bad kisser? It was totally possible. I wasn't the most practiced in the field.

"We shouldn't have done that." Jay glanced straight ahead, severing our connection. "It was a mistake."

Ouch. I mean, really. *Ouch.*

Mortified, I couldn't form a response. The word *mistake* replaced *beautiful*, and my face burned with humiliation and hurt.

"You shouldn't get tangled up with a guy like me, Casey," Jay warned gruffly, and I couldn't tell if he was just making an excuse to let me down easy.

I raised my chin. "I guess we have something else in common. No one is harder on you than you, right?"

"Except for my probation officer." His sardonic smile indicated he meant it as a joke, but I didn't feel like laughing.

Tonight was a weird mixed bag of some of the best and worst moments I'd ever had, and the extreme highs and lows left my body feeling wrung out.

Now I just wanted to go home.

Jay waved down to Charlene, and the wheel started moving again.

Just as we made it to the bottom, I turned to him. The only repayment I could give him for his kindness was some encouraging advice.

"Are you doing your best, Jay?" I threw his question back at him.

He clenched his jaw, all serious and brooding. Sexy. "Yes."

"Then maybe it's time you stopped thinking of yourself as a failure, too."

CHAPTER 10

Jay

What the hell had I been thinking, kissing Casey like that?

That damn Ferris wheel was to blame.

Like the weak man I was, I got caught up in the magic of the atmosphere. Our heart-to-heart conversation reeled me in, and the way she looked at me—like I wasn't complete garbage—sealed the deal.

Casey made me feel worthy. Better. Because that was her way—she improved everything around her, even at the utter destruction of herself.

I kept picturing the teardrop prism on her neck. Worn but resilient. Tragic and beautiful. Weathering every storm, while throwing indiscriminate rainbows on ugly things.

I still felt her.

Days later, all the places she touched me tingled as if she became a part of me, but now she was a phantom limb.

Running my thumb over my lower lip, I remembered the way she sucked on it. How she tasted like powdered sugar. How strong the urge had been to keep going.

To never stop.

Past memories of physical intimacy in my pre-prison years were difficult to recall. Details were all muddled in my mind because I was drunk or high or both. Sensations were dulled. Faces were blurred.

Not with Casey.

I'd been on sensory overload. So sweet. Smooth. Wet.

Adorably sexy dimples.

Long, dark eyelashes.

The warm skin on her neck.

The way the smooth strands of her hair tickled between my fingers.

When she'd reciprocated with enthusiasm and passion, it took everything I had not to push for more. To put my hands on places they had no right to be.

And when I felt my balls draw up tight, I knew I was in trouble.

The first time I kissed someone sober, I almost nutted in my pants.

A bit embarrassing, but it was the reality check I needed.

I hated getting off that ride. Dreaded walking Casey and Gus to the parking lot. Loathed letting them go.

But I did it anyway.

I didn't ask to see them again. Didn't get a phone number before watching them drive away.

I hadn't seen the object of my obsession since then.

Scratch that—I'd seen her. She just hadn't noticed me lurking.

When I wasn't working, I was in my apartment, watching her through the back door.

Saturday morning, Casey went grocery shopping. It took her three trips to and from her car to carry in the bags. I could've gotten them all in one. I briefly thought about going over to offer my help, but that would've defeated the purpose of trying to stay away.

Then, yesterday she and Gus played in her small yard. They dug with shovels in their turtle-shaped sandbox and drew on the sidewalk with chalk. Several neighbors said hello as they passed by, but no one stayed for a visit. It was just the two of them, making memories together. Memories Gus was probably too young to remember later.

Funny how things we can't recall shape the kind of people we turn out to be. Every kiss she gave him, every sandcastle they built, every doodle they drew—the seemingly insignificant moments were making impressions on his mind and heart.

And I knew without a doubt that he was going to be okay. They both were. Come hell or high water, they'd succeed.

Which was why I needed to leave this place. Being this close was too tempting for me.

And for her.

Every now and then, Casey had glanced over at the apartments, searching the darkened windows. Probably looking for me, wondering which unit was mine.

But I was hiding inside, cloaked in shadows like a stalkerish asshole. Just sat in my recliner while my dick got hard for the last person I should be with.

Some fucking creepy shit.

Morning light filtered in as I kicked my legs up on the recliner footrest and took a sip of coffee.

The newspaper crinkled in my lap as I combed through the 'For Rent' section. I circled a couple possibilities with blue ink. They were more expensive than I'd like, but they weren't in Brenton. Major plus.

Maybe I could find something in Daywood near my mom. Or maybe I should go somewhere farther. I wasn't allowed to leave the state while I was on probation, but distance was the only thing that would keep me from Casey now.

Glancing at the time, I noted that it was almost seven, and I was surprised she hadn't left for work yet. She was always out the door by now on Mondays.

Leaning so close to the window my nose was almost touching it, I squinted at Casey's home. Her white curtains were closed. Her bike was propped up against the porch. Her beige car was parked in the same spot it always was.

There was an eerie stillness about the place, and suddenly a bad feeling came over me.

Call it intuition. My instincts had always been on point. My mom used to call it my Spidey sense. It was a sickening feeling in my stomach. A rapid pulse. A tightening in my chest.

Honestly, it felt a lot like a panic attack.

If I'd listened to my gut the night of my arrest, I never would've gotten caught in the first place. I would've stayed away from that fight because I could tell something was off.

But the warning bells blaring inside my body now? This was different, because it wasn't about me. I didn't like it at all.

Calm the fuck down. She probably has the day off.

Draining my mug, I went to the meadow in my mind. My safe place full of wildflowers, butterflies, and the smell of dirt baking in the hot sun.

It helped a little.

Eyeing the trailer, I stood up. I was just about to start pacing when I saw Casey's mom slowly striding away from her house toward Casey's. She let herself inside, and less than twenty seconds later, Casey flew out of her front door at an impressive speed.

Ah. Running late, then.

She flung her purse into the passenger seat of her car as she jumped in. Gravel kicked up when she hit the gas, and I saw a pinched expression on her face as she sped away.

Yikes. She was pissed.

I let out a sigh of relief.

Everything was fine, and I was glad Casey's mom was helping, even if she made Casey run behind.

I should've been able to relax then, but the uneasy sensation continued nagging at me.

To distract myself, I did some laundry and dishes, made my bed, and picked up some cluttered coffee mugs. There wasn't much to clean—I didn't own a lot of shit.

While I mopped the linoleum floor, I turned on some bad talk shows about paternity tests and cheating spouses for background noise. The orange scent of the cleaner was pleasant, but it seemed like no matter how much I scrubbed at some of the spots on the tiles, they always looked dirty.

In all honesty, this was a pretty crappy place to live. These complexes had been poorly built decades ago. They were riddled with structural issues and bottom-of-the-line materials. Cracks in the drywall decorated the ceiling, and the white walls wore smudges and scratches by former residents.

But for how cheap it was, I couldn't complain. Besides, I'd lived in worse conditions.

Around noon, I made myself a sandwich and went out to the balcony to eat my lunch while perusing potential jobs in the paper.

The career search wasn't going well. Nothing could change the black mark on my resume.

Felon. Having that word branded on me was an ugly scar I would carry around forever. I'd served my time, but the consequences of my actions continued to echo throughout every aspect of my life.

It seemed like temporary work was all I could find. The carnival job was great, but it was short-lived.

Frustrated, I let out a growl as I turned to the second page of the help-wanted ads.

Banks were a no-go. Schools were definitely out. I actually liked the idea of being a cop, but any type of law enforcement wouldn't take me. I'd been turned away at an animal shelter earlier in the summer. Apparently, I wasn't even fit to be around dogs and cats.

I was willing to do dirty work and I wasn't against a short commute, but even janitorial jobs at the university in the city thirty minutes away were extremely hard to snag; I'd applied three times.

I hated feeling stuck.

And I also hated the bad feeling from earlier that I still couldn't shake.

In fact, it'd gotten worse. My anxiety was higher, and my stomach was in knots. But despite my nonexistent appetite, I couldn't let a good sandwich go to waste.

Haphazardly folding the newspaper, I dropped it in my lap and picked up my food.

At least I could enjoy this—the freedom to sit in the sun and leisurely eat a meal of my choosing.

I'd only taken two bites when movement over the trailer park caught my eye.

Smoke.

Not regular smoke. Fire smoke.

Shooting up from my chair, I just about choked on the bite in my mouth when I saw streams of the gray clouds curling out of Casey's front windows.

Fuck.

The bread, lunch meat, and cheese fell to the wooden planks with a *splat*.

I didn't think—I just acted.

Climbing over the balcony railing, I jumped down to the parking lot below and broke out into a sprint.

Good thing I had socks on. The debris on the asphalt surface would've shredded the bottoms of my feet. Dirt, gravel, and broken glass flew behind me as I ran faster than I ever had in my life.

Tunnel vision took over. All I could see were the dark billowing clouds pouring from the trailer.

Asthma. Even a person with healthy lungs couldn't be in there for long without serious damage. I needed to get Gus out.

In total, it probably took less than thirty seconds to make it to the front porch, but the trip from across the street seemed like a lifetime.

My feet pounded up the steps, and I wrapped the bottom of my T-shirt around my hand, protecting my skin as I turned the hot doorknob.

When the door opened, I was hit with a wall of smoke.

Coughing, I stepped back. "Gus!"

Covering my face with my shirt, I waved my other arm, attempting to clear my vision. Some of the haze dissipated as the smoke escaped.

I took a deep breath, and I crossed the threshold of the burning building.

My eyes teared from the fumes, but I could see.

To my right, the floor-length curtains were ablaze, and Casey's mom was there, trying to put out the flames by hitting them with a towel.

"Where's Gus?" I asked, but she was too busy swatting at the fire to answer me. "Laura!" I shouted, and that got her attention.

We'd never been introduced, but thanks to my investigating back in the day, I knew her name. She was tan, bleach-blonde, and thin. Although she was only in her thirties, she looked much older. The only characteristic she and Casey shared were their eyes.

Remorseful blues full of panic flitted to me. "Help me put this out!"

"Where the fuck is Gus?" I roared urgently, and she

pointed in the opposite direction toward a closed door at the end of the hall.

I got there in four long strides. As soon as I turned the knob, I heard one of the best sounds in the world—crying.

Good. If Gus was wailing that loud, that meant he could breathe, and right now, that was all I cared about.

I opened and closed the door as fast as I could, hoping to keep the smoke out. It was a little hazy in here, but so far, the flimsy wood had been an effective barrier.

Not for long, though. This place was old, the materials cheap, and the walls thin. It was about to go up like a box of matches.

"Hey, dude." I crossed the small room.

Gus was standing in his crib, looking at me with sharp skepticism as I picked him up. He started crying again.

There was no time to make sure the kid remembered who I was, but he let me know of his displeasure in a series of high-pitched screeches. I didn't know if he was terrified of the strange man busting into his house or if his lungs were hurting. Of course I didn't want him to be scared of me, but I preferred that over the latter.

I carried him to the window. It was the only way out of the bedroom; I wasn't about to go back the way I came in.

As I shoved it open and kicked at the screen, Gus let out a few tiny coughs.

Shit, shit, shit.

"Okay, hang on to me." I put his hand on my shirt collar, imitating what I'd seen him do to Casey a hundred times. "We're gonna get out of here."

The window was a tight fit, but I was able to maneuver us through the opening without so much as a scrape to Gus. My long legs had no trouble reaching the ground, and then we were out.

To safety. To clean air.

Adrenaline pumped through my body as I breathed deeply and took us farther from danger. A maniacal laugh burst from me because I'd never been more relieved in my entire life.

"We did it. You're okay, Gus. You're okay."

Concerned neighbors had gathered across the street, and several let out grateful cries when I ran over with Gus.

I turned back to the trailer, and I could see Laura still inside. Now she was tossing cups of water on the wall, but the fire had spread. Orange flames were licking up the siding, and the roof was looking charred.

"I already called the fire department," one woman said. "Is he hurt?"

I glanced down at the little boy.

His face was streaked with tears, but he was clean. Sticking my nose by his hair, I sniffed. A little smoky, but not bad.

"I don't think he was in there for too long, but I'm not a medical expert." Patting Gus, I checked his body parts. Feet. Legs. Stomach. Arms.

All seemed good. Physically, at least.

He was a little shaken up, but not nearly as bad as I was.

Fucking terrifying. That was the only way to describe the past few minutes.

"You saved that baby's life," someone said to my left. "You're a hero." The woman cupped her hands around her mouth and yelled, "Laura! Honey, come out of there. Let the firemen handle it."

"What is she still doing in there?" I hissed to no one in particular.

I didn't want to go back in to haul her ass out, but I'd do it.

"That lady's always been a few bricks shy of a full load," a random pre-teen boy answered, shaking his head.

His mom clung to him as she viewed the tragedy,

sympathy in her eyes. Casey had just lost her home. In a matter of minutes, everything she owned was gone.

Well, not everything.

Casey's most important possession was in my arms, safe and sound. He'd even stopped crying because he was busy studying my earrings.

My tone was light when I joked, "Man, you just can't seem to stay out of trouble, huh?"

He gave me an incredulous look so appropriate for the moment that it made me laugh.

"Okay, okay. This one wasn't your fault."

"Shit. Shit." Laura's cussing drew my attention back. Abandoning her mission, she swore like a sailor on her way down the porch stairs. She jogged over, a light film of gray soot covering her from head to toe. "Casey's gonna be so mad at me."

No shit, Sherlock.

"Maybe you should be concerned about your grandson," I snapped. "Did you even check to see if he was out of the house?"

"I saw you got him."

"And what if I hadn't been here?" Voicing the question caused an unpleasant sinking in my gut. "How long would he have had to stand there, stuck in his crib, while you tried to save your own skin?"

"I was trying to save Casey's house," she shot back. "The fire could've been put out by now if you'd helped me."

Oh, hell no.

"The first thing you should've done was make sure he was safe." I clenched my jaw so hard my teeth hurt. "End of story."

As if to prove my point, Gus began coughing. I patted his back, feeling completely helpless. I didn't know anything about asthma. No clue about what signs to look for, or how to make him better.

"Can you breathe, buddy? Like this?" I inflated my middle, exaggerating the motion.

Laura outstretched her arms. "Give him to me."

"Absolutely not." I moved away.

Her expression turned outraged. "Why?"

"Look at yourself. You're a walking chimney. It's not good for him."

"Who the hell are you?"

"A friend."

Her eyes narrowed. "Well, I'm family and I'm the babysitter. Gus is supposed to be with me today."

"I can't speak for Casey, but I'm pretty sure you're *fired*, no pun intended."

She opened her mouth to respond but didn't get the chance because sirens blared in the distance. A fire truck sped down Main Street, lights flashing as it passed the small business district.

Including Gloria's Diner.

Casey.

God. What the hell was she gonna do now?

I glanced back at the trailer. There was no way it'd be livable after this.

As the noise of the fire engine got louder, Gus began to cry again.

"It's okay." I pressed the side of his head to my shoulder while covering his other ear with my palm. "They're just here to help."

We all moved back, clearing a path for the truck. It slowed to a stop just past Casey's house, and Laura ran over to talk to the fire chief. I could hear her filling him in on what happened, but I couldn't make out the words over Gus's wailing.

Three firefighters emerged from the truck. After quickly assessing the situation, they got the hose going. Powerful jets of water soaked the front of the house, spraying inside through the open window and door.

The sound of squealing tires grabbed my attention. I looked to the entrance of Brenton Estates to see Casey's car hauling ass around the corner.

I held up a hand to signal that Gus was okay, but she didn't get the memo. Slamming on the brakes, the car skidded to a stop in someone else's driveway. The driver's side door swung open with an unnerving screech.

Casey's eyes were wild when they zeroed in on her distraught son in my arms.

She ran to us, her hands pressed to her unusually pale face. "What happened?"

Handing Gus over, I quickly relayed the last five minutes. Told her about how I'd been sitting on my balcony when I saw the smoke and how I'd gotten Gus out as fast as I could. I didn't know what started the fire. I left Laura out of it, since I didn't want to start shit between Casey and her mom.

"How much smoke did he breathe in?" she asked, checking him for injuries the same way I'd done.

"Not much, I think. From the time I saw the smoke to when we climbed out the window, I'd say it was a minute or two. Fortunately, his room was fairly clear since the door was shut."

"Has he been short of breath? Wheezing? Turning blue?" She put an ear to his chest.

"Turning blue?" I asked, alarmed. Seriously, what the fuck?

She nodded, still listening to Gus's breathing. "It can happen during an asthma attack if it's bad."

Okay, that was some scary shit.

"No, none of that," I reassured her. "Just a few coughs."

"Okay, good. That's so good." She looked relieved for about two seconds before her eyes searched the crowd. Her voice became high with panic when she asked, "Is my mom still inside?"

She started to pass Gus back to me, as if she was planning to run in there herself.

"She's out. She's fine, Casey."

Deflating, she closed her eyes and inhaled slowly. I was afraid she might have another panic attack, but she took a few more deep breaths while hugging Gus snugly to her chest.

"My bubbie," she murmured, raining a few kisses onto his head. "I was so scared."

Laying his head on her shoulder, Gus sucked on his thumb and rubbed Casey's shirt collar against his cheek.

Anyone could see how much he loved her. How she was his everything. He gazed up at her like she was all he needed to be happy.

I wanted that. Someday, I wanted someone to look at me that way.

Casey turned to her crumbling home. Most of the flames were out now, but not gonna lie—it was in bad shape.

The front part of the house where the fire began was completely blackened. Dark rings from smoke damage lined the windows, and the roof appeared to be caving in on one side. Not to mention, everything was soaked, inside and out.

"My house. My house. My house," Casey chanted, her voice wavering.

I didn't know what to say, but I couldn't stand to see her upset. Doing the only thing I could, I engulfed Casey and Gus, looping my arms around them. "Don't look. Just don't look, okay?"

Casey became still as I rubbed her back and pressed my

nose to the top of her head. She smelled like pancakes, French fries, and coffee.

Gus was wedged between us, a hand on each of our collars. I looked down at his fingers, the way he clung to me.

And it felt like he was squeezing my heart instead. Something about seeing him connect the two of us made me ache for a dream I'd written off a long time ago.

A family of my own.

A lifetime kind of love.

A chance to give a child the trust and security I didn't have growing up.

Tilting her head back, Casey peered up at me. "What are you doing?"

Hell if I knew.

What, exactly, was she asking? Why was I touching her? Why did I run into a burning building for her son? Why couldn't I leave her alone?

Her long ponytail tickled my forearm, and I briefly let go of her to wind the strands around my finger.

"I don't know," I answered honestly. "Distracting you?"

Inching closer, she didn't question my motives further, but then her tennis shoe crushed one of my toes.

I winced. "Ow."

Casey stepped back and frowned down at my feet. "You're not wearing shoes."

I tried to grin but a grimace was all I could manage. "Like I said—got here fast."

"I don't understand how this happened." Shaking her head, she glanced back at her wrecked home.

I didn't understand it either. Only one person could explain that story.

And speak of the devil…

"I got burnt pretty bad." Laura came over, clutching her

right arm. "I'm so sorry, honey. It was just one cigarette while Gus took a nap."

Any hope I had that there wouldn't be drama between the pair evaporated.

"What?" Casey's voice was deadly calm, and something in her tone sent chills down my spine. Her eyes were wide as saucers as she stared at her mom. "What did you say?"

"You know the window that doesn't have a screen? I opened it to air out the room while I had a smoke. When I was finished, I tried to toss the butt outside, but I guess I missed. I didn't realize it got tangled in your curtain. Must've been there for several minutes, because I went to go make myself lunch. Before I knew it, I turned around and there were flames everywhere. I tried to put it out." Laura extended her arm to show us the evidence of her battle scars. Blisters were forming on her wrist. "See? I'm hurt."

Playing the victim. Not cool. If she wanted sympathy from me, she wasn't going to get it. Apparently, she wouldn't get it from Casey either.

"You were smoking in my home?" she asked low, the color coming back to her cheeks. A red flush of anger started at the base of her neck and worked its way up.

Laura started to cry. "I said I was sorry."

"Sorry doesn't fix this." Casey threw a hand toward her trailer. "How did the fire get so out of control? Didn't the smoke detector go off as soon as it started?"

Grinding her teeth, Laura guiltily glanced away. "I took the battery out. I didn't want it to go off while Gus was taking a nap."

Oh, fuck.

Shit was about to get real. My eyes volleyed back and forth between the women, wondering what level of hell was going to break loose.

Fortunately, the ambulance showed up, interrupting the tension-filled moment. Gus jerked at the loud siren, covering his ears as it got closer. It parked two trailers away from us, and a paramedic came out.

"Does someone need medical attention?"

"I do." Laura raised her injured hand.

"He does." I pointed at Gus. "He might've inhaled some smoke and he has asthma."

They all went over to the ambulance to get checked out. While they talked about medical history and what happened today, I paced the gravel road as I looked at what was left of Casey's house.

I had no idea how she was keeping it together. Maybe she was in shock. She sounded calm and collected as she quietly murmured responses to the EMT. Gus started screaming when they tried to take him from her arms.

My stomach dropped at the gut-wrenching sound, and I was surprised by how much it affected me.

Realizing Gus would cooperate much better if he was with Casey, they let her get into the back of the vehicle with him while they strapped on a baby-sized oxygen mask.

"We'd like to bring him in, just in case." I heard them tell Casey.

"Yeah, of course," she responded. "Can I ride with him?"

"Yes."

"Can I go, too?" Laura cut in. "I don't think I can drive with my hand all burnt up."

"But my car…" Casey protested. "Can't you drive it? How am I supposed to get home later?"

"I'll ride with Gus in the ambulance," Laura countered. "You meet us there."

"No, I'm not leaving him."

"I'll take care of him. He'll be safe with me."

Casey barked out a humorless laugh. "Do you have any idea how crazy that sounds coming from you right now? I trusted you. Of all the selfish, irresponsible things you've ever done—"

"I'll drive your car," I intervened, stepping closer.

All eyes turned my way and I sheepishly rubbed the back of my neck, feeling like an intruder.

I silently begged Casey to say yes. In all honesty, I wanted to go. Wanted to see this through.

It'd been a long time since I was this worried about someone other than myself, and it wasn't just about Casey or my infatuation with her. Gus had unknowingly wormed his way into my heart when he held onto my collar.

Casey didn't argue with me. In fact, she didn't hesitate to dig her keys out of the pocket of her jeans and toss them my way.

I was glad she didn't put me through the 'are you sure' and 'you don't have to do this' dance. This wasn't a time for politeness.

"I'll meet you at the ER," I told her with a reassuring nod. "I'll be in the waiting room when you're done."

"We can call in a second ambulance for you," one of the paramedics said to Laura.

"Unless you'd like to ride with me," I piped up, jingling the keys.

The only response I got was a scowl. I'd take that as a no, then.

Casey's momma didn't like me. Noted.

CHAPTER 11

Jay

I didn't go straight to the hospital. After going home to put on some damn shoes, I made a pit stop at Walmart.

Mentally checking off all the basic necessities Casey and Gus might've lost, I walked the rows in the baby section. He needed diapers and wipes, definitely. Rash cream, probably. Shampoo. Lotion. A teething toy that squeaked.

God, this shit was expensive.

Maybe prices had gone up since I was a kid.

Because ten dollars for a bottle? It was the most expensive one and it had a crap ton of parts, but the package said it was doctor recommended. Did kids Gus's age even use bottles? Better safe than sorry. I got a couple sippy cups, too.

I tossed them into the cart along with some groceries—milk, bread, applesauce, crackers, jarred baby food, frozen pizzas, and cookies.

How the hell did single parents afford all this?

I remembered how things were for my own mom. Bare cupboards and empty stomachs were common in our house. My sister and I wore second-hand clothes until holes formed and seams gave out. Christmases and birthdays were bittersweet. Mom scraped up as much money as she could to give us each something special, but too many of those days ended with her crying herself to sleep.

I shook my head to clear my thoughts. Now wasn't the time for a trip down memory lane.

What else did I need?

Toys. Kids loved those.

I felt like a complete idiot as I checked each package for the correct age range. The decision came down to a dump truck with some colorful balls and a plush puppet set with a king, a queen, a dragon, and a fairy.

I couldn't choose, so I went with both.

Placing them in with the rest of the merchandise, I paused.

I knew what Gus really wanted.

Rings.

I headed to the jewelry section and found a cheap set of a dozen rings. They varied in color and size, but most importantly, they all sparkled. Perfect.

When I saw a plain silver chain, I thought of Casey and that nylon band she used for her prism. It was probably weird for me to buy her a necklace, but I couldn't stop myself.

Pushing the cart forward, I headed to the clothes.

The clearance aisle had a few racks of baby outfits. I held up a baseball pajama set that looked like it was the right size. Over the chest of the shirt, it said 'Daddy's Little Slugger.'

A lump formed in my throat. Gus would have to grow up seeing other kids wearing stuff like this when he couldn't. And that sucked.

I put it back and chose one with dinosaurs instead. After snagging a few more mix-and-match shirts and shorts, it was Casey's turn.

I went to the women's clothes and picked out some black yoga pants and a couple plain T-shirts in a size small.

Underwear. Casey needed that, too, but I didn't know her bra size. If I had to eyeball it, I'd have guessed a solid B cup, but I didn't want to get it wrong. I picked up a multi-pack of sports bras and smiled to myself. I was a genius.

Next, lacy panties taunted me from the racks.

I tried—really tried—not to get a boner as I fingered the black silk, but I pictured it on Casey's body. I imagined the way it would curve over her ass cheeks if she bent over.

Adjusting the front of my pants, I quickly knocked a few bikini-cut panties into the cart.

I was about to head for the checkout when I realized I almost forgot one of the most important items: a crib.

And talk about sticker shock.

I chose a basic one with a white frame, but it didn't include the mattress. Together, the two items cost more than a month's rent.

By the time I made it out of the store, I felt a little sick at the amount of cash I'd just dropped. Years ago, I wouldn't have blinked at five hundred dollars. Hell, I used to blow that much on beer and other recreational substances nightly.

And what did I have to show for it? Twenty-one months in the big house.

At least this was a good investment, even if it was making a huge dent in my bank account.

CHAPTER 12

Casey

Your house is on fire.

I'd never forget what it felt like to hear those words.

When Gloria told me I had a phone call from a neighbor, I immediately knew something was wrong. People didn't call me at work unless it was an emergency.

Now, I felt like I was stuck in a nightmare.

This wasn't real. I'd wake up any second. We'd be back in our home instead of the emergency room. But no matter how many times I pinched myself, that didn't happen.

Numbness settled over me as I trudged out to the waiting room with Gus on my hip. He was wearing the hospital gown they let him have, because his smelly clothes had to be thrown out. His hair was still damp from when I'd rinsed it out in the sink.

But he was okay.

Sleepy from missing his nap, but okay, nonetheless. The doctor said he was extremely lucky. It was literally a difference of a minute. One more minute in the smoke, and today could've had a very bad outcome.

They'd given Gus a breathing treatment just to be safe, but thanks to Jay, the smoke inhalation was minimal.

I couldn't say the same for my mother.

The burns on her arm weren't as bad as her lungs, and the state of her poor health wasn't caused by the fire.

Smoking two packs a day for over fifteen years had taken its toll. I overheard the doctor tell her if she didn't quit, she probably wouldn't live to see fifty. Her blood pressure was sky high, and they were concerned about her cardiovascular health. They wanted her to make an appointment with her primary doctor for additional testing.

Angry or not, the thought of completely losing my mother was terrifying. No one wants to go through life without their mom, regardless of how strained the relationship may be.

Glancing around the waiting room, I spied reddish-brown hair. Jay's head was hanging down, his elbows resting on his knees.

He must've sensed my presence somehow, because his shoulders stiffened before he looked up. A strange sense of comfort cloaked me when his worried gaze met mine.

For some reason, having him here zapped the numbness away and replaced it with so many emotions.

Fear and relief.

Gratefulness for him, and grief over the unmeasurable loss.

My eyes stung, and tears threatened to appear. I blinked to clear the wetness, mustering all the inner strength I had to get myself under control. I didn't want to cry in front of him. He'd witnessed my train wreck of a life too many times already.

"Sorry you had to wait so long," I said quietly, pacing over to him.

Shaking his head, he stood. "I didn't. I had to make a stop first, and I just got here about twenty minutes ago." His attention went to Gus, who was dozing off on my shoulder. "Everything okay?"

I gave him a nod, and my voice trembled when I replied, "Because of you."

Reaching out, his hand paused a few inches away from Gus's head. His questioning eyes asked permission, and I nodded.

His fingers softly sifted through my son's blond strands.

"I was so fucking scared today," he rasped, then he cringed. "Sorry. The F-bomb just slipped out."

"I don't think he heard you." Tilting my head down, I looked at Gus's sleeping face. "He's pooped."

"You free to get out of here?"

"Yeah," I sighed. "I'm really glad you were there today, Jay. Thank you doesn't cover it."

His lips rolled inward, pressing the lush flesh together before he blew out a breath and said, "You're welcome."

I was pleasantly surprised that he allowed the praise. I'd expected him to downplay his heroic actions, but I was happy he didn't.

Moving his hand upward, his fingers left Gus's hair and found their way to mine. Some wisps had escaped my ponytail, and he smoothed them away from my face, tucking them behind my ear.

Lingering a few seconds longer than necessary, he grazed my cheek as he pulled back.

Gah. Why did he have to touch me like that? If I wasn't careful, I might start to believe he had feelings for me. Judging from the way he recoiled from our kiss Friday night, that was unlikely.

He'd called it a mistake.

Honestly, I was still butt hurt about that.

Just then, my mom came out. Her right arm and hand were wrapped in bandages, and her eyes were red rimmed from crying.

"Casey, I'm so sorry," she said for the thirtieth time. "I feel really bad about this."

"You should feel bad," I bit out. "Accidents happen, but this was more than that. You had one rule to follow. One. And you broke it. You endangered my child, and you destroyed my home."

"Can you ever forgive me?" She started sobbing again, but I knew I couldn't give her the reassurance she wanted.

"Honestly, I can't right now." Maybe I could get past this someday, but the events were too fresh.

"I have some money in savings. We can fix this. I can buy you a new trailer. A real nice one."

"It's not just about the trailer." Exasperated, my voice came out louder than I'd intended, and several people in the waiting room took notice.

This wasn't the best time or place to air out our personal issues.

I lowered my volume. "Right now, we're homeless. We have nowhere to go. Nowhere to stay tonight. Do you understand that?"

"Stay at my house."

Surprised she'd even have the audacity to offer, I gaped at my mom. "No. We've been over this—"

"I mean, without me," she clarified. "I'm going to stay in town with my boyfriend for a while. You can have my place until we figure out what to do."

I didn't even know she was dating someone new, but that wasn't unusual. She'd never shared details about her love life with me.

"I need some time to think." Fatigue caused my words to come out mumbled as I adjusted Gus to a more comfortable position. "And I can't do it at your house."

"All right." Mom pulled her wallet from her purse and took out sixty dollars. "This is all the cash I have, but I can get more. Get yourself a hotel tonight."

She slipped the money into my hand. The amount wasn't enough to stay somewhere nice, but it was a temporary solution.

And then there wasn't anything left for us to say to each other. I knew she was sorry, and she knew I wasn't ready to accept her apology.

Yet, my heart twisted painfully as I watched her walk out the sliding doors.

Today had been my mother's chance to prove herself as an ally. Someone I could count on. When I'd mentioned needing a sitter, she'd begged for the chance to be with Gus for the whole day.

And now I was so mad at myself for agreeing. For getting my hopes up. For trusting her.

Yes, I lost a lot of material things today, but more than anything, I felt like I'd lost my mom.

Our relationship would never be the same.

If it came down to choosing her or my son, Gus would win every time, no contest. That's how it's supposed to be when you're a parent. I just didn't know why my mom didn't feel that way about me.

"Your carriage awaits, milady." Jay held up an empty hand, as if something invisible was dangling from his fingertips.

Despite the seriousness of the situation, my lips twitched with a small smile. "Where are my keys?"

"Oh, I guess you'll need those," he replied with an over-dramatic, showman-like tone.

Reaching out, his hand went to the side of my head, and I suddenly heard a jingle by my ear. When he pulled his arm back, my key ring sat in his palm.

"Very impressive, magic man."

"Magic man?" Amused, Jay cocked his head at the nickname.

"Yep. That's you." I swiveled to the side, jutting my hip out. "Can you put them in my back pocket?"

He gulped when his eyes fell to my butt. I hadn't thought about the fact that he'd have to touch my ass to put them in there, and his hesitancy only reinforced my suspicions that he wasn't attracted to me.

Before I could retract my request, he reached out and pinched the material of my pocket. Stretching it, he opened it wide enough to drop my keys in without touching me.

"Let's get out of here." Jay's hand went to the small of my back as he led me to the exit. His thumb rubbed up and down my spine, and my confusion over his physical affection mounted.

So, he didn't like kissing me, and he didn't want to touch my butt.

Maybe he felt sorry for me. Hell, I felt sorry for me, too.

"How much is that ER visit gonna cost you?" Jay's arm snaked around my waist and he drew me closer, protecting us from the traffic as we crossed the busy street.

"Nothing."

"Nothing?"

When we got to the sidewalk, I put some distance between us. These mixed signals made me feel like I was on an emotional rollercoaster.

"The hospital has a financial assistance program." I flushed with embarrassment over my need to rely on such things. "I'm poor enough to qualify."

"Casey, you don't have to feel bad about having a low income. I'm about to be unemployed after next week." Jay's hand found its way back to me. This time, strong fingers splayed over the nape of my neck and goose bumps skittered over my skin. "Where are you staying tonight?"

"A cheap motel, I guess."

When we got to the parking lot, I almost walked right past my car. I didn't recognize it with the trunk propped half-way open. A large white box was sticking out, and a bungee cord held it in place.

My footsteps quickened as I hurried over to it. Holding Gus to my chest, I bent down a little to peer inside. I saw all the brand-new stuff, and a ball of emotion formed in my throat.

"You got all this for us?" My voice cracked as I straight-ened. "I'll pay you back, I promise."

"Consider it a gift," Jay ordered, his tone bossy.

"But you said you won't have a job next week."

"So?"

I opened my mouth to argue, but he cut me off.

"Let me do this for you. This saves me the trouble of hav-ing to start an online fundraiser." His lips quirked up. "I detest social media."

"But this is a lot of money. I've never bought anything new. Ever. It's all been from garage sales and hand-me-downs."

"You didn't buy it. I did."

Since I was too dumbstruck to move, he grabbed the keys from my pocket. He started the car and cranked up the air conditioning. Then he opened the back door so I could put Gus in his car seat.

Apprehensively chewing the inside of my cheek, I gently placed Gus in the rear-facing seat. Carefully moving his little limp arms, I strapped him in.

I didn't think it was possible to be more confused than I already was, but what Jay said next rocked me to my core.

"I don't want you sleeping in a motel tonight." That bossy voice again. "You can stay with me until you get back on your feet."

The last buckle snapped into place and I stood so fast I almost hit my head on the roof of the car. "What?"

"See, we have a problem," he continued, casually leaning against the taillights. "Because all the motels are in Champaign."

"And you need to get back to Brenton. I know. I'll drive you."

"Sixty bucks isn't gonna get you very far. What about tomorrow night? And the night after that? Best to crash at my place."

"You mean, like, live with you," I deadpanned.

"Yeah."

"I—it could be a while," I sputtered. "It could be weeks."

"I know."

Was he for real? "I'm not sure you realize what you're inviting into your home. Toddlers are very rude house guests. They demand a lot and pretty much never say thank you."

He shrugged. "I've known some adults like that."

"Gus doesn't sleep well. He'll keep you up at night."

"I already have trouble sleeping, so at least it'll keep my routine going."

Stunned, I blinked at him for several seconds.

Shacking up with a man I barely knew was impulsive, reckless, and uncharacteristic for me. But… it was my best option. The most affordable choice. Safer, too.

Despite what Jay believed about himself, he wasn't a bad person. Bad people didn't go around giving money to pregnant teenage girls, and they certainly didn't risk their lives for children who didn't belong to them.

If Jay had ill intentions toward me, he'd had ample time and opportunity to carry out a sinister plan.

The truth of it was, he saved Gus's life and now he was opening his home to us.

I glanced at the trunk, which was literally bursting with merchandise, then my eyes went to Jay's stubborn expression.

He wasn't taking no for an answer, and my faith in humanity was restored. The guy with the rough exterior and hard look in his eyes was our hero.

I took a deep breath, and on my exhale, I said, "Okay."

Jay's auburn eyebrows shot up, like he'd expected a bigger fight. "Yeah?"

"Yeah." I moved to the driver's side door but paused before I got in. "Have you ever lived with a woman before? I've never been a roommate, but I might be terrible at it."

"You can't be worse than my sister."

"Is she younger or older?"

"Younger. She's only two years younger than you. You'd probably get along great."

Oh. Comparing me to a sibling. So that's how Jay saw me? Like a little sister? Well, that explained his lack of romantic interest.

Huge bummer. "If you get tired of us, will you tell me? You can kick us out at any time."

"I'm not going to."

"You're not going to tell me? Or you're not going to kick us out?" I asked for clarification.

"Either. We can stand here and bicker about it, or you can get your ass in the car," he said playfully, tilting his head toward the trunk. "I've got milk and frozen food back there. It'll go bad in this heat if we don't get it home."

Home.

The word was like a punch to the stomach, but knowing we had a place to go—for now—was good enough for me.

CHAPTER 13

Jay

"Tell me how you ended up in jail." We were barely a
block away from the hospital when Casey hit me with
that doozy. "I've heard the rumors, but I want the real
story. The history behind it."

It was a fair request. If I wanted her to feel safe with me, I
needed to tell her about my past, even if it was a conversation
I didn't care to have.

Ashamed, I looked down at my lap. "I can start from the
beginning, but it's a sad story. You sure you want to hear it?"

"I'm sure."

I nodded. "All right."

Reaching for the volume knob on the radio, Casey made
sure it was silent, then she gave me an expectant look.

My chest expanded with a steeling breath, then I went back
to a time when I had the potential to be so much more than I
became.

*My alarm clock woke me, and just like any twelve-year-old boy
during a summer of freedom, I wanted nothing more than to shut it
off and go back to sleep. But it was Saturday, and that wasn't the plan.*

It was yard sale day.

*After getting out of bed, I stood and poked my sister in the top
bunk. "Nora."*

She shot up, like she hadn't just been dead-asleep. "Is it time?"

"Yeah," I whispered, amused by the six-year old's lisp caused by her missing teeth. "Meet me in the kitchen."

The clock over the stove read just after 4 a.m.

I grabbed the last two granola bars for breakfast. I handed one to Nora before I wrote a note to my mom telling her we were spending the day at Chris Burwash's house and we'd be home by dinner.

We'd probably make it back before she did.

In addition to working as a medical office assistant during the week, Mom had a second job at a store in the mall on the weekends. She had to go in extra early today for a big inventory event, and I was in charge of Nora.

The note wasn't a complete lie—we were going to Chris's house. Just not to stay.

We ran the three blocks in the dark to his house and crept into the backyard. He'd been letting me use his old garden shed to store a bunch of stuff I'd picked up for free. Some of it was leftovers from garage sales. Some was stuff people threw away. All of it was going to be money in my pocket.

Dumpster diving was gross, but it paid off.

I'd been collecting the items for a month. The summers were tough because food was scarce. I hated school, but at least when we were there, we got lunch every day. My mom tried her best to provide, but sometimes it wasn't enough. She never complained about our father, but I knew he didn't pay child support after the divorce.

"Come on," I whispered to Nora as I handed her the wagon handle. "We'll probably have to make a few trips."

I carried the card table and a duffle bag full of baby clothes, while Nora pulled the wagon full of toys.

"Can we keep some of them?" she asked, looking longingly at the loot behind her.

"If they don't sell, yeah. But let's hope they do, because we need the money more."

We made the four-block trek to my dad's brick ranch-style house. He was out of town this weekend, and we planned to use his drive-way. After all, you couldn't have a yard sale without the yard.

By the time we made it back with our third load of things, the sun was peeking over the horizon and Nora was starting to whine.

"My feet hurt," she complained. "I'm hungry."

"I'll go into Dad's house to see if there's anything to eat."

She grabbed my arm. "But we're not supposed to be in there when he's not home."

This was the part I hadn't told her. "Don't worry. I'm only go-ing in for a second."

"Can I come, too?"

"No." I didn't want her getting in trouble if he found out. "Just stay here and I'll be right back."

I punched the code into the control panel to open his garage door. Bypassing the kitchen, I went straight to Dad's room. My hands shook with fear as I opened the lowest dresser drawer.

I wasn't supposed to know about the money my dad had hidden away.

Lifting the false bottom, I eyed the stacks of cash inside. I took out thirty dollars in fives and ones. I needed to borrow some so we'd have change to give back to people.

After the sale, I'd replace it, and it'd be like it was never missing.

The sale was a success. We priced everything low so we'd sell out. It wasn't even noon yet when I took down our signs and started folding up the card table.

"Jay!" I glanced over to see Nora pointing down the road, her face as white as a sheet. "He's supposed to be gone."

My stomach dropped when I spotted Dad's black BMW coming toward the house. "Go home, Nora."

"But—"

"Now!" I shouted. "Run."

With tears in her eyes, she ran in the direction of Mom's

apartment, her long blond curls flying behind her. She didn't stop to look back. I was glad, because I didn't want her to see what was about to go down.

Dad had been known to use his belt when he was mad, and it was safe to say he was going to be pissed. I was small for my age and I'd barely hit puberty. There was no way I could fight him off.

The thunderous look on his face when he pulled up next to me in the driveway had me swallowing hard and rethinking my recent decisions.

"Jay, what are you doing here?" He slammed the door.

"Having a yard sale." I was proud of myself for keeping my voice steady.

"With what stuff?" Looking around, his gaze landed on the card table laying flat on the grass, the empty wagon, and the neon green sign lodged under my arm.

"We sold all of it."

He narrowed his eyes at me. "You been stealing?"

"No." I shook my head. "It was all throwaways. Stuff people didn't want anymore." Digging into my pocket, I tried to keep my hands steady as I counted out the thirty dollars that belonged to him. "I borrowed some money for change, but I swear I was going to put it back."

"How much did you make?"

"Huh?"

"How much money did you make today?"

"Um…" I counted the bills in my hand. "Thirty-eight dollars."

"You made thirty-eight dollars profit from nothing?" His face was impassive.

He'd never been an outwardly expressive man. He didn't tell us nice things just for the sake of saying them. Exclamations of love were non-existent, and praise was few and far between.

That's why his next words surprised me so much.

"A little hustler, huh?" He chuckled. "That's my boy."

I could barely believe my ears. "You're not mad?"

"How can I be mad when I'm so impressed? You're a real go-getter. Just like me."

He ruffled my hair. Dark red—the same shade as his. And when he smiled at me, pride shining in the blue eyes we shared, I felt a connection with him I'd never had before.

"How'd you like to make some real money?" he asked. "I'm not talking about chump change."

I nodded my head enthusiastically. I'd do anything if it meant I had his approval and enough cash to feed Nora.

I just had no idea what I was agreeing to at the time.

"After that day, he had me running drugs for him." I slid a glance at Casey. I saw sympathy on her face, not judgment, so I kept talking. "He never asked what I needed the money for and I didn't tell him it was for things he should've been helping us with all along. He paid me a flat fee every time I delivered a product while he waited in the car. He'd have me dress up in nice clothes. Khakis and button-up shirts. No one would ever suspect the all-American kid of doing something like that."

"Wow. That's awful, Jay."

"The twisted part about it is that I loved doing it. And my mom was happy because my dad was spending time with me. Nora was happy because I could buy her food and toys. Most of all, my dad was proud of me. It seemed like a win for everyone."

"He pulled you into a life of crime," Casey said sadly. "And you were so resourceful, too. You could've been…"

She trailed off, so I finished that sentence for her. "So much more. I know. I'm a classic case of potential gone to waste. The real kicker was how disappointed my mom was when she found out the truth. For years, I'd been telling her my dad was giving me money for us. She thought he was being a standup guy. And the guilt she felt... That was the worst. For a while, she blamed herself for my mistakes." My voice was hoarse with emotion when I added, "I'm not sure I'll ever forgive myself for breaking her heart like that."

"You took on a lot of responsibility at the age of twelve. No kid should have to do that, and your intentions were good."

"In the beginning, they were," I agreed. "But don't make me out to be an innocent in this. When I was eighteen, my father got caught. After he was convicted, I kept doing it. I took over the clients he'd been working with."

"I never said you were innocent, but it was all you knew." Casey paused. "Is he still in jail?"

"Nah. He got out a year or so ago, but I don't know where he is now."

"Did he ever come to visit you?"

I shook my head. "To be fair, though, I never went to visit him either. We just didn't have that kind of relationship."

"Did anyone come to visit you?"

"Yeah. My mom and my sister came every chance they got."

"That's good." The line between Casey's eyebrows lessened. "I don't like the thought of you being all alone there."

I didn't know why she cared, but her concern made me feel good. "I'm lucky to have family who loves me. Not everyone does. Remember those rude roommates I told you about? I had dozens of them there. A lot of them didn't get visitors."

"Was it terrible?" Concerned eyes briefly bounced to me. "Were people mean to you?"

I chuckled, because she sounded like such a mom then. Like she was asking about bullies on a playground.

"Not as much as you'd expect. I had something to offer."

Reaching into my back pocket, I grasped the ace of hearts

I always kept on hand. With quick movements, I rolled it through my fingers and flashed it between us, before flipping it out of sight again.

Casey's mouth popped open, her eyes quickly moving to me before focusing back on the road.

"Entertainment is a commodity," I continued. "My magic tricks made me popular. The guys who have family on the out-side—kids, even—want to learn anything they can to impress them when they get out. Nothing can make up for the time they spend away, but they sure can try."

"Pretty smooth, Jay." Casey's lips tipped up, then she quietly asked, "Are you mad at your dad? I mean, I just don't understand how someone could do that to their kid."

I thought about how to explain why I didn't hold a grudge against my father. Bitterness was a weakness. A toxin I didn't have room for in my life.

"When I think about him, I feel nothing. No anger, no resentment, no love. He doesn't deserve to get any of those things from me." I shrugged. "Sometimes we fall in love with people on accident. It's like a runaway train that can't be stopped. I'm not only talking about romantic love, but all kinds. Like the love I have for my sister. There isn't anything she could do that would ever make me turn my back on her. And sometimes love takes work—we have to choose to love someone on purpose."

"That's an interesting way to look at it—love can be intentional or unintentional."

"Or neither. Some people just don't have the capacity to love. My dad falls into that category." I looked over my shoulder at a sleeping Gus in the back seat. "Not all parents love their kids the way you love yours."

Casey was silent for a few seconds.

"I didn't know how I was going to feel about him when he

was born," she admitted. "I mean, I wanted him, but I didn't know what being a mom felt like."

"What did it feel like?" I asked, suddenly wanting to know the answer so badly. Wanting Casey to reveal some inner part of herself that I hadn't seen yet.

Smiling, she sighed.

"It was more than just love at first sight. When they gave him to me, all wrapped up, bald, and wrinkly…" She let out a soft giggle, and her eyes went misty. "It was like dying and being reborn. That sounds really dramatic, but it's true. I changed in one second. I became someone else. Before him, I didn't know it was possible to love someone so much that who I was ceased to exist. But every heartbreak I'd had in the past disappeared, because he made my heart new."

"Wow." What she described sounded amazing, and my desire for that experience became so overwhelming that it physically hurt.

I rubbed at my sternum. I didn't believe in magic—the real kind.

But Casey talked about love like it could wipe away the past, which was nothing short of a miracle.

Sometimes I felt that way about her. Because when I was with her, it was so easy to forget who I used to be.

"My mom—" Casey shook her head. "I'm pretty sure she loves me, but she has a crappy way of showing it. I've often wondered if she resents me. If she hadn't gotten pregnant, she could've gone to college. She could've done whatever she wanted. Instead, she got a job in construction. Life hasn't been easy for her. Several years ago, a bad shoulder injury put her on disability, and she's just seemed kind of aimless since then. As soon as I was old enough to be home alone—twelve or thirteen—she was gone most of the time. She started dating a lot. Spending nights away from home. I never met any of her boyfriends. I guess she didn't want me to be included in that part of her life. Maybe she thought having a teenaged daughter would scare guys off."

No wonder Casey had been such easy prey for Jaxon. A lonely teenager with no supervision was a recipe for disaster.

I didn't know what to say. It felt wrong to give my opinion on her family shit, so I just said, "That sucks."

"God, she really fucked up this time." Her hands tightened on the wheel. "You know, all that stuff Charlene said about putting your trust in people—it made sense. I wanted to give my mom another chance to be in our lives, and now…"

She didn't have to finish that sentence. Now their relationship might've been irrevocably fucked.

"I hope you two can get past it," I told her sincerely.

"Which one do you think is better?" She stole a quick glance. "To love on accident or on purpose?"

"I think they're both great in their own way. There's something amazing about being so consumed by a feeling you never meant to feel. Then again, the act of choosing love is special, too, because it takes effort."

Our conversation stopped as we exited the interstate, and I could practically feel the dread oozing from Casey.

The closer we got to Brenton, the more anxious she seemed.

She tapped her fingers on the steering wheel. Nibbled the inside of her cheek. Held her breath as we drove down Main Street.

When we neared my apartment, she took a left and parked next to my building instead of heading toward the trailers on our right. Facing forward, she stared at the rough brick exterior.

"I don't want to look," she stated softly. "Not yet."

I glanced behind us across the street. I could see the

charred remains of her house and the yellow caution tape around it. The building was no longer safe to enter.

"You probably shouldn't right now," I agreed. "Give it a day to sink in."

"It's that bad, huh?"

"Yeah." I grimaced. "Is your landlord cool? Will they help you find a new place or cover any of the stuff you lost?"

"I don't have a landlord. The trailer is mine."

She was a homeowner? Casey never ceased to amaze me. At the young age of eighteen, she was the definition of having her shit together.

"Do you have insurance?"

She nodded. "I know for a fact that it covers fire damage, but I don't want to think about that right now. We were settled, you know? Starting over sounds so daunting." Her eyes moved my way, and one dimple appeared when she gave me a half-smile. "If we're getting technical about it, the trailer is actually yours. I bought it with the money you gave me."

My eyebrows shot up. "Four hundred dollars goes that far in Brenton?"

"Four hundred? No. But five grand does."

Tilting my head, I paused. "Where'd you get five grand?"

"Um, you? At the diner… a few days after you came to my house, you sent an envelope of cash while I was working…" Her words tapered off when I slowly shook my head.

"Casey, I don't know where that money came from, but it wasn't me."

Sitting back, her expression was confused. "Then who was it?"

Good question. And the answer came to me quickly.

CHAPTER 14

Casey

"I have a pretty good idea." Jay rubbed the stubble on his jaw.

"Who?"

"Mackenna Connelly. Or I guess it's Johnson now, since she married my buddy Jimmy."

My jaw dropped. "I know her. Well, not really. But I know her name."

Mackenna was my ex's ex. The one who'd sent him to jail the first time.

When we met, Jaxon had made her out to be some kind of evil witch. I realized now that his inability to stop talking about her wasn't just a grudge. It was an obsession. He was fixated on her, even after three years of zero contact.

I got the facts straight after he went back to prison. People told me he'd abused her when they were dating in high school. She tried to break things off with him, and it all came to a head one night when he broke into her house and attacked her. She'd shot him in self-defense.

Looking back, I wasn't surprised. Although Jaxon had never been overly violent with me, sometimes his temper scared me. There were times when he'd grabbed me a little too hard, resulting in bruises on my arms. When he got really pissed, he usually threw the nearest object across the room.

Thankfully, we weren't together long enough for me to see it escalate to him throwing *me* across the room.

"Why would Mackenna give me that much money?" I wondered, baffled. "I'm no one to her."

"Honestly? She's the reason I checked in on you that day. She asked me to find out who you were. I think she felt bad for you when she heard you were tangled up with her ex. Plus, she's kind of loaded. I wouldn't be surprised if what she gave you was just pocket change to her. I can take you to meet her sometime if you'd like. She has a son about Gus's age. I bet they'd be good friends."

Bewildered, I nodded.

Friends.

I didn't have any of those anymore, and neither did Gus. In fact, he'd never had a friend his age. The plus side to him going to Doreen's instead of daycare was one-on-one attention and no exposure to viruses that could cause an asthma flareup.

But was he missing out on vital social interaction?

"I'd really like that," I told Jay. "The least I can do is thank her in person."

"I'll set it up, then." His eyes went to the back seat. "Will he wake up if you move him?"

"Probably not. Although he's not great at sleeping for long periods of time, he's usually out cold for the first couple hours."

Satisfied, Jay gave me a nod. "Good. You guys can take a snooze while I assemble the crib."

I didn't even get a tour when we got inside Jay's place. After ushering me over to the couch and setting Gus's detachable car seat next to it, Jay left to bring all the stuff inside. He put the groceries away, then went to the bedroom to tackle the crib.

Curious about the kind of man Jay was, I studied his

home. The walls were bare and there were three unpacked boxes sitting in the corner. The kitchen had basic white appliances and it lacked storage space. Only two cabinets separated the fridge and the stove. It was furnished with a rectangular dining table, and the living room had a gray couch and a brown recliner. A modest flat screen TV sat on an old wooden console.

His apartment was completely void of personality. Either Jay was a minimalist, or he didn't plan on staying.

My trailer was about the same size, but it was way cozier than this.

Well, it *used* to be.

I didn't want to think about the place that housed all our memories. All our pictures. All Gus's favorite toys and the tiny newborn outfits I'd planned on keeping forever.

It was where Gus had so many important firsts.

First word: Mama.

First steps—he'd surprised me in the kitchen one night when I was cooking macaroni and cheese. One second he was sitting across the room. The next he was wobbling over and hugging my legs.

Sighing, I told myself to suck it up. We were lucky. Gus was healthy and he still had a lot of firsts left. We could make new memories somewhere else.

Swallowing around the lump in my throat, I lay down on my side and looked at the most precious thing in the world. Gus's face was squished from being slumped in the seat, and his breathing was even and deep.

I was so thankful for those breaths. So incredibly grateful for every intake of air. That was more important than anything else.

I placed my hand on his thigh, then exhaustion caught up with me. I only meant to close my eyes for a second.

A high-pitched whine woke me with a start. I sat up quickly and blinked at Gus, who was trying to Houdini his way out of his straps.

It was getting dark out now. Bright orange clouds were streaked in the sky over the balcony. Not a bad view for such a plain apartment.

Unhooking Gus's clips, I asked, "You hungry, buddy?"

His thumb went to his mouth as I picked him up. "Nyuk."

"Milk it is."

There was a brand-new bottle sitting next to the coffee maker, and an unopened gallon of milk in the fridge. I'd just screwed the cap back on when Jay emerged from the bedroom with a wide grin on his handsome face.

"All set." He was a little sweaty, and his hair was sticking up in random places like he'd wanted to pull it out at some point during the construction. "Wanna see?"

He was so proud of himself. He was jumping up and down with excitement, and it was strange to see him like that. It made him look younger. Less burdened.

I grinned. "Yes."

With Gus propped against my hip, I puttered across the kitchen with the nipple firmly planted in his mouth. As soon as we made it into the bedroom, I gasped.

But not because of the crib—which was beautiful, by the way.

I was too busy staring at the monstrous bed taking up most of the space.

I pointed at the California king. "That's the biggest mattress I've ever seen."

"It was my gift to myself when I got out. In prison—" Jay stopped, and his gaze darted to Gus. I could tell he wasn't sure if I was comfortable with him talking about it in front of my son. I urged him on with a nod, and he continued. "In prison, I slept on a mat. That's what we got. Not even anything with springs or support. There was no room to roll over and my feet hung off the end. I hated it."

"Then it makes sense why you'd want something this gigantic." I tilted my head back to look at the door frame. "I just can't believe you got it to fit through here."

"It wasn't easy," he confirmed. "There was a lot of grunting and shoving on my part."

I bet there was.

My face heated with a sudden hot flash.

Jay wasn't describing anything sexual, but I couldn't stop my mind from going there. Thrusting hips. Straining muscles. Erotic noises.

What the hell was wrong with me? Clearing my throat, I fought the urge to fan myself as I experienced an out-of-this world level of arousal.

Luckily, Gus was here to bring me back to Earth.

He spotted his new sleeping spot. It was decorated with soft toys along the back, and there was an old-looking quilt spread over the mattress. The blue and white fabric was faded. There were bunnies on it, and the edges were frayed.

I shot Jay an amused look. There was something incredibly endearing about a guy who kept his baby blanket.

Wiggling until I put him down, Gus forgot all about his milk he toddled over to the crib. There was only a foot between it and the end of the bed, and he wedged himself into the tight space. Groping at the bars, he tried to climb in.

Jay snickered at Gus's enthusiasm.

"I think it's safe to say he likes it," I announced, going over to lift him up and set him inside.

Sinking onto the end of the bed—oh my God, it was the most comfortable thing my butt had ever touched—I smiled over my shoulder at Jay.

"You spoke too soon." Smirking, he gestured toward the crib.

I turned back to see Gus reaching for me because, apparently, he was only interested in one thing—toys. He'd grabbed the dragon puppet, and now he wanted back out. I put him on the big bed, and he rolled onto his back while poking at the shiny fire tongue.

My eyebrows pinched together as a realization came to me. "Wait, where will you sleep?"

"On the recliner," Jay replied.

"But it's tiny. You won't be able to roll over and your feet will hang off. You said you hate that."

"Actually, I happen to love my recliner. Every man should have one."

He sounded so sure, but I didn't feel right imposing.

It was one thing to let him ease a panic attack. It was another to allow him to treat me to a night at the carnival. It was necessary to have him meet me at the hospital with my car.

But this.

This was taking the man's get-out-of-jail gift to himself.

"You could put the crib out in the living room," I suggested. "I'll take the couch."

"That would mean I have to take this thing apart." Pointing at the crib, he chuckled. "I'd rather sleep on a concrete floor."

"Okay," I conceded. "Well, I'll be in touch with my insurance company tomorrow, so hopefully we'll be out of your hair soon. You might even be rid of us by the weekend."

"Frozen pizza sound good for dinner?" The change in subject was abrupt, but the mention of food made my stomach growl.

I nodded.

Jay sent me a sexy wink, but I could've sworn I saw a hint of disappointment in his eyes before he left the room.

CHAPTER 15

Jay

I didn't want them to leave.

They'd only been in my place for a few hours, and now I couldn't imagine going back to my solitary existence. They brought life and color to this drab place.

And noise. A lot of noise.

I winced at the screaming coming from inside the bathroom.

After wolfing down half the pizza, Casey and Gus had decided to get washed up. I could hear the happy splashing sounds when Gus was taking a bath, but as soon as the shower started, so did his wailing.

There'd been a brief reprieve when the water shut off, but the crying continued when the hair dryer turned on.

I stood outside the door, wondering if I should intervene or offer some help. A particularly loud screech made me cringe.

Fuck it.

Rapping my knuckles loudly on the wood, I knocked. The dryer quieted and Gus's cries lowered to whimpers. A couple seconds later, Casey opened the door a crack. Gus was clinging to her as she wore nothing but a white towel and an apologetic expression.

"I'm so sorry." She ran a hand through her half-dried hair. "Nothing's wrong, I swear. This is totally normal."

"Seriously?"

She nodded, letting the door open wider as she adjusted Gus on her hip. "He doesn't like the noise, and I can't hold him while I'm doing it." She shrugged. "So he cries. Is it okay that I'm using your dryer?"

"It's not mine."

Her mouth opened and closed, then opened again. "Oh. Um, a girlfriend?"

It took me a second to realize she was asking if it belonged to someone I was dating. "No. The people who lived here before me left some things behind. That was under the sink when I moved in."

Deflating, she seemed relieved, and I wondered if she realized how transparent she was. She was attracted to me. She wasn't good at being aloof.

This was a problem.

If she made a move on me... all bets were off.

I was trying to be good, but I wasn't a saint, damn it.

I motioned behind me. "Want me to hang out with Gus while you finish up?"

"You don't have to do that." Casey shook her head. "He'd just be crying out there instead of in here."

"Can I dry your hair for you?"

Her eyes went wide with shock. "What?"

I gestured past her to the sink. "You hold him. I'll dry your hair."

"Um." Glancing behind her, she seemed totally thrown off by the question. She looked at Gus, and her eyes softened. "Okay."

"Yeah?" I hadn't actually expected her to say yes. "Yeah. Let's do this."

I tried to seem confident as I picked up the dryer, but I didn't know shit about girls' hair.

Setting Gus on the side of the sink, Casey wrapped her arms around him and made eye contact with me in the mirror. "I don't have a brush. You'll just have to use your fingers."

My hands. In Casey's hair. Fuck, I didn't think this through. *Here goes nothing.*

Warm air blasted from the nozzle, and I pointed it at Casey's head. I was clumsy and uncoordinated as my fingers sifted through her silky strands. But at least Gus stayed silent, and Casey's hair wouldn't be dripping when I was done.

My fingers caught on a tangle, and Casey grimaced.

"Sorry," I said over the loud hum, massaging her scalp.

A shudder racked her body and we locked eyes in the mirror again. Heat crackled between us. I saw her throat work with a swallow, and her lips parted on a sigh.

"Feel good?" My voice came out deeper. Huskier.

Casey gave me a brisk nod, so I continued the gentle strokes.

The moment was surreal. Here she was, standing in front of me, practically naked. She was letting me take care of her as we watched each other.

She looked at me like she was trying to solve a puzzle. A puzzle she wanted to fuck.

My cock thickened, and I tried not to think about the towel falling off her body.

All too soon, my mission was complete, and I left her to get dressed.

When she came out in the white T-shirt and yoga pants I'd bought her, she brushed past me to the bedroom. "We'll just watch some cartoons on my phone until bed. We'll stay out of your way. Goodnight."

The latch clicked before I could respond, and I stood outside the door for several minutes, debating.

Should I ask her to come out here? There was no reason

why we couldn't all watch cartoons together. Obviously, she felt like she was intruding, which was the furthest from the truth.

But spending time with Casey was a bad idea. It was inevitable, now that she was living here, but distance was better, even if every cell in my body rebelled at the thought of avoiding her.

I was about to back away when I heard her singing.

It was one of the silly songs she'd made up just for Gus. The melody was simple, starting low and climbing high as she sang, "Everybody loves a Gus. Everybody loves a Gus." Then she'd repeat it, going from high to low.

So fucking adorable.

Pacing over to my recliner, I told myself it was better to leave her alone. Like she said, they'd be gone soon.

Until then, I could rest easy knowing they were safe under my roof.

~

It was the best night of sleep I'd had in years. Even Gus's cries jolting me awake at one a.m. didn't fuel my ever-present insomnia. I'd pretended to be asleep while Casey quickly retrieved a bottle from the fridge, but I promptly passed out after she went back to the bedroom.

That term 'slept like a baby?' Yeah, that was me last night.

Now the sun was coming up.

As I stood over Casey's sleeping form, I was stunned by how pretty she was in the morning.

She was on her back, and Gus was cuddled up to her side. His hand was wrapped around her collar. Long, dark strands fanned out on the pillow, and the memory of how it felt to touch them made my dick twitch.

God, I wanted to kiss her again.

But I wouldn't.

For once in my life, I'd do the right thing.

"Casey," I whispered, kneeling next to the bed. She didn't move, so I gently nudged her shoulder. "Casey."

She startled, her eyes snapping open. Blinking rapidly, she was obviously confused by the unfamiliar ceiling above her.

I knew what it was like to wake up somewhere new, disoriented because you forgot where you were. Scared because you weren't home like you thought.

Reacting on instinct, I soothed her by running my fingers through her hair.

"It's just me," I said low.

"What's going on?" The question came out groggy. "Is everything okay?"

"Yeah. I just didn't know if you needed to get ready for work." My hands got clammy from nerves when I said, "I, uh—if you need a babysitter, I can do it."

I'd rehearsed the offer in my mind at least a dozen times, bracing myself for the inevitable rejection.

I knew she'd say no, but I desperately wanted her to let me help somehow. I didn't know much about babies, but I was willing to do whatever it took to keep Gus safe and happy until Casey returned.

My hope deflated when she shook her head.

But then she said, "You're the best, you know that? But I have the day off. Gloria heard about the fire, and she sent a text last night telling me to take my vacation time."

Oh. Not exactly a rejection, then. "So, what are you doing today?"

"I have to call the fire chief. Then the insurance company. After that…" She shrugged with her free shoulder. "Shopping, maybe. Everything you bought for us is great, but we have a lot to replace."

"You want some company while you do that?"

Fuck me. So much for not spending time with her.

Just then, my phone chimed with a text.

Jimmy: Sorry to hear about your friend's house. We have a shit ton of baby boy clothes. Please, for the love of God, come take some away. I want my closet back.

Me: What size are they?

Jimmy: Fucking tank-size. Will is busting out of his 2t clothes now.

Me: Yeah, that'd probably work. I have something I need to talk to you about anyway.

I pocketed my phone and glanced at Casey. "You wanna go see Mackenna and Jimmy this morning? If you want to meet them, now's your chance, and you might not have to go shopping after all."

CHAPTER 16

Jay

C asey wouldn't let me drive on the way to Jimmy's. I'd suggested it because my car was in better shape than hers.
She'd made the excuse that it'd be a pain to switch over
Gus's car seat, but that didn't explain why she tried to convince
me to drive separately.

She didn't want to ride in a car with me? What'd changed
since yesterday?

Confused, I'd told her it didn't make sense for us to use
twice the gas when we were going to the same place.

But…

I wasn't confused anymore.

The ungodly wailing from Gus had been going on for a
solid ten minutes. Nothing calmed him down. I'd handed him
toys and tried to talk to him with no success. If anything, my
efforts only made it worse.

The contrast between the ear-splitting sound and the
cheerful classical baby CD playing through the speakers was
almost comical.

With her hands firmly placed at ten and two on the wheel,
Casey sighed and loudly said, "I'm so sorry."

It was the fifth time she'd apologized. We really needed to
work on that. "You don't need to be. It's fine."

"He just hates being in the car," she explained, hitching

a thumb behind her. Seeming stressed, her fist fell to her lap. "You got lucky yesterday because he was asleep."

"Does he do this the whole time?" Because holy shit. That'd make going anywhere hard for her.

"He usually stops after fifteen minutes or so. Just gotta wait it out. I'm so—"

"It's okay," I cut off her apology, reaching over to grab her hand.

Bad. Fucking. Idea.

Because once my skin was on hers, I didn't pull away. Instead, I curled my fingers around hers and kept them there.

She stiffened, bit her lip, and squeezed me back. Watching her profile, I adjusted my fingers, sliding them to lace with hers.

Casey's lips parted, like she wanted to say something, but no sound came out. Giving in to the weak moment I was having, I ran my thumb over the skin on the back of her hand. So soft and smooth.

And that was how we ended up holding hands on a deserted country road on the way to Jimmy's house.

Despite the pissed off kid in the back seat, it was a pretty good time.

Casey was right—after a few more minutes, Gus quieted down, just in time for us to drive past the 'Welcome to Tolson' sign.

"Are you sure Mackenna wants to meet me?" Casey sent me an apprehensive look.

"Positive. She'd probably be upset if you didn't come. I told them about what happened yesterday, and they want to give you some of Will's clothes."

Groaning, her head fell back. "Mackenna must think I'm pathetic. First, she gave me pity money. Now pity clothes. Next, we'll be pity friends."

"Turn right here. It's the house with the porch." I pointed at the beige bungalow. "And pity friends? I don't think that's a thing."

"Isn't it?" She gave our hands a pointed stare before relinquishing her hold on me to put the car in park.

"You think I'm doing all this because I feel sorry for you?"

"Well, yeah."

"You want the truth, Casey?"

Turning her head, she locked eyes with me. "Yes."

"I'd like to say I'm doing this out of the goodness of my heart, but if I'm being honest, it's because I like you, and not in a pity-friend way." I lowered my voice to a whisper, because what I was about to say wasn't appropriate for young ears. "Holding your hand makes my dick hard. Smelling you makes my dick hard. Talking to you makes my dick hard. Thinking about you—"

Sucking in a breath, Casey pressed her fingers over my mouth. "Okay. I get it."

Grasping her wrist, I pulled her hand away from my face while caressing her palm. "I don't think you do. If you knew about the fantasies I've had—starring you—you'd run."

Eyes widening, she licked her lips.

Shit. She looked intrigued instead of scared.

Loud knocking broke us apart, and we looked out the driver's side window. Mackenna was there holding a brown-haired boy. Both were smiling and waving at us, unaware of the moment they'd just interrupted.

Casey got out, and I followed her lead.

"Hi." I heard her say shyly as she opened the back door to get Gus.

Mackenna gave her a warm smile. "Hi. I'm so glad you decided to come over."

"Of course. I wasn't sure if it would be awkward because…"

"Because we dated the same psycho?" Mackenna concluded, her tone light.

Lifting Gus out, Casey laughed. "Yeah. Exactly that."

Now that the women were standing side by side, the resemblance between the two was uncanny. They both had dark hair and light eyes. Casey was several inches shorter than Mackenna, but they had slender bodies and pretty faces. Mackenna even had one dimple on the left side of her mouth when she smiled.

It was safe to say Jaxon had a type, and I was reminded again how calculating he'd been when he chose Casey as Mackenna's replacement. It pissed me off. Casey was one of a kind, and she deserved to be treated as such.

"So this is August, but he goes by Gus." Casey ruffled her son's blond hair.

Mackenna smiled down at her own little boy. "And this is William. We call him Will for short."

"How old is he?"

"Sixteen months."

"Oh, he's only a month older than Gus. And wow, he's so much bigger." Casey glanced back and forth between the boys as she noted the size difference.

Jimmy wasn't kidding—the kid was a tank.

"You're telling me." Mackenna laughed. "I pushed for two and a half hours to get him out."

"Yikes." Casey cringed. "Gus was a little less than seven pounds, but it felt like a lot more at the time."

Not having anything to contribute to a conversation about birthing large objects, I stuffed my hands in my pockets while they went into some of the nitty gritty details of labor.

The girls were so absorbed in meeting each other that I hadn't been acknowledged yet.

It didn't bother me, though. Actually, I was pretty pleased

with their interaction. Casey needed this—another mom to talk to.

When they came to a break in their conversation, I jokingly complained, "I guess I don't count since I'm not in the psycho ex club. I'm just an old high school acquaintance."

Mackenna's gaze finally bounced my way, and she smiled softly. "It's so good to see you, Jay. Jimmy and I thought you'd come visit sooner."

I shrugged, still feeling bad about what'd happened the last time I saw Jimmy. I'd already apologized to them both and done what I could to make amends. Didn't stop the guilt, though.

Sensing my discomfort, Mackenna let me off the hook. "Jimmy's grilling out back. You can just walk through the yard."

I smirked. "Is that woman-code for 'leave us alone?'"

"You've always been a smart guy. I'm happy to see that hasn't changed," Mackenna quipped before pivoting toward the house.

Before Casey turned to follow, she sent me a look full of questions, and I knew she was thinking about what I'd confessed in the car. That conversation would have to wait, and I had no idea what I'd say when that time came.

I shouldn't have told her all that shit.

Admitting my true feelings might've opened a door neither of us should walk through.

Carrying the kiddos, the girls made their way up the porch steps, and I heard Mackenna offer condolences about Casey's house as they went inside.

I caught the scent of burning charcoal and hamburgers, and I followed the smell to the backyard. I found Jimmy sitting at the patio table. He was shirtless, his tattoos and piercings on full display as he sat under the shade of the green umbrella.

It felt good to see someone familiar. Someone I had something in common with. Like me, Jimmy had an ornery streak. It was why we got along so well. But, unlike me, he never took it far enough to let it ruin his life.

The grin on his face let me know he didn't hold a grudge over our history.

"It's hot as balls." The first words he'd said to my face in two years. No finesse at all, this guy.

I laughed, because he wasn't wrong. Been out here for three minutes and I was already sweating. "Yeah, it is."

Jimmy leaned down to reach into the red and white cooler next to him.

"Want a cold one?" He extended his arm to me, holding a brown bottle.

I shook my head. "Thanks, but I don't drink anymore."

Chuckling, he twisted his wrist so I could see the label. "It's root beer. You really think I'm gonna get tanked at eleven in the morning?"

I grinned, accepting the beverage. "Wouldn't be the first time. Remember homecoming weekend when I visited you at Ohio State?"

"Nope." He bent down to get one for himself. "But I do recall the midterms I failed the week after."

Just as I took a gulp, Jimmy made a displeased sound. Rummaging around in the cooler, he discovered that most of the ice had melted to slush.

"Hey, would you mind running inside for me? I gotta stay out here and flip the burgers." He tipped his head to the back door. "The kitchen is just on the other side of the dining room. There's a bag of ice in the freezer."

"Sure thing."

After setting my root beer down, I headed to the screen door. Cool air and feminine giggles blasted me when I got inside.

Mackenna and Casey were out of sight in the living room, but I could hear them laughing over something the boys were doing.

Glancing around the dining room, I realized just how well Jimmy had done for himself in the past couple years.

The exterior of the house was nice, but the inside was even better. Deep amber-colored walls gave it a warm atmosphere, and the hardwood floors appeared to be original to the house. A nice mahogany table was surrounded by six sturdy chairs, plus a highchair. There was a basket full of baby toys in the corner.

This was a far cry from the rebel Jimmy used to be, and it gave me hope.

A family. A nice home in a quiet town. Was it possible for someone like me to have a life like this?

Just as I was reaching for the freezer, I heard my name uttered in the other room. I paused.

Nothing stood between me and the ability to hear every word the girls said. Was it wrong to listen in? Probably. Was I going to do it anyway? Yep.

Silently moving closer to the doorway, I stood out of sight around the corner and eavesdropped.

"A few days after Jaxon went to jail, I was given a large amount of money from an anonymous person," Casey said. "Jay told me it was probably you."

"Jay has a big mouth," Mackenna replied, humor in her voice. "Yes, it was me."

"Why would you do that for someone you don't know?"

"Because I was financially stable—you weren't. And to be honest, I feel partly to blame for your situation."

"What? Why?"

"Well, I should've had better aim when I shot that bastard." Mackenna chuckled. "But now I'm glad I didn't kill him.

If I had… well, you wouldn't have your son. And I have a feeling our boys could be really good friends."

A few seconds passed before Casey whispered, "Gus has his eyes. And his hair. What if—what if—"

"Hey." Mackenna's tone was soothing. "Don't even go there. You have nothing to worry about."

"I'm terrible for even thinking Gus could be anything like Jaxon."

"No, you're not. We all have irrational fears. It's a mom thing. At least, that's what my mom tells me. Listen, genetics only go so far, okay? Some people are just wired wrong."

"I know you're right."

"Plus, by the time Jaxon gets out, Gus will be an adult. He's *your* son. Look at him. See how good he is at sharing? He already knows how to be a friend. When I look at him, I see a lot of you."

"Seriously?" Casey asked, happiness bleeding through.

"Seriously. And I'd be glad to have you guys come over any time. Jay can come, too."

"Thanks."

I was about to back away, but Casey's next question had me halting.

"Do you think I'm crazy for liking Jay? Because I do. I like him a lot, and I don't exactly have the best track record with men. To be honest, I'm not sure I trust my own judgment."

Finally. Someone was going to talk some sense into Casey.

Bracing my hand against the wall, I held my breath as I waited to hear what Mackenna had to say.

"No, I don't think you're crazy at all. Jimmy wasn't exactly a boy scout when we got together, either. I was scared. Sometimes a person can make bad choices, but it doesn't make them a bad person. Deep down, Jay has a good heart." She paused. "You know, when we were in fifth grade, Jay used to share his lunch with another boy who didn't have much to eat. Not like he had a lot to give. I always thought it was really sweet, though. Jay might've lost his way for a while, but that generous kid he used to be? That's who he really is."

I'd forgotten all about that, and the reminder left me with conflicting feelings. I was glad someone remembered me for something good. On the other hand, Casey was right to be hesitant about me, and Mackenna had just given her a stamp of approval.

As quietly as I could, I retrieved the ice and went back outside.

"So how've things been?" Jimmy asked as he filled the cooler.

"As good as can be expected. It's good to be out, but life is a lot different now." I sat down and rubbed at the condensation on the side of my root beer. "I did things the wrong way for so long, it's like I don't know how to do it right. I don't have any real job experience, aside from the carnival. Getting hired is damn near impossible."

"Shit, man. I wish there was something I could do to help."

His comment was the perfect segue to the subject I wanted to broach. "That's one of the reasons I wanted to talk to you. You guys wouldn't happen to be hiring at the shop, would you?"

Jimmy worked as a mechanic at Hank's Auto Shop here in Tolson. He loved it, and the idea of working on cars—fixing things and making them better—appealed to me.

With an apologetic expression, he shook his head. "I wish I could say we have a spot for you, but things have been slow. Hell, I'm having a backyard barbeque on a Tuesday because I'm only needed three days a week right now. If it weren't for the fact that Mackenna has a good income, we'd be screwed."

"I get it." I tried not to let my disappointment show. "Just had to ask."

"If I hear of anything, I'll let you know." Scratching his inky black hair, he cocked his head to the side. "Actually, there's a shop in Daywood that might be hiring."

"Burwash Auto Repair?" I guessed, since it was the only one I knew of in my small hometown.

"That's right," Jimmy confirmed. "One of their guys quit a few weeks ago. I could have Hank put in a good word for you."

I grunted out a hesitant sound. "I dunno. Jordan Burwash probably hates my guts. His son Chris and I used to hang out a lot when we were kids. That is, until Chris got caught drinking at a party with me. He was grounded for the rest of the year, and we haven't spoken much since."

Grimacing, Jimmy opened the grill and started plating the burgers and hotdogs. Thankfully, he decided to change the subject.

"So, you and Casey, huh?" His playful tone suggested he was a hundred percent sure we were banging.

"Nah, it's not like that," I denied. "I'm just helping her out."

"Really," Jimmy deadpanned, seeing right through my bullshit.

"Yep."

"Is it because she's too young? Because I gotta say, I can't imagine how hard these past couple years have been for her. I think she's earned the right to be considered an adult."

"It's not that."

"Is it because she's got a kid?"

I shook my head. "No. God, no. That's one of my favorite things about her."

"Then what's wrong? I know you like her." He waved the

spatula in my direction. "I saw you two in the car when you pulled up. You look at her like…"

"Like what?"

"The same way my grandma looks at top-shelf liquor. Grandma Beverly loves good whiskey."

I barked out a laugh before seriousness took over again.

"I don't deserve her," I sighed. "And don't even get me started about all the shit I have in common with her ex."

Jimmy's face darkened at the mention of Jaxon. "What the hell are you talking about? You're nothing like that asshole."

"We're the same age." I held up a finger. "He and I went to the same high school." A second finger joined the first, ticking off the reasons. "We both got arrested for drug possession. And I'm obsessed with Casey. I scare myself, man. I've never wanted someone the way I want her."

Fuck, it sounded even worse when I said it out loud.

"First of all," Jimmy started, butting into my self-loathing. "The first two things you said aren't anything you had control over. So what if you know the guy from school? And second, would you ever hit a woman?"

I jerked back at the question. "Hell, no."

"Would you ever abuse Casey?"

"Not ever." My voice was low, certain, with a dangerous edge to it.

The very thought of harming Casey—or any woman, for that matter—made me feel physically ill.

Jimmy smiled wide. "See? You're not like that mofo at all. And, hello." He pointed at himself. "I'd know a thing or two about being with someone who's way too good for me. Mackenna, superstar songwriter for one of the biggest punk bands in the world? She literally makes eleven times more than I do. I did the math. It ain't pretty."

"Wow."

Jimmy really hit the jackpot, but I wondered if it made him feel weird that he wasn't the main provider in his house. Yeah, these were modern times, and there was nothing wrong with a successful woman. But Mackenna already went through unimaginable pain birthing Jimmy's gigantic kid. She was the baby maker and the breadwinner.

What did Jimmy have to offer her in return?

"We'd be lost without each other," Jimmy went on, basically answering my inner thoughts. "I'd do anything for Mack, and I'm probably the most pussy-whipped guy in history. She's got me by the balls, and she knows it." He grinned and waggled his eyebrows, like he thoroughly enjoyed that aspect of their relationship. "And you know what? She makes me better without even trying. I was really down on myself when we met, but I didn't feel like a loser when I was with her."

I sat up straighter. "That's how I feel with Casey."

"Then don't blow it." Coming over to sit next to me, he took a long swig of his root beer. His face was serious when he said, "You're not in lockup anymore, Jay. Quit acting like it."

He was right.

Maybe the forgiveness I was seeking had nothing to do with anyone else. No one was mad or bitter about my past. On the contrary, everyone was wishing good things for me.

That meant I had to forgive myself, which was easier said than done.

Just then, the back door opened. Mackenna came out first, her arms full of chips, ketchup, and a jar of pickles. Will was trailing behind her carrying the mustard.

Casey was next. Gus was on her hip, his thumb in his mouth. His other hand was wrenching at her white shirt, rubbing the material against his cheek.

Twin dimples appeared when Casey smiled at me, and the last of my resistance melted away.

You know what? Fuck it.

I was done fighting my attraction to her.

It was time to stop living as though I was still being punished.

CHAPTER 17

Casey

Light from the streetlamp filtered through the blinds as I gently set Gus down in the crib. His body was lax, his breathing deep. His nap had been shorter than usual this afternoon, so it hadn't taken me long to get him to sleep tonight.

I walked over to the door, but I hesitated, my hand hovering over the knob.

It was just after nine. I wasn't tired yet. Actually, it was the opposite. I was wired. My energy levels were through the roof, like I'd just had a couple cups of coffee.

But caffeine wasn't the cause.

Jay was on the other side of this door, and I knew we needed to talk. Aside from our brief time on the Ferris wheel, it was the first time we'd be hanging out just the two of us.

I was nervous.

Maybe he'd be wearing the same beat-up jeans and black T-shirt from earlier. Or maybe I'd get to see him in something more casual. Gym shorts or sweatpants.

Oh, God. What if he was shirtless? For all I knew, Jay might be used to walking around his home half naked.

I might legit die.

Blowing out a shaky breath, I yanked the hair tie from my messy bun, letting my still-wet hair fall around my shoulders.

Earlier, when Jay said he could dry my hair again, I promptly declined. After what he'd said today, I couldn't handle another eye-fucking session in the mirror.

I probably should've taken him up on it, though. Because I looked like hell.

Self-conscious about the ratty knots on the back of my head, I finger combed my hair to the best of my ability.

Then I slipped out the door, closing it behind me until it was open just a crack.

When I turned and saw the kitchen, my jaw dropped. Two lit votive candles and a vase of peonies sat on the table. Jay was standing on the other side of it, and he wasn't wearing jeans or sweatpants. He was in a gray suit.

Not what I was expecting to see.

"What's all this?" I looked at the flickering lights, then back to Jay's face.

"You and I both missed out on our proms. I figured I could give you a taste of it." He spread his arms in a shrug, causing the jacket to stretch over his muscular shoulders.

I glanced down at my outfit.

It was the opposite of prom attire.

The purple T-shirt and flower-print leggings were from Mackenna. Crazy leggings weren't really my style, but she seemed to have an endless supply of them.

Beggars can't be choosers, and I had to admit they were super comfy. Along with enough pants and shirts to last me two weeks without having to do laundry, Mackenna also insisted on me taking two garbage bags full of clothes for Gus. We'd be set for the rest of the year.

But she didn't stop there. She also gave me a wicker basket full of toys. And shampoo. Conditioner. Soap. Tampons. Makeup samples she'd never used. Pretty much any women's product was covered.

I felt like I had more stuff now than I did before the fire. Well, except for formal wear, but I never had that in the first place.

Realizing Jay was waiting for me to answer, I awkwardly rubbed my bare toes together. "I'm not dressed for prom."

"I got you covered." Jay held out his empty hands, cupping them together.

Giddy, I stepped toward him. He was about to do a trick.

He swirled his hands, then a small plastic grocery bag appeared out of nowhere. It was balled up, no bigger than both of his fists put together. Studying his pockets and sleeves, I tried to figure out how the illusion was done as I moved closer.

"How did you do that?"

"Ah, ah." He shook his head. "A magician never tells his secrets."

"You taught the inmates," I pointed out.

"That was different—I wasn't taking them on a date."

My heart jumped. "Is this a date?"

"If you want it to be." Jay's face was so serious. So vulnerable. Hopeful.

I smiled a little. "I want it to be."

Grinning, he handed me the bag. "Then go put this on."

I shuffled to the bathroom, and once I was closed in, I peeked into the crinkled plastic. A purple dress was neatly folded into a ball. Holding it by the shoulder straps, I let it unravel. The material was thin and shiny. Slinky and sexy.

After removing my clothes, I slid into the silky fabric.

"Holy crap," I whispered to myself.

This was more like a nightie than a prom dress. It was formfitting, and the hem barely reached mid-thigh. If it wasn't for the built-in bra, my nipples would've been very visible.

Fluffing my hair, I gazed at myself in the mirror over the sink. I couldn't see below my waistline, but such a fancy dress looked out of place against the dinginess of the nylon band around my neck.

My face looked plain without makeup, but there was no time to fix that.

Jay was waiting for me out there.

I pinched my cheeks to get some color and firmly pressed my lips together to plump them up a bit. It would have to be good enough. Besides, it wasn't like he'd never seen me look like crap before.

Apparently, my concern about my appearance was all for nothing, because as soon as I stepped out of the bathroom, Jay's jaw went slack. His eyes perused me from head to toe. Then he clamped his mouth shut and swallowed with an audible gulp.

Snapping out of his stupor, he shook his head and grabbed his phone. He fumbled with it, almost dropping it, before setting it back on the counter.

It was cute.

Poor guy was more nervous than I was. "All of Me" by John Legend played quietly through the room as he faced my direction. He opened his arms in invitation.

As my bare feet padded across the linoleum, I fought a giggle. I had to dig my teeth into my lower lip to keep the hysterical sound from bubbling out.

I didn't know why I felt like laughing—it wasn't really funny. Jay was trying to be romantic, and he was succeeding.

My lungs felt big. My stomach, light. Something strange was happening inside of me—like I might burst—and I didn't know what to do about it.

Was this happiness?

Not the kind of contentment I experienced when I looked at my son. Not the kind of satisfaction I felt at the end of a shift when I earned a good amount in tips.

This was fulfilling in a different way. A feeling I'd experienced only once before.

At the top of a Ferris wheel.

The common denominator between the two was the man standing in front of me.

As soon as I was close enough to place my hand on his chest, a snort escaped. I tried to cover it with a cough, but I couldn't get anything past Jay.

Quirking his eyebrow at my outburst, he chuckled. "I'm that bad at this, huh?"

"No." Another giggle. "I'm not laughing at you, I swear. Spontaneity isn't something I get a lot of. I just feel… good. I feel pretty, and it's crazy because I'm so *not pretty* right now."

A crease appeared between Jay's eyebrows. "How can you say that? How can you even think that?"

He threaded his fingers through my damp strands.

Well.

He tried.

His hand got caught in a net of waves, and I winced as I reached up to help untangle him.

"I need a haircut," I mumbled, embarrassed.

"You're beautiful this way." His sincere compliment sucked the humor out of the moment.

In awe, I looked into his eyes and saw myself there—the way he saw me. "I like it when you tell me I'm beautiful."

"I mean it. You know I've watched you, Casey—I'm not hiding that fact. I've seen you at work. I've watched you play with your son in your yard. I've seen you in the middle of the night. Exhausted, determined, persistent. It doesn't matter what you're doing or what mood you're in. You're always gorgeous, no matter what."

"Thanks." Beyond flattered and a little shy, I glanced down.

He put his finger under my chin and tilted my face up. "But I've never seen you look more beautiful than you do right now."

"Because of the dress?"

"Because you're mine."

Time seemed to stop as I processed his words. He declared it with so much conviction, such confidence.

"I am?" I asked quietly.

Grabbing my waist, he drew me in until there was almost no space left between us.

"In here, you are." Without breaking eye contact, he pointed at his chest. "For so long, you've been my happy thought." His gaze dropped to my prism necklace. "My rainbow. You brought me light and color after my darkest times."

Well. I certainly didn't feel like laughing anymore.

"You've been that for me, too," I confessed. "You have the ability to make me smile when it's the last thing I feel like doing."

"Then I'm yours."

Did we seriously just agree to be in a relationship? It almost seemed too good to be true. In less than twenty-four hours, I went from assuming Jay thought of me as a little sister, to him talking about how hard I made his dick.

Sliding my palms up his chest, I linked my hands behind his neck. We automatically started swaying to the music, and a surge of affection for this man overtook my heart.

I could fall in love with him.

The thought came out of nowhere, but it was true. Logically, it was too soon for love, but what I felt wasn't just infatuation either.

Lust was purely physical. This was more than that.

Yes, I was insanely attracted to Jay, but I liked who he was on the inside. He took everything in stride. He was brave, laid-back, and he handled a crisis like a boss. Most importantly, he accepted me as I was, Gus included.

"Did you raid Mackenna's closet, too?" I joked, my gaze flitting down to the dress while I tried to direct my thoughts away from my growing feelings.

Jay flashed me a grin. "And Jimmy's. He thought the suit would help me on job interviews. You're not the only one who left with a loot today."

"What else did you get?"

"Some more clothes. The candles and flowers." He cleared his throat. "Condoms."

My lower belly tightened. Warmth spread through my core, and my nipples stiffened.

Just the possibility of sex put my body on high alert.

"You're not going to start talking about your dick again, are you?" I kept my face serious, but mirth bled through my tone.

Jay laughed. A deep, rich sound.

"I hadn't planned on it. At least, not tonight. I'm sure it will come *up* in the future."

"Did you just make a boner joke?"

Grinning, he nodded. "I totally did."

I giggled again, and this time I didn't try to hold it in. It felt so good to laugh. I liked this undiscovered side of Jay—light and funny.

"What would *you* like to talk about?" he asked, our bodies still swaying to the music. "I'm rusty at this dating thing, but I'm pretty sure listening is part of the deal."

The ball was in my court now, and I wasn't sure if I had anything interesting to say. Dating wasn't my expertise either. I didn't have much life experience to speak of. He already knew where I worked, and I'd talked about my kid way too much as it was.

Sensing my inner turmoil, Jay rubbed his thumbs back and forth on my sides before hooking his hands behind my back. The action pressed us together even closer, and now my breasts were smashed against his stomach. My nipples were so hard, I wondered if he could feel them through the layers of fabric and padding.

"Just say whatever comes to mind," he urged.

I want to fuck you.

Holy shit. I would *not* say that.

I searched my brain for a topic that didn't include how turned on I was.

"I have a meeting with someone from my insurance company on Friday." It wasn't the most enthralling conversation, but it was better than admitting I wanted to bang his brains out. "They're going to assess the damage, but according to the fire chief, it isn't salvageable. It's not even structurally sound, which really sucks. There were some things of Gus's I'd hoped to get, but it's not safe to go inside."

"I'm sorry." Jay frowned. "I figured that was the case."

"The trailer wasn't worth much to begin with. I paid cash for it. The woman who lived there before had to go to a nursing home, and her family was eager to sell. I offered three thousand and they sold it to me on the spot."

The current song playing ended, and "Fix You" by Coldplay came on as we continued to dance. How fitting. Because Jay was my fixer. He seemed to have a solution for every problem.

"So what will you do now?" he asked. "Get another trailer?"

Slowly, I shook my head. "I've been thinking about it all day, and I keep coming to the same conclusion. I don't want to live in Brenton forever. It's so easy to get stuck here. Maybe this is my way out. A blessing in disguise."

"That's a good way to look at it."

"Daywood is nice," I mused. "There are more jobs and it's closer to the city. I'd like to go back to school at some point."

A smile ticked up on Jay's face. "Yeah? What do you want to do?"

"Cosmetology, maybe? There's a program in Champaign. It's only nine months long and they offer night classes. And the course would pretty much pay for itself in the long run. Do you know how much money I'd save over the years if I never had to pay for Gus's haircuts? Speaking of that, he needs one."

"No," Jay burst out, as if I'd just suggested poisoning my own child.

His reaction made me lift an eyebrow. "Why not?"

"You can't chop off his mullet. Business in the front, party in the back."

He stated it so seriously. Like it was a matter of life or death. His dramatics threw me into another giggling fit.

Leaning my forehead against his chest, my lungs convulsed with silent cackles.

And as Jay chuckled along with me, I had a weird out of body experience. I didn't recognize this girl. This happy, sexy, beautiful girl.

But Jay did. He knew who I was, even when I'd forgotten.

When I finally got myself under control, I thought about all the other stuff I wanted to know how to do. "I'd also like to learn to sew—how to mend clothes when they rip or get a hole. And gardening. That's a useful skill, too. I could grow my own food. Oh, and also maybe some trade schools, like carpentry or HVAC? So I can fix things around the house when they break."

"You're very ambitious."

I hiked a shoulder. "I want to be self-sufficient. I probably won't be able to do any of it until Gus is older, but it's good to have goals."

"You know," Jay started, taking a deep breath, like what he was about to say was hard for him. "I'd be happy to hang out with Gus anytime you're busy."

"Are you sure?" I asked, skeptical. It was the third time he'd brought up the subject of babysitting today, but I wasn't sure he knew what he was signing up for. "Have you ever watched a little kid?"

Blowing out a breath, he loosened his hold. It wasn't enough for us to separate, but I could sense him emotionally distancing himself.

"You don't trust me to be alone with your son." Jay sounded resigned and defeated as he averted his gaze, staring blankly at some spot on the stove. "I can't say I blame you."

I moved my head to the side until I caught his eye. "Hey. I don't trust *anyone*, but I *do* trust you."

Surprised, he blinked at me. "What?"

"I know Gus is safe with you. It's not *him* I'm concerned about."

"You're worried about me?" He huffed out a laugh. "He's a baby. What could he possibly do?"

"Scare you away," I replied honestly, before I could stop myself. "Nothing like a raging toddler tantrum to make you have second thoughts about me."

"I'm not that fragile. Give me some credit."

"I do, Jay. You deserve all the credit in the world." My voice came out in a whisper when I admitted, "I barely know you and I'm already scared to lose you."

Intensity and candlelight flickered in Jay's eyes as his hands flexed on my waist. "How do you do that?"

"Do what?"

"Make me feel like I'm… good."

"Because you are."

How could he not be proud of who he was today? Jay's struggle with his conscience was something he wore like a giant caution sign. With traffic cones and flashing lights around it.

It was unnecessary. He'd already paid the price for his mistakes.

Sympathy for him overflowed as I stroked the back of his neck with my fingers. My nails scraped over his scalp, and he briefly closed his eyes at the pleasant sensation.

"But how can you be so sure?" he pressed, dipping his forehead until it bumped mine.

The song on his phone switched to "All I Want" by Kodaline, and I replied, "It's the little things that show me the type of person you truly are. Your acts of kindness. Like how you rode in the back seat on the way back from Tolson today, just so Gus wouldn't cry."

That'd been a huge shock to me.

I didn't ask Jay to keep Gus entertained, but that's exactly what he'd done. In the rearview mirror, I could see him busting out magic tricks with the rings he'd gotten from Walmart. Gus was a happy camper all the way home.

"And the pseudo prom in your kitchen," I went on, glancing around the small space. In the warm glow, our shadows danced together against the wall. "And it's the big things, too. You've literally saved us more than once."

The tightness in Jay's jaw eased, and I could tell he was finally starting to believe me when I complimented him.

Still, I didn't want to give him the chance to deny it.

"What does your tattoo mean?" I asked, switching the topic. "The one on the inside of your arm."

He visibly flinched, and dread passed over his features.

"It's dumb. I got it when I was wasted out of my mind. I don't even know why I chose it. I barely remember that night."

Okay. So, he was weird about the tattoo. I guess ink regrets happened, especially if someone wasn't sober.

"So, what do you want to do, career-wise?" I changed the subject again, letting him off the hook.

He shrugged, seeming to relax now that we were talking about something else. "Honestly, I don't know. I enjoy the magician gig, but it's not something I can live off of long-term."

"You could start your own business," I suggested.

"And do what? Children's birthday parties? I'm not exactly the kind of guy parents want to hire."

Well, he had a point there. I knew he'd be great at something like that, but a quick background check was all it would take for people to judge him.

"Would you say you're more trustworthy now, or before you went to jail?" I asked.

His eyebrows furrowed. "Now, of course. I don't do the things I used to."

"But you didn't have a record then."

"Yeah." He let out a humorless chuckle. "Because I hadn't gotten caught yet."

"Exactly. Sometimes the squeaky-clean ones only look great on paper because they've never been caught. It doesn't make them innocent or harmless."

We stopped moving.

"Casey," he breathed out, his tone a bit tortured as he buried his face in my hair. "If I was a better man, I'd walk away from you and your son. I'd leave you alone. I'd let some other guy—a doctor or a teacher or *anyone* who's not me—sweep you off your feet and give you everything you've ever wanted."

"But you're not *that* good, right?" I asked lightly, a smile spreading over my lips.

Jay pulled back slowly, his scruff scraping against my cheek along the way. Tingles spread over my skin as he gave me a heated look.

He cupped the nape of my neck, and his gaze fell to my mouth. "No, I'm not."

And then his lips were on mine.

Dizziness made me sway, and I held onto Jay's shoulders to stay upright. It felt like we were back on the carnival ride, because I could've sworn the room was spinning.

Wait.

The room wasn't spinning.

But I was.

Jay was moving us toward the kitchen counter, and suddenly I was lifted up. My butt landed on the edge, and the cool surface felt good against my overheated body.

Without disconnecting the kiss, Jay's strong hands pushed my knees apart.

Oh, boy.

He nestled his hips between my thighs, and I could feel the massive bulge behind the zipper of his pants.

"I really like your knees, baby," he murmured, his lips brushing mine as his fingers drew lazy circles on my legs.

Baby. He called me baby.

I had no idea how one word could affect me so much, but the pulsing in my core became unbearable as his tongue plunged into my mouth.

Hang on a sec.

"My knees?" I questioned, pulling back as his strange compliment registered.

A slow smile spread over his face. "They're cute. Knobby."

"Knobby?" I sounded a bit insulted as I parroted the word.

Jay's thumbs caressed my skin, and we both looked down at my knees. Sticking my legs out, I studied the way my bones protruded a little more than the average person. I'd never thought much of it.

"They've always looked like that. It's just the way they're shaped," I defended, letting my legs fall. My heels thumped against the cabinets.

"It's not a bad thing." Bending down, Jay pecked one knee-cap, then went over to the other to give it the same treatment. "Just gives me more places to kiss you."

When he straightened, his lips went back to mine. Hooking his hands behind my knees, he yanked my body forward until my core collided with his prominent erection.

Gasping into his mouth, I groped at the lapels of his jacket, wanting him closer.

Whatever playlist we'd been dancing to had run its course, and now the room was completely silent except for our ragged breathing and wet kisses.

To hell with the jacket.

I started peeling it away, and Jay let it slide off his shoulders. It fell to the floor.

Jay's palms moved to the top of my thighs, but they didn't stay there for long. His fingertips skimmed up the sensitive skin of my inner leg. Higher. Closer to where I wanted him.

My lower belly clenched when he was just an inch away from my pussy.

The anticipation was killing me.

How far would he go? How far would I let him get?

All the way. That was the answer. There was no way I'd be satisfied with anything less.

"Please, please," I begged, my words muffled by his mouth.

Pushing away, he separated himself from me.

No, no, no.

I leaned forward, chasing him with my lips and groping at his arms to bring him back.

"Don't worry. I'll give you what you want." Letting out a deep chuckle, Jay flipped my dress up.

The fabric crumpled over my stomach, baring my damp panties. Brushing his thumb over the lace, he found my swollen clit. I nearly fell backward when he pressed down.

"There," I gasped, bracing my palms on the counter to hold myself up. "Touch me right there."

Jay did what I asked, but he stayed on the outside of the thin material, driving me wild as he lightly teased the area. There wasn't enough pressure for me to come, and I needed more.

I made a wordless, impatient sound as I bucked my hips.

Spreading myself wider for him, I hooked my ankles behind his ass, digging into his muscled flesh. "Please."

"Okay, baby. Okay." He gave me what I wanted when he slipped his hand under the waistband.

His fingertips trailed over the trimmed patch of hair before cupping my pussy. I moaned, and the back of my head hit the cabinet with a thud.

"Shit," Jay groaned. "You're so wet."

"Only you," I told him, breathless. "It's all for you."

No one had ever made me this crazy. I didn't even know it was possible to want someone so badly, but Jay had me questioning my sanity.

The things I'd do for an orgasm right now.

So many questionable, desperate things.

I was pretty sure it'd take an earthquake to pull us apart.

Jay nipped at my chin before his lips traveled down the column of my neck, kissing and sucking along the way. Flattening his tongue on the hollow of my throat, he licked upward. Chills racked my body when he blew on the dampened skin.

I was panting now. My inner muscles spasmed when Jay's

fingers grazed my slit. The tip of his middle finger played at my opening. Slowly circling. Gently stroking. Awakening nerve endings I didn't know I had.

Suddenly, two thick fingers pushed inside, causing both pain and pleasure as he buried them deep.

I cried out, and my eyes slammed shut.

"Am I being too rough?" Jay asked gruffly, his stilled fingers lodged deep inside my pussy. "Want me to slow down?"

"Don't you dare," I puffed out, ready to issue threats if he stopped.

"Yes, ma'am." It sounded like Jay was smiling, but I couldn't open my eyes to look, because those fingers started moving.

In and out. Slowly, at first. Priming me for what he was about to do next.

Cradling the back of my head, he protected me from banging my skull on the cabinet as he began hooking those fingers in a 'come here' motion.

When his thumb pressed down on my sensitive clit, my entire body jerked.

I moaned loud and low, and I didn't recognize my own voice. The carnal sound coming out of my mouth was a noise I'd never made before.

"Shh," Jay hushed, his hand moving from behind my head to close over my mouth. "Gotta keep quiet."

Opening my eyes, I looked at him. He was watching me, his darkened eyes bouncing from my covered face to between my legs where his hand pumped into me.

I was completely at his mercy, pinned in place.

It turned me on.

In my life, I was always in charge. Every decision was up to me. It was oddly refreshing to let someone else take control for once.

And hot. Really fucking hot.

I could hear how wet I was. Scandalous, slick sounds were coming from my pussy as Jay worked my body like an expert.

Needing something to do with my mouth, I bit down on his finger before sucking on the flesh.

He gasped, then growled, "Fuck, yes. Suck on it."

He stuck his thumb into my mouth, and I did as he commanded, enjoying being filled by him in more ways than one.

But it still wasn't enough.

Clumsily pulling at the bottom of his shirt, I tugged it up. Jay stepped away long enough to whip it over his head.

I whimpered, feeling so empty without him touching me.

Plus, the sight of him without a shirt did nothing to help the situation. The candlelight transformed his skin into liquid gold, accentuating every dip and indent, making his six-pack pop.

His chest heaved as his gaze fell to my spread legs. He licked his lips, then his eyes traveled to my breasts, which were still concealed by the dress. Stepping close, he tried to pull the fabric down. It wouldn't budge.

He frowned, and the look of utter frustration on his face made me smile. Tugging the straps off my shoulders, he yanked a little too hard, and I heard a rip.

Oops.

I hope Mackenna didn't want this thing back.

Cool air caressed my hardened nipples, making them tighten painfully.

"These tits," Jay said reverently, cupping and squeezing both breasts at the same time. "You fucking kill me, baby. So perfect."

Then he was back inside me. The stretch caused a sting, and I looked down. He was using three fingers now.

Moaning, I raked my nails over his chiseled pecs. It wasn't

hard enough to break the skin, but I could see red lines forming in their path.

Grabbing me by the back of the neck, Jay pushed his mouth to mine in a rough kiss. Tongues dueled and teeth clacked as he grinded his erection against my inner thigh.

He growled, and the sexy sound vibrated in my mouth.

This wasn't like before. Jay's control was unraveling. We were losing our restraint, and I thought for one brief, glorious second that I might actually get to see Jay naked tonight.

A faint wail zapped me out of the moment, popping our sexy bubble like one of the balloons at the carnival.

Gus.

If anything could ruin the mood, it was the sound of my baby crying.

Jay must not have heard it, because he began undoing his belt.

"Wait, wait." I pushed at his shoulder and he immediately backed away.

With his hands up, he looked like he'd gotten caught doing something he shouldn't. His expression was horrified. Guilty.

He thought he'd hurt me.

I quickly shook my head as I righted my clothing and hopped off the counter. "Gus woke up."

Jay visibly deflated with relief when he realized I wasn't upset with our hot-as-hell encounter.

His fingertips grazed my arms as he slid the dress's straps back into place. Delivering one last kiss to my lips, he ordered, "Go."

As soon as I turned, he playfully swatted my butt. I squealed, giggling as I dashed to the bedroom.

Making it to the door, my hand went up to idly toy with my prism, but something didn't feel right. It took me a second to realize it was because it wasn't on the nylon band anymore.

Glancing down, I held the prism out and saw it on a shiny silver chain.

"Momma's coming, bud," I called through the crack of the door, and Gus's cries quieted. I looked back at Jay, my eyes wide with disbelief. "What is this?"

Jay grinned. "Do you like it?"

"You switched it without me noticing." The sneaky devil. Sometime during our 'prom' he'd removed my necklace, put the prism on a new chain, then put it back on. "How did you do it?"

"Ah, ah. A magi—"

"A magician never tells his secrets. So I've heard, magic man." I smiled wryly. "Will you at least tell me when?"

Jay closed the distance between us and lowered his face next to mine. His warm breath tickled my ear when he replied, "Maybe it was when I was knuckle-deep in your pussy. You were a bit distracted."

I gasped, a new heat wave rolling through me.

Pissed that I was taking so long, Gus shouted out a garbled string of impatient grunts. Pretty sure that was baby-speak for *get the fuck in here*.

I sighed and turned, checking the clock on the nightstand as I traipsed to the crib.

Ugh. It wasn't even ten o'clock yet. Gus never woke up this early. Either we were being louder than I thought, or he could somehow sense that I was having fun without him. Babies seemed to have an uncanny way of knowing when they weren't invited.

Picking Gus up, I swiveled toward the bed, ready to lie down with him. My eyes found Jay standing in the doorway, casually leaning against the door frame.

Still shirtless.

The gray slacks hung low on his hips, and even in the

shadows, I had a great view of the V lines disappearing into the waist of his pants. And his abs. Pecs. Broad shoulders and chiseled arms.

Gah.

It seriously wasn't fair how handsome he was.

"I can get him back down," I said, wanting to continue whatever it was we were about to do.

But Jay shook his head. "Catch up on some sleep. It's probably a good thing we got interrupted."

"Why?"

"Because I wouldn't have stopped unless…"

Unless I asked him to. "I know."

An unspoken communication passed between us as we both processed what that meant.

We were in this now. Committed.

We wanted each other, but the relationship was still was so new.

It was probably too soon to have sex.

But how were we going to avoid the inevitable when only a wall separated us at night?

CHAPTER 18

Jay

T urns out, toddlers make for really good cock blocks. Casey wasn't joking when she'd said Gus didn't sleep well, and his sleeping patterns had only gotten more disrupted with all the changes.

New place. New routine. New guy hanging around all the time.

For the past two nights, Casey and I hadn't even had a chance to finish what we'd started. Gus was staying up well past ten, and by the time she got him down, she was exhausted.

Last night, she came out to the couch to chill with me. While I picked out a DVD for us to watch, she passed out. After watching her sleep for way longer than what was socially acceptable, I'd carried her to the bed and tucked her in.

Tonight I'd be working the carnival in a town forty-five minutes away, and she'd most likely be asleep by the time I got home. Same for tomorrow.

Oh, well. It was best this way.

Casey was a temptation I couldn't resist. The other night I'd been *this close* to fucking her right there on the kitchen counter.

Not the romance she deserved. Maybe I couldn't take her on expensive dates, but at least I could try to make our first time worth remembering.

"I'm declaring this a total loss," the insurance agent said to Casey, giving the trailer a wide birth as she carefully walked around the perimeter in her high heels.

"That's what I thought," Casey responded, sounding forlorn as she trailed after the woman in the spiffy pantsuit. "So what do I do now?"

"I'll run some numbers and we write you a check."

"Just like that?"

The woman gave her a reassuring smile. "Just like that. It'll probably take me until next week, but I want to make sure I take your personal items into account, since they're covered under the policy. If you can make a list, that would be great. Furniture, electronics, jewelry…"

"Dewey?"

I smiled down at Gus. We were in the neighbor's yard across the street, staying occupied with their small swing set while Casey ironed out her business.

After finding out the hard way that Gus fucking hated the swing—seriously, my ears were still ringing—I sat him on top of the little red slide. He didn't like going down, but he enjoyed being up high.

"Yeah, little man. Jewelry. Like this." Digging in my back pocket, I pulled out one of the rings I'd bought for him and did a quick trick.

His eyes went comically wide when he saw the silver band appear on my pinkie finger. Diving forward, he almost plummeted to the ground when he snatched it.

"Whoa." I caught him, amused by his lack of self-preservation. He had zero chill when it came to shiny things. "All right, all right. There's more where that came from."

I had several more at home, but I wanted to spread the gifts out. They were perfect for distracting him from unpleasant situations like the one Casey was dealing with now.

I tried to set him back on the slide, but he clung to me instead. One hand closed tightly around the ring, and the other went to my shirt collar. Gus tugged at it, rubbing the soft cotton material against his cheek.

My heart warmed. I loved it when he did this.

Kids, man. Their innocence was humbling. He had no idea about all the bad shit I'd done in my life, and he didn't care. There was no judgment in his eyes when he rested his head on my shoulder and smiled up at me.

We were best buds now.

Even Casey was astonished by how fast he'd taken a liking to me. Yesterday, I'd kept him occupied while she had some time to herself in the bathroom. She emerged looking refreshed, and she was beyond ecstatic when she realized Gus had been happy the whole fifteen minutes she was out of sight.

Most surprising of all was his freely given affection. Yesterday morning, we'd been playing with his rings on the floor when he leaned over and kissed my arm. I'd been so shocked by it that I didn't talk for five minutes. I just stared at him, wondering if I'd imagined it, or if it'd been a mistake.

But when I'd looked over at Casey, I saw remnants of unshed tears in her eyes as she smiled at us. Since then, I'd gotten countless hugs and kisses from the little guy.

"I'll be in touch, Miss Maxwell." The insurance agent said her goodbyes to Casey, offered her sympathy one more time, then drove away in her Mercedes.

Casey trudged over to us, arms crossed and head down.

"How do you feel about all this?" I asked, waving my hand at the rubble. "You okay?"

She shrugged, kicking a pebble with her shoe.

"I'm glad I'll have money to get a new place, but I guess you're stuck with us until next week." Her tone was apologetic, and she wouldn't look up from the ground.

Aw, fuck.

In a time like this, she was still worried about imposing? Sweet girl. When would she learn that it was never a burden to have them around?

"Hey." I outstretched my free arm. "Come 'ere."

She closed the distance willingly, and my hand found her waist as I reeled her in. My thumb slipped under her tank top, rubbing the smooth skin on her hip, and I recalled how it felt to have my fingers in her pussy the other night.

Really inappropriate time for that to happen, considering there was a youngster sandwiched between us.

I placed a kiss on Casey's temple. "You two can stay at my place as long as you want. I like having you there."

In fact, I was selfishly hoping the insurance company might take their time with that reimbursement check.

I felt the tension ease from Casey's muscles, and she nodded, accepting what I said as the truth.

She looked longingly at her trailer. "It just sucks that I can't get in."

"What do you need from inside?"

"Just a few things in the bedroom. The fire didn't spread there, and I bet they're still in good condition." Her gaze went to the collapsing roof. "But there's no getting through that door."

Assessing the structure, my nose hovered over Gus's hair while I formed a plan. I took in a whiff of his powdery baby shampoo before passing him to his mom.

Then I strode toward the trailer with purpose.

"What are you doing?" Casey sounded alarmed as she followed after me.

"Getting your stuff. What is it that you want?"

"You can't, Jay. It's not safe."

"It'll be fine." Ducking under the caution tape, I went

to the same bedroom window I'd climbed out of with Gus. I opened it. The air inside was hot, musty, and definitely smelled like a campfire. I glanced at Casey over my shoulder. "Just tell me where the stuff is."

Anxiously chewing her lip, she stood a good distance away, scrutinizing the building like it might cave in on me.

"This won't take more than a couple minutes," I insisted. "Better tell me before I go in there blind and start throwing everything out the window."

"Gus's bucket of rings," she rushed out. "It's under his crib. And the two picture frames on the nightstand. Then in the closet, there's a plastic storage bin on the top shelf. I want his go-home outfit from the hospital. It should be the first thing you see when you open it. Yellow striped onesie, with a matching hat. Actually, you know what? Just bring the whole container out. It has important papers in it."

"Anything else?"

"Nope."

"None of your clothes or shoes…?"

She shook her head. "I don't think I'd be able to get the smell out."

"Got it." I threw her a wink before hopping inside.

The air was heavy and silent as I scanned the dim room. Last time I was in here, I was in too big of a hurry to look around.

It was a little weird seeing Casey's personal space, everything exactly how she'd left it Monday morning.

The comforter on her twin-sized bed was thrown back, and the cheerful design made me smile. Blue sky and fluffy clouds. It was the kind of blanket a child might have, and I was willing to bet my last dollar that she'd had it since she was a kid.

I went over to it and sniffed.

Whoa. Rearing back, I rubbed at my nose, wishing I could get the funky smell out of my nostrils. Definitely wouldn't be able to salvage that.

Putting my hands on my hips, my eyes searched the room for anything I might be able to save for her. But after seeing how little she had in the first place, it was obvious that I should just stick to the items she listed off.

Living with Casey had made me realize something: she was the most low-maintenance girl ever. It was actually fascinating to watch her scrape by with the bare minimum. Only one pair of shoes? No problem. Those sneakers could work with any outfit. Makeup samples only meant to be used once or twice? She could stretch it for days. Low on groceries? She'd dig around the cabinets until she found enough ingredients to fix dinner.

She hadn't complained once. Just kept chugging along, working with whatever she had.

I'd never met anyone so resourceful and selfless.

Approaching the nightstand, which was crammed in the small space between the crib and the bed, I studied the two pictures Casey wanted. One was of Gus. It must've been when he was just born, because he was bundled up in a hospital blanket.

My lips twitched with a smile. He looked so mad. His tiny face was scrunched, like he was about to cry.

Chuckling, I tucked it under my arm.

The other frame held a selfie of the two of them on Gus's first birthday. It was here in the kitchen. Gus was licking a cupcake while Casey was smiling over his shoulder. I wondered if they'd celebrated alone. Considering there was no one else there to take a photo, I could only assume that was the case.

Never again. If I had anything to say about it, they'd never have to spend another special event snapping selfies.

After the second frame joined the first in my hold, I crouched to peek under the crib. I spotted the Disney princess bucket right away. Grabbing it, I stood and pivoted toward the closet.

I set everything on the floor so I could drag the small blue storage bin off the shelf. Kneeling, I put it down. Curiosity got the best of me, and I snapped off the air-tight lid.

Casey was right—the yellow outfit was on top of everything else. I ran my fingers over the impossibly soft fabric, bumping over each button, ending at the little feet. Gathering the material, I brought it to my nose.

No smoke. In fact, it carried a hint of the baby scent I liked so much.

As I inhaled a second time, a strange sensation tugged at my heart—a mixture of longing and regret.

I wished I'd been there for this.

Impossible. Even if I hadn't been busy serving my sentence, Casey and I couldn't have been involved then. We'd been on two different paths, not to mention the age difference.

I just hated the idea of her coming home with Gus all by herself.

The hospital blanket was next on the pile. Under that, Gus's birth certificate. No father was listed, and he had Casey's last name. Good.

"Jay? You've been in there for a while." Casey's worried voice carried through the window. "Are you okay?" Pause. "Jay?"

"Day?" That was Gus. It was the first time he'd ever tried to say my name, and excitement ran through me.

"Yeah, buddy," I responded, packing up the box. "I'm almost done."

"Oh, you answer him," Casey snarked. "I see how it is. Tell Jay to come out."

"Day!"

"Who's in there?" she asked in the cute voice she only used for Gus.

"Day."

"That's right, bud." She seemed just as excited as I was. "Say it one more time."

"Daaay."

I'd never get tired of hearing that.

Smiling so wide my cheeks hurt, I piled the bucket and pictures on top of the storage bin. Then I climbed out the window, juggling everything as my feet touched the ground.

Casey's dimples were prominent, her elated expression mirroring mine, when she saw her recovered belongings.

She was so beautiful in the mid-morning sunlight.

Her dark hair was falling around her shoulders, long and straight. She'd quickly become a fan of the stretchy leggings Mackenna had given her. Today it was zebra print. On anyone else, I might've thought they were tacky, but Casey was so fucking sexy in the form-fitting black tank top she'd paired with the pants. Gus was wearing the new dinosaur shirt I'd gotten for him.

I took a second to admire the two people who'd become so important to me, and I had a surreal moment, where I felt like I was looking at someone else's life. How'd I get so lucky?

"Day." Outstretching his arms, Gus made grabby hands at me.

Couldn't say no to him.

The same bewildered look—the one Casey got every time Gus wanted me—appeared on her face as we traded. She passed Gus to my arms while I transferred all her stuff to her.

Gus added his new ring to the bucket, then he grasped my collar.

I lifted a shoulder and sent Casey a cocky grin. "I'm just a likeable guy."

"Yes, you are," she agreed, bumping me with her shoulder.

We started walking back to my apartment, close enough for our elbows to brush. Extending his arm, Gus grabbed Casey's shirt with his other hand.

Tethering us together.

Like a family.

I thought about my tattoo—the one Casey asked about.

I didn't know why I clammed up when it came to revealing its meaning. Maybe because it was so personal. I wasn't lying when I'd said I was really messed up the night I got it—that much was true.

But I remembered why I chose it.

It was a desperate man's wish. One I'd gotten permanently etched into my skin.

"Watching the sky, I wish for a family," I said quietly.

Casey looked at me. "What?"

Embarrassed, I glanced away. "That's the translation of my tattoo. Like I said—it's dumb."

She stopped in her tracks. "That's not dumb, Jay. I think that's beautiful."

I held my arm out and scanned the black lettering. "Back when I got this, I knew deep inside I wasn't doing life right. The path I was on wouldn't give me what I really wanted." I dropped my arm. "When I was a kid, I used to make wishes on clouds, not stars. I'd lie down in my backyard and watch the clouds go by, and that's what I always wanted when I grew up. A family."

Twisting her lips to the side, Casey studied my face before saying, "I think I like you a little more than I did five minutes ago."

I chuckled at her blunt honesty. "The feeling is mutual then. Seems like the more time I spend with you, the better this thing between us gets."

She gave me a brilliant smile, and I wanted to kiss those dimples. Leaning over, I caught one with my lips in a loud smooch. She giggled.

Jealous, Gus demanded one, too, glaring at me while pointing at his cheek.

"All right." I laughed before placing a peck on his baby-soft skin.

Casey and I resumed our walk, but we'd only gone about twenty feet before my phone started buzzing in my back pocket. Anchoring Gus to my side, I tried to dig it out.

Casey noticed my struggle, set down her things, and held out her arms. "I can take him."

The two of them returned to the slide while I answered the call.

I expected to see my mom or sister's number on the screen. They were the only ones I talked to these days. So I was surprised to see a number I didn't know. It was a Daywood area code.

"Hello?"

"Can I speak with Jay, please?" The voice was deep and gravelly. I didn't recognize it, and it brought back memories from all the times I used to get random calls back in the day.

People were always coming to me for their next fix.

I'd cut all ties with connections from my old life. Gotten a new phone number since regaining my freedom.

The thought that someone might've tracked me down had sweat trickling down my temple.

"This is him," I replied warily, wiping my brow as I distanced myself from Casey and Gus.

"This is Jordan Burwash. Jimmy Johnson told me you're looking for a job."

Disbelief made my feet stop so abruptly that I nearly tripped. "H-hi. Yeah, I am."

"We're having an event at the shop this Sunday," Jordan went on. "It's an annual promotion called Single Parent Sunday. All single parents get half-priced oil changes and a free car detailing. I've got the oil changes covered, but my cleaner quit without notice. If you're up for it, I'd like to pay you fifty dollars for the afternoon. We can call that your interview. If you do the job well, I'd like to hire you on full-time."

"I'm in," I told him without pause, unable to hide my enthusiasm.

"It's dirty work," he warned.

"I'm fine with that."

I used to clean my cell from top to bottom daily. I'd get into cracks and crevices with an old toothbrush, assuring every inch of it was as sanitary as possible. I liked having control over my space and keeping it clean made me feel a little better about being there.

Who would've thought I'd acquire honest skills in prison?

"Thank you, Jordan," I said. "I won't let you down."

"Good," he responded jovially. "Can you be here at noon?"

Carnival teardown was that morning, but we always finished by midday. Plus, it was the last weekend of the season. No one would be pissed if I had to leave a little early.

"Yes, sir. I'll see you then." Hanging up, I grinned at Casey, who was not-so-conspicuously eavesdropping.

"What's going on?" Her smile grew when she saw how happy I was.

"I think I just got a job."

CHAPTER 19

Casey

I didn't like being at Jay's apartment when he wasn't here. After we got back from the trailer park, he left to go to the carnival, and he wasn't supposed to return until after midnight.

I'd actually gotten Gus to sleep on time tonight. Go figure. The one evening when I had free time and Jay was gone working.

Now I was all alone.

A week ago, this would've thrilled me. I would've had a snack by myself, enjoyed some sitcom reruns, and gone to bed early.

Letting out a sigh, I turned a full circle in the dark bedroom. It just wasn't the same knowing Jay wasn't on the other side of that door.

The rain pouring down outside only added to the gloomy atmosphere. A thunderstorm had rolled in about an hour ago, and the heavy drops were still pelting the windows as lightning flashed outside. As a child, I'd always been uneasy about storms, and being a mom hadn't given me any kind of special bravery.

At least Gus always seemed to sleep heavier with the constant rushing noise.

Maybe I had a chance at getting some time with Jay.

It was a little ridiculous how quickly I'd started to depend on him. Household chores had been divided according to what we hated the least. I mostly cooked and did the laundry, and Jay did… well, pretty much everything else, including entertaining Gus while I was busy.

Jay was seriously getting the short end of the stick. I wasn't even a great cook. It was like that area of my brain wasn't wired right. I could boil pasta and stick a frozen pizza in the oven, but that was the extent of my skills.

I stepped out into the living room and looked around. The only light source was the dim bulb on the range hood over the stove. Colorful blocks and balls were scattered on the floor, because the basket of toys Gus had been playing with earlier was tipped over.

Other than that, the apartment was spotless.

I'd never lived with a man before, but it wasn't what I'd expected. I thought guys were supposed to be messy, but Jay was the tidiest dude ever.

No complaints here. I wouldn't argue with someone if they wanted to do the dishes and hang up my wet towels after I was done showering.

After putting all the toys away and setting the basket in its rightful place next to the couch, I went to the fridge. I took out the plate of leftover pizza, popped it into the microwave, and grabbed a can of soda.

Caffeine. That was what I needed.

If I was still up when Jay got home… It. Was. On.

∽

Sometime later, I heard the lock turn, and that was when I realized I'd fallen asleep in the recliner.

The kitchen light switched on as Jay came through the

door. Blinking to adjust to the sudden brightness, I quickly wiped at my face to make sure there was no drool on my chin. I smoothed down my hair and straightened my tank top.

So much for that caffeine. The empty soda can was still sitting between my legs where I'd put it while I rested my eyes. The plate of pizza crusts was almost falling off my lap, so I leaned over to set it on the coffee table. It landed with a clatter, and Jay looked surprised when he saw me.

"Hey," he said quietly. "Didn't realize you were still up."

Squaring my shoulders, I tried my best to sound seductive, not groggy. "I've been waiting for you. What time is it?"

"Just after ten. We had to close up early because of the rain."

Oh. Maybe thunderstorms weren't so bad after all.

Jay smirked as he held up a brown paper sack. Some dark spots bled through it, and even before he announced what it was, I knew. I could smell the grease and sugar from fifteen feet away. My mouth watered.

"I brought you a funnel cake," he announced, clearly pleased with himself. As he should be. If I hadn't already been planning to jump his bones, I certainly would've been now.

Getting up, I crossed the room with quick footsteps.

"Gimme. Thank you," I sang, snagging the bag and returning to my spot to dig in.

"Oh, it's like that, huh?" Jay chuckled as he watched me return to my comfortable spot. "Is that chair yours now?"

Breaking off a piece of the funnel cake, I shoved it in my mouth, and my answer came out garbled when I replied, "I'm willing to share it with you."

Amused, he shook his head and edged toward the bathroom. "I need to shower real quick."

Jay was the fastest shower-taker ever. I swear he was only in there for forty-five seconds. He came out wearing a white

T-shirt and gray gym shorts, scrubbing a towel over his wet hair.

Striding across the room, he dropped the towel to the coffee table. Suddenly, his arms were under me, lifting me up. "I think you said something about sharing."

Startled, I let out a squeak as he rotated us and lowered himself onto the cushion with me sideways on his lap. Looking ornery as hell, he grinned before opening his mouth.

I tore off a piece of the funnel cake and brought it to his face. I paused, pulling back before I could reach my destination. "Don't bite me."

I placed it between his teeth, and some of the white sugar smeared across his lips.

"I would never." He chewed and waggled his eyebrows. "Unless you wanted me to."

My stomach did a somersault at the mental image of him branding me with love bites.

Adjusting my position, I wiggled until I was straddling him. A groan escaped him when his eyes fell to my spread legs.

"My turn." I opened my mouth and waited for him to feed me.

His eyes darkened and his face turned serious as he obliged. When he pulled his hand away, I caught his wrist. Sugar coated his thumb and pointer finger. Couldn't let it go to waste.

Closing my mouth around his thumb first, I sucked. Jay's breath caught in his throat. His finger was next. I licked them clean before grabbing another morsel for him. After he swallowed it, I held out my sugary hand to him.

He didn't disappoint. The tip of his tongue swirled my fingers, and I imagined what it would feel like to have that tongue somewhere else on my body.

Heat flooded my core, and it was difficult not to squirm and seek the friction I craved.

Our sexy game went on like that for at least five min-utes—us feeding each other while making one hell of a mess.

It was impossible to eat a funnel cake without getting powdered sugar everywhere. The white stuff had rained down between us, landing on Jay's shirt and dusting the skin of my chest.

Which presented a convenient opportunity.

"You're all dirty," I said, pinching the bottom of Jay's shirt. "Better take this off."

Deciding we were done eating, Jay rolled up the paper bag and tossed it to the coffee table where it landed on top of the towel. Then he peeled off his shirt.

As I skimmed my fingertips down his sculpted torso, I could feel the massive erection beneath me. I wanted to rock against it. Rub myself on him until I came.

"You're dirty, too," Jay rasped.

Gripping my hips, he dragged me forward so my chest was just an inch away from his mouth. Jay's hot breath fanned over my skin before he licked my cleavage. Keeping his tongue flat and wide, he tried to cover as much area as possible.

My toes curled. My heart went wild. My hips gave an in-voluntary jerk, and his hardness nudged my clit. It felt so good my eyes nearly rolled back in my head.

"Mmm. So sweet," he mumbled against my collarbone.

Bringing my hands up to his hair, I threaded my fingers through the reddish strands.

As he lapped at my skin, he moved up to my neck.

I knew for a fact that there was no sugar there, but he went at me like I was his favorite dessert. Teeth nipped my pulse point. Lips dragged over my throat. Fingers dug into my back, pulling me closer.

Jay sucked at a spot under my ear, sending chills down my spine.

And this was the point where I just couldn't wait any longer.

We were beyond foreplay.

I needed sex.

So what if it was too soon? We'd been playing house for four days now. If you added up the hours we'd spent together, that equaled like a month's worth of dates.

"Jay," I breathed out.

"Yeah, baby?" he murmured before nibbling my jaw.

"Need you now." Sliding off his lap, I stood. My center was throbbing, and I felt like I could combust at any moment.

At least I wasn't alone in this. Jay seemed just as worked up as I was. Jaw clenched, lips parted, chest heaving.

Air whooshed out of him when my fingers grabbed the bottom of my shirt and started to lift it up. With heavy-lidded eyes, he didn't even blink while I got rid of my tank top, like he didn't want to miss one millisecond of the show.

I wasn't wearing a bra. As the clothing dropped to the floor, Jay's focus was glued to my breasts, and his hands grasped the arms of the chair so hard I thought he might rip it to shreds.

Hooking my thumbs into the waistband of my leggings and panties, I tugged them both down until they pooled at my feet.

I kicked them off to the side.

It was weird to be standing in front of someone totally nude, but the way Jay looked at me made me feel powerful.

Beautiful.

"Take off your shorts." My voice didn't even sound like my own as I made the command. It was low and husky, and I felt like Jay was unlocking a new side of me that I'd never been aware of until now.

Lifting his ass, he pushed his gym shorts and boxer briefs

down. And when his cock bobbed up, I couldn't stop myself from gaping at it.

It was long and thick. So unbelievably thick. The swollen head was slightly wider than the shaft, and I visualized what it would look like entering me, spreading my opening as it pushed inside.

On my next exhale, a whimper escaped. My pussy was so damp I was afraid I'd start dripping.

Jay crooked a finger at me, and I obeyed, closing the distance. Putting a knee on either side of his hips, I resumed my position on his lap. Only this time it was different. Because we were both completely naked.

And his giant dick was mere inches away from my aching core.

Jay still had sugar on the corner of his mouth, so I leaned forward to lick it. Sweetness danced on my taste buds. Taking his bottom lip into my mouth, I sucked at his flesh, unable to get enough of it. Of him.

Jay groaned. "I can't believe this is happening. Are we really doing this?"

"Oh, yeah." Lick. Suck. Bite. "We're doing this."

"Right here?"

"Right here."

His large hands cupped my breasts, and when he rubbed his thumbs over my nipples, I gasped. He squeezed each mound, testing their weight in his palms.

Then all of the sudden, his hands were gone. Hooking an arm around my waist to keep me from falling, Jay bent over the side of the chair. He groped for his shorts and retrieved a condom from the pocket.

I raised an eyebrow. Looked like I wasn't the only one prepared for sex tonight.

Throwing me a smirk, Jay rolled on the protection, then

stroked himself. His tight grip traveled from the base to the tip in a smooth, practiced motion.

Once. Twice. Three times.

The sight caused another gush of wetness to coat my inner thighs. Totally fixated on the erotic scene, I almost didn't want him to stop.

Almost.

"You ready?" Jay asked, bringing his hand to my soaked pussy. He made a sound when he slid through my folds. "Holy shit."

I wasn't sure if I should be embarrassed by my body's reaction.

"Can't help it." I glanced away. "You always do this to me."

"Hey." Jay's tone was gentle but firm. I looked back at him, and he took my chin between his thumb and forefinger. "If you knew what you did to me, you'd be scared."

"Try me," I baited him.

"Feel how hard I am."

My mouth went dry as I gripped his dick. I couldn't even get my fingers all the way around the girth.

"I could come right now," he grunted out. "Then I could come again. And again. Whenever I jerk off, I think of you. I've lost count of how many times I pictured your face when I came. I'm addicted to you, and I haven't even fucked you yet."

"I love it when you say things like that." I squeezed his stiff cock, earning a moan from him. "So dirty and honest. I'm not scared of how much you want me. It only makes me want you more."

Connecting our lips, I tasted his sweetness again.

"I need you to know something else," he said, his words muffled by my mouth.

"What?" I asked distractedly, licking his bottom lip.

"I've never done this sober."

Huh?

Putting enough distance between us so I could look into his eyes, I tilted my head. "Done what sober? Sex?"

"Any of it," he clarified. "This is a first for me. It feels… important that I tell you." Letting out a humorless laugh, his head dropped back. "I don't even know what it'll be like. I might come in two minutes. I might be too rough. If I hurt you, you need to say so—"

I cut off his worries with another kiss. It was chaste and quick, meant for comfort.

"We'll figure it out together," I reassured him. "Just be you."

Nodding, he yanked the lever on the side of the chair. The footrest popped up, and Jay reclined backward.

My hand was still holding his dick. He wrapped his fingers around mine and began guiding my movements. Making me jerk him off. Gliding up and down. Up, down. Up, down.

Meanwhile, his other hand started softly circling my clit. Running the tip of his finger over my entrance, he slid around the opening, but he didn't go inside. He repeated the teasing caresses several times.

"I want you so bad it hurts," I admitted, peering down at the man at my mercy.

"Come 'ere, then." Holding his cock at the base, he pointed it up. "I'm all yours."

Shifting so my pussy hovered right over the broad head of his dick, I braced my hands on his shoulders. As soon as his hot flesh touched mine, I gasped.

Acquainting myself with the feel of his erection, I rocked my hips. His cock slid through my folds, sparking nerve endings with every pass. When the tip nudged my clit, I was surprised to feel the little spasms I always got before an orgasm. My inner muscles were already fluttering, and we hadn't even gotten to the good stuff yet.

Jay let out a sexy growl as he massaged my upper thighs. "I've got the best view in the world. If only you could see how fucking hot you look right now."

His thumbs found purchase on either side of my pussy. He spread the lips apart and cool air touched my clit.

Holy shit.

I blew out a shaky breath.

Jay's hungry gaze bounced from between my thighs to my breasts. To my stomach. To my arms. To my knees.

He roamed my body, looking like he wanted to touch every inch at once.

When Jay's eyes finally locked with mine, I saw a pure vulnerability there, filled with adoration.

"I've waited so long for you," he said on a reverent sigh.

Any coherent response I could've formed got caught in my throat. My chest tightened, overwhelmed with an emotion I couldn't describe.

I didn't know a man could make me feel worshiped with his eyes. Jay looked at me like I held the key to his happiness. Like I had the power to make all his dreams come true.

Sex was a big deal. I didn't know what laid on the other side of this or how our relationship would change after such an important step.

All I knew was that I needed him inside me.

I rose up, positioning his cock at my entrance.

We both moaned when the tip slipped in, and I slowly sank down.

The pressure alleviated the aching emptiness, but it was replaced with a slightly painful stretching sensation.

"Oh my God," I moaned. "You're so big."

I lifted myself, then I let my weight do some of the work for me as I came back down. It was still a tight fit.

We both glanced to where our bodies were joined,

and I was shocked to see that I still had a few inches to go. Seriously?

"Hurt?" Jay grunted.

I gave a nod. "A little."

"Let me help."

His hand was shaking when he brought it to my clit, and I was humbled by how much I affected a guy like Jay. He outweighed me by almost a hundred pounds. He was strong. Intimidating.

Yet, I made him tremble.

The tight, quick circles he drew on my sensitive bud made me wetter. Made my body want to take all of him.

"Better?" Jay's husky voice wavered.

Nodding, I dropped to my elbows, placing our faces just inches apart. My nipples dragged up his chest, heightening the pleasure as his cock went deeper.

Jay kissed my nose.

The tender action twisted me up inside.

This wasn't just a physical act for either of us, and that fact both thrilled and terrified me. I'd been waiting for this kind of connection my whole life. A part of me had started to doubt it even existed.

Now that I knew it was real, now that I'd experienced it, I didn't want to lose it.

And I wanted to try *everything*.

Jay's body was like my own personal amusement park, and I couldn't wait to go on every ride.

Anchoring his hands to my waist, Jay jerked his pelvis, shoving his cock all the way in.

Despite the fact that I was biting my lip hard enough to hurt, a small cry escaped my mouth as my pussy clenched a couple times. It was almost like I had a mini orgasm.

"Fuck, baby." The calluses on Jay's palms felt good on my

skin as his hands slid up my back. "You have no idea how great this feels."

I made a sound of disbelief. "I'm pretty sure I've got an idea. You were worried about coming in two minutes? I think I'm going to beat you to that finish line."

"Oh, you're under the impression you're only coming once?" he quipped, smirking. "That's cute."

"Why are we talking when we could be fucking?" I whispered playfully.

Turned on by my words, Jay groaned, and his dick twitched inside me. "Fuck me, then."

No more holding back.

Smashing my mouth to his, I parted his lips with my tongue while I began to move.

I quickly found a good rhythm. I rolled my abdomen, tilting my hips as I rocked back and forth. My clit kept rubbing against his pelvic bone, while his cock hit deeper than I ever thought possible.

The dual sensations pushed me to the edge embarrassingly fast.

Every time I rose up and sank back down, Jay let out a raspy sigh. The sexy sound turned me on more.

Unable to concentrate on kissing, I rested my forehead against his while I chased the elusive explosion I'd only experienced by myself.

My motions got faster. Ragged breathing became panting. Panting turned into high-pitched whining.

Jay's hands traveled to my ass, and as he squeezed the flesh, I was vaguely aware of the whispered obscenities and dirty encouragements flying from his mouth.

"Shit. That's it, baby. So fucking sexy. Ride my cock."

I'd never imagined someone would speak to me that way. And that I'd like it.

Love it.

Coming. Coming. Coming.

I wasn't sure if I was speaking it out loud or if I was just thinking it, but the buildup was so strong that I lost all rational thought.

A scream lodged in my throat as my walls clamped down. The orgasm tore through me, affecting every single muscle in my body.

My fists clenched, my toes curled, my abs locked up.

I couldn't breathe.

Oh my God, I couldn't see. Was it possible for an orgasm to rob someone of their eyesight?

After the last spasms tapered off, I realized I wasn't blind—my eyes had slammed shut. When I opened them, I found Jay staring at me again with that expression, so full of wonder and awe.

Gah. A girl could get used to being looked at like that.

Holding eye contact, I rode out the aftershocks while trying to catch my breath. My motions got slower, more languid.

Then I lost the ability to hold myself up.

I collapsed, burying my face between the cushion and Jay's neck.

CHAPTER 20

Jay

I didn't know if Casey could tell, but my whole body was practically vibrating.

The feel of her skin against mine was too much and not enough at the same time. We were as close as two people could be, but uncontrollable need still thrummed through my veins.

I wasn't sure if I would ever be sated when it came to Casey.

This was what happened when a man went years without sex. When he finally met the one who made it more than just sex.

I was the luckiest motherfucker on the planet.

First, Casey had trusted me with her safety. She let me protect her, taking refuge under my roof.

Now she was trusting me with her body.

Next, I'd conquer her heart.

She'd be mine, in every way possible.

Stroking a gentle hand down her back, I let her catch her breath as my fingers combed through her hair. My cock was still lodged deep inside her, and my balls demanded release.

"You're not falling asleep on me, are you?" I asked gruffly, trying to keep my voice steady.

"Are you kidding?" Casey mumbled, her breath tickling my ear. "You promised me multiple orgasms."

I chuckled. "That I did. Considering I haven't even had one yet, I'd say the outlook is good on fulfilling that promise."

Pulling herself up, she let out a ragged sigh. Her chest heaved, and her amazing tits bobbed up and down.

God, she was perfect.

Even with just-fucked hair she was regal and classy.

But as much as I loved having her on top of me, this position wasn't going to work when she was weak as a kitten.

Reaching to the side of the chair, I tipped the lever over. The footrest popped down and I shot up.

Looking startled, Casey's arms went around my neck. "What are you doing?"

"Moving to the couch."

Without removing my dick from my new favorite place, I stood. I carried Casey a few feet across the room and gently deposited her on the cushions.

I brushed some of her hair out of her face and caressed her cheek with my thumb.

She cupped the side of my face with her palm. "You don't have to be so careful with me. Don't get me wrong—I like it when you're cautious and considerate, but I'm not going to break."

I smirked. "I'm glad to hear you say that, because I wasn't planning on going easy on you."

She licked her lips, and her pussy tightened involuntarily, responding to the threat.

She wanted it hard, liked it rough. Which was good, because I had a lot of pent-up desire clamoring to get out.

Maybe sometime in the future I could take my time. Go slow. Be sweet.

Tonight wasn't that night.

Removing her hands from behind my neck, I put them up against the arm of the couch above her head.

"Hold on," I told her, before giving a hard thrust.

Arms tensing, her mouth popped open as she closed her eyes.

"Look at me," I demanded. "Watch."

Gripping her left leg, I lifted it up and draped it over my shoulder. I gave her a wicked grin before turning my head to lightly bite her knee.

I really loved her knees.

I also loved how she let out a scandalized gasp when my teeth met her skin. I kissed the spot before I pumped into her again.

The new angle felt fucking good, and I shuddered as pleasure tingled up my spine. She was so fucking tight. So warm and wet.

Withdrawing my dick, I let my tip hover at her drenched entrance, then I plunged into her heat. Harder. Deeper.

She cried out.

I paused because I couldn't tell if it was too much.

"Don't stop," she begged desperately, her fingernails clawing at the fabric of the couch. "Please."

Okay, then.

Surging forward, I set a rhythmic pace, reveling in the snug grip her pussy had on my cock.

Every time I went deep, our pelvises bumped and Casey's tits bounced.

I was fascinated by how her dusky pink nipples stood out against her creamy skin. I liked watching her become even more disheveled, her hair in complete disarray. I enjoyed seeing her fight to keep her eyes open.

Eventually, sensation won out and her eyes slammed shut. One of her hands went to my shoulder, and her nails dug into my skin.

It hurt, but I enjoyed that, too.

I liked sober sex. A lot.

Everything about it was fun.

Only problem was, Casey was being loud. The last thing I wanted right now was to have her wake a certain someone up. Being interrupted at this moment would've been terribly inconvenient.

I remembered how she'd responded the other day when I pinned her against the cabinets. How her pussy gushed on my fingers when I put my hand over her mouth.

"Shhh." I covered her swollen lips with my palm.

Blue eyes filled with desire snapped open. A low moan reverberated in her throat as I drove my cock into her over and over again. I fucked her so hard her entire backside would probably have rugburns tomorrow.

Muffled whimpers continued behind my hand as I pumped my hips, and I wanted to kiss her so bad.

Since her mouth was unavailable, I kissed her nose instead.

Just when I didn't think Casey's pussy could get any tighter, she brought her other leg up, basically asking me to fold her in half.

I could feel myself filling her completely. Stretching her to the limit.

"Too much?" I gritted out, fighting off the signs that I was about to come.

She couldn't answer me in words, but she gave a shake of her head.

Greedy girl.

I didn't slow down as I snaked my other arm between her thigh and stomach. I slipped my hand to her clit and strummed it with my fingers.

I'd told her I'd get her off more than once, and I meant it.

Unfortunately, my deprived body didn't agree.

My balls drew up close and my heartrate accelerated.

I tried not to think about how good Casey felt. How she smelled like femininity, sweat, and sex. How she literally surrendered to me.

But every time I closed my eyes, it enhanced the sensations.

The wet sounds of me sliding in and out of her. Her uninhibited moans. Our rhythmic breathing.

Every time I opened them, I could see those perfect tits jiggling. Her hair askew. Legs up.

Fuck, fuck, fuck.

Suddenly, Casey's whimpers stopped, her eyes widened, and her body stiffened. Her thighs shook violently, and her back arched. I felt her pussy contract, strangling my dick in a vise-like hold.

Her high keening sound echoed through the room as she thrashed beneath me, and that was all it took for me to let go.

I uncovered her mouth and replaced my hand with my lips.

She wasn't the only one who'd have trouble being quiet.

A quiet roar started in my chest as jets of cum shot from my cock. The low rumbling traveled up my windpipe. As I rutted my dick as far as it could go, a shout erupted from me.

Casey swallowed up my sounds, and I felt like I was giving over another piece of myself to her.

I'd never come this hard in my life. I was actually shocked at how long and powerful it was.

Jerking one final time, I let Casey's legs slip off my shoulders. I lowered her trembling limbs to the couch and dropped down, pressing our chests together.

I stayed propped on my elbows so I didn't crush her. "Holy shit, baby."

Slender fingers threaded through my hair as our faces met in a lazy kiss. Her tongue stroked mine. I sucked on her bottom lip. Nipped her chin. Kissed her nose.

We made out for a few minutes, both of us trying to calm our racing hearts.

Finally, Casey let out a satisfied hum. "I didn't know it could be like that."

"Neither did I," I admitted.

"I wanna do it again."

Agreed.

I was still rock-hard. I hadn't even pulled my dick out of Casey yet, and I was already thinking about ways to get back in.

Maybe slow and sweet could happen tonight after all.

CHAPTER 21

Casey

I blinked, disoriented by the brightness in the room. Had I forgotten to turn out the light before I fell asleep?

I rolled onto my back, looking for the source. When I saw sun streaming through the window blinds, I realized it was daylight that woke me up.

Daylight.

Which meant Gus slept through the night.

For the first time ever.

I smiled as I stretched. My body was still sore from the other night with Jay, but my libido came alive when scorching-hot memories of our sex marathon flooded my mind.

The first time was wild and explosive. Desperate and passionate.

But the second time we did it, Jay made love to me. I'd always thought that phrase seemed so cheesy, but I didn't know how else to describe it. It was plain old missionary position, but there was nothing plain or old about it. The steady, unrushed pace Jay set as he thrust into me was so... loving. He'd laced his fingers with mine, pinning my hands above my head while he kissed me over and over again. We looked into each other's eyes the entire time, and after what seemed like an hour, I was begging him to go faster.

The third round, however, was much like the

first—rough and unrestrained. Jay took me from behind, and I had to smother my screams by burying my face into the couch cushion.

In total, I came four times.

Four. Times.

Despite the signs that my body needed to recover, I'd been up for a repeat last night. Unfortunately, the weather was perfect, and Jay worked late. I'd tried to stay awake for as long as I could, keeping the bedroom door cracked so I might hear him when he came home. But apparently, I slept through any ruckus he made.

I guess I wasn't mad about that. I hadn't had an uninterrupted eight hours of sleep since the second trimester of my pregnancy. I needed this.

Feeling rejuvenated, I sat up, expecting to see Gus in the blue footie pjs I'd put him in before bed.

But the crib was empty.

Panic struck me as my head whipped toward the door. It was halfway open, and the sound of complete silence in the apartment was alarming.

Gus had never climbed out of his crib before. He was big enough to do it if he really wanted to, but he would've gotten in bed with me. He would've made some noise, at the very least.

Nightmarish scenarios pummeled me as I threw off the covers. What if he wandered out of the apartment? My rational side reminded me that he couldn't reach the deadbolt but fear overpowered logic as I ran from the bedroom.

"Gu—" My shout was cut short when I saw the scene in the living room.

Jay was lying on his back on the floor. He was halfway in a blanket that had been folded to make an uncomfortable looking sleeping bag. The pillows and cushions from the couch had been strategically placed around him, caging in the area with safety 'bumpers.'

And Gus.

My little boy was asleep on top of Jay's chest. He was sprawled out, face-down, cheeks squished. Some drool was dribbling onto Jay's gray shirt.

Jay's hand lifted in a silent wave, his eyes questioning and concerned. Groping around for his phone, he found it on one of the cushions. He picked it up, then started typing out a text. My phone buzzed on the nightstand.

Jay: Is this okay?

Me: Yeah. I was just scared because I didn't know where he was.

Jay: Gus was awake when I got home last night. He was standing in his crib when I checked in on you guys. He was cool with coming out here to hang with me, so I thought I'd let you sleep. Sorry. I should've asked you first.

Me: No, it's okay.

To show my sincerity, I smiled as I leaned back on the wall.

Me: I really appreciate it. Did he keep you up long?

Jay: Nah. I changed his diaper, gave him a bottle, and put on a weather channel. He was out within five minutes.

Me: You're the best. I'll go take a shower while I have the chance.

Jay: Cool. We'll be right here.

A goofy smile was plastered on my face all the way to the bathroom.

So this was what it was like to have a partner. A co-parent. A teammate. Someone to pick up the slack when I needed a break. Someone to make the days and nights less tedious. Someone to make life more enjoyable.

I'd just turned on the shower when my phone vibrated on the counter.

Jay: Any chance your car needs an oil change?

The random question made me pause. When was the last time my car had work done? I honestly couldn't remember. I didn't pay attention to that sort of stuff since I didn't drive often.

Me: Yeah, probably.
Jay: Come to Single Parent Sunday at the shop later while I'm working. I'll clean out your car.

Single Parent Sunday. The event at Burwash Auto Repair was well-known in the area, but I'd never taken advantage of the deal.

I wanted to go, and not just for my car—I missed Jay. He'd been gone so much lately and I wanted any opportunity to see him.

Me: Okay, we'll try to make it.

CHAPTER 22

Jay

So many Cheerios. Old French fries. Crayons. Spare change. Long lost sippy cups with dried-up milk crusted inside.

These were the treasures lurking under the seats of every vehicle that came through here.

My hands were sweating inside the rubber gloves, and I was pretty sure the smell of disinfectant and cleaning solution was permanently burned into my nostrils.

But I felt good.

I enjoyed this kind of work, and it was a bonus that everyone was impressed with the condition of their car when they got it back. Some even insisted on tipping me.

As I crawled on the floor of the fifteenth mini-van I'd been inside today, I ran the vacuum along the carpet, sucking up dirt and debris under the back seats.

I had a methodical way of doing things—working from top to bottom. Windows and windshield were first. Dashboard and steering wheel second. Doors. Seats. Carpets.

Satisfied with my work, I climbed out and turned off the Shop-Vac. The constant hum quieted, and I peeled off the gloves. On my way to the office, I put them in a bucket filled with all the other cleaning supplies by the bathroom.

Damn, it was hot in here. With the garage doors open to

the hot afternoon air, it had to be over eighty degrees. I was in desperate need of a cold shower.

Wiping the perspiration from my forehead, I went to hang the key ring on the board that indicated the vehicle was ready to go. Jordan was sitting behind the desk in his office, and he looked up when I came through the door.

"All done with that one," I announced. "What's next?"

His chair creaked as he leaned back. "That was the last one. You did a heck of a job today. I'm really impressed."

"Thanks. I had fun," I told him honestly.

"The job's yours if you want it."

A grin stretched over my face. "I want it."

"Can you start tomorrow?"

I nodded eagerly. "Just tell me when to be here."

"Nine a.m." Standing, he grabbed his wallet and dug out three twenties. "Keep the change. I'll want you Monday through Friday. Day ends at four."

"Sounds great."

After accepting my pay, I turned to leave, but I stopped before I could make it through the door.

I faced my new boss, noting how much he'd aged since the last time I saw him.

The wrinkles on his clean-shaven face had deepened, and he had a full head of white hair. His brown eyes were the same, though—kind. What I remembered most about Jordan Burwash was his kindness. I'd spent a lot of nights at his house when I was a kid, and I'd been envious of Chris for having such a good dad.

Of all the mistakes I'd made in high school, getting Chris tangled up in one of my messes was one of the worst. He and his dad had been good to me, fed me, provided a safe environment.

And how did I repay them? By almost getting the kid arrested.

"Jordan… I really appreciate you giving me a chance. You of all people have no reason to trust me—"

"Clean slate," he cut in, sending me a genuine smile. "I'll trust you until you give me a reason not to."

A lump rose in my throat. His forgiveness was unexpected and surprising. All I could manage was a nod before I strode away.

As I walked outside, I saw Casey approaching the shop with Gus on her hip. Her long ponytail was swishing in the breeze and a bright smile lit up her face when her eyes found me.

My heart gave a happy thump.

"Am I too late?" she asked, meeting me under the main opening. She glanced at the big clock on the wall. It was after five. Technically, the event was over. Disappointed, she shrugged. "Gus's nap went longer than I thought it would."

I was about to tell her I'd make sure her car got taken care of sometime this week, but Jordan sidled up next to me before I had the chance.

"We can squeeze another oil change in. You mind doing one more detail, Jay?"

"I've always got time for her," I replied seriously, tucking a flyaway strand behind her ear. "Jordan, this is my girlfriend, Casey."

"Nice to meet you." Grinning, Jordan shook her hand and looked at Gus. "And who's this small gentleman?"

Tickling Gus's tummy, Casey whispered, "What's your name?"

"Gus." His toothy grin was adorable.

"Well, Casey and Gus, it's nice to meet you." Jordan pointed at the door to the lobby. "We have a small waiting room through there. It's air conditioned and there are toys to keep him occupied. Help yourself to the coffee."

"Great. Thank you," Casey said, passing her keys to Jordan. Once she was behind him, she turned around, gave me a thumbs up, and mouthed, "Nice place."

Her approval caused a warm feeling in my chest.

Once she was out of sight, I took fifteen dollars from my wallet and extended it to Jordan. "I'd like to pay for her oil change."

He gently pushed my hand away. "This one's on the house. Call it a family discount."

There was that word again. The one that echoed in my mind like my heart was shouting it from the bottom of an empty canyon.

Family.

As Jordan shuffled out to get Casey's car, I looked at the lobby door, knowing my whole world was on the other side of it.

I didn't know how or when Casey and Gus had become so important to me. Maybe it started on that porch two years ago. Maybe it began the first time I saw Casey with Gus.

Either way, the kind of love she'd talked about in the car last week—the kind that was unfathomable to me—was real. It'd snuck up on me, but I could finally admit the truth.

I was in love with Casey, and I was a new man because of her.

CHAPTER 23

Casey

T he past week had been a dream come true. I wasn't used to things going my way, but luck had been on my side.

Doreen got back from her trip Sunday night, so she was able to start watching Gus again Monday. And for the first time ever, he didn't cry when I dropped him off. Beginning my day without crippling guilt weighing on me made a huge difference. I was happier at work, which resulted in better tips from my customers.

Then I got my reimbursement check from the insurance company. They gave me $5,675, plus they were going to cover the cost to have the damaged trailer removed from the lot.

Financially, I was back in the same place I started two years ago, almost to the exact dollar amount.

Gus and I could start over.

But between work and hanging out with Jay, I hadn't had time to contemplate our next step.

To be honest, I was okay with that.

I was too shy to admit it to Jay, but I wasn't in a hurry to leave his place. Having him around was extremely convenient, for many reasons.

In the past week, we'd had sex so many times I lost count. We'd kept up our cleaning and cooking routine, which made my life a lot easier. Plus, Jay liked getting up with Gus in the middle of the night.

I was well-rested and sexually satisfied.

How crazy would I have to be to leave a situation like that?

"You're checking your phone again." Jay's amused observation cut into my thoughts, and I glanced down at the blank screen in my palm.

I hadn't even realized I was holding it.

"Sorry." I shrugged. "Habit."

"You know they'll call if something's wrong, and you'd hear it ring. That's how phones work."

I scowled at his playful tone.

Yeah, I was being nuts, but I couldn't help it.

"I'm just nervous about being away from Gus. I've never had someone watch him because I wanted to…"

Be selfish.

"Go out?" Jay finished for me. "Have fun? Get some adult time?"

"Yeah," I sighed.

We were supposed to be having fun, but I was pretty crappy company.

It was Saturday evening, and Jay had arranged a date for us. He took me by surprise when Jimmy, Mackenna, and Will showed up at his apartment this afternoon. They were going to let the boys play together for a few hours while Jay and I went to dinner.

I'd assumed we'd go to Gloria's, but nope. Jay wanted to go to a Mexican restaurant in Daywood. Said they had the best chips and salsa.

And he was right. The burritos were pretty dang amazing, too.

"I won't look at this again," I promised, dropping my phone into my purse.

Just then, it chirped with a text and I lunged for it so fast I almost tipped over in the booth seat.

Mom: Hey, how are you?

"Everything okay?" Jay asked, concerned lines appearing between his eyebrows.

I nodded, putting the device away again. "It's just my mom."

"You two talked at all lately?"

"We texted a few days ago. She offered to give me money, but I told her I didn't need it." Guilt churned inside me as I picked at my napkin. "She hasn't returned to her house yet."

"And you feel bad about that?"

Reluctantly, I nodded. "I know I shouldn't feel sorry for her, but I do."

I was still really mad, but I missed my mom. We'd never gone this long without seeing each other. Even if we didn't spend much time together, being neighbors guaranteed the occasional run in.

"I'd be willing to bet she feels terrible about everything, too," Jay said before adding, "And she should. That's why she hasn't been back. Why don't you see if she wants to meet up tomorrow? I'll watch Gus and you two can iron things out."

"Really?" I asked, grateful.

My mom and I needed to have an unpleasant conversation, and I didn't want Gus to witness it. Nothing would get resolved until we sat down and got the serious chat out of the way.

And I wanted real talk. Woman to woman.

I wanted to know more about her. Not as my mother, but who she was as a person. I wanted to know who she was dating, why she never talked about her childhood, and what she wanted to do with the rest of her life. She was still young. Surely she had goals.

We'd never discussed any of those things, and I was old enough now to handle some hard truths.

Jay dipped his chin toward my phone. "Text her back."

"Thanks." I smiled.

Me: I'm good. What are you doing tomorrow? Wanna get together?

Instead of putting my phone back in my purse, I set it on the tabletop. Thirty seconds later, I couldn't resist checking for new missed calls or texts, even though I knew I didn't have any.

Jay caught me looking. He just gave me a knowing grin as he scraped the last chunk of burrito off his plate.

When the waiter came by to drop off the check, Jay slipped some money inside the black book. Then he stood and held his hand out to me. "Come on. Time to go."

I guess the date was over, and I wanted to kick myself for not being more mentally present.

"We don't have to go back right now," I insisted, slinging my purse over my shoulder before lacing our fingers. "Seriously. I'll be fine. We could go get some ice cream."

Considering how full I was, it was a bad suggestion. My stomach cramped in protest at the mere mention of more food. I wasn't sure I could eat anything else, but I was willing to try if it meant I could salvage this date.

We exited the double doors and walked out into the cooling temperatures. The sun was setting, throwing bright pink on the clouds in the sky.

I took a deep breath through my nose.

Late summer air in the Midwest was one of the best smells in the world. It would be September soon, and I was looking forward to fall. This year, Gus would be old enough to have fun at pumpkin patches and go trick-or-treating for Halloween.

And we'd have Jay with us, which would make it ten times more fun.

"The ice cream store is that way." I hitched a thumb behind us.

"You really want dessert?" Jay asked skeptically. "Do you seriously have room for it?"

Okay, so he'd seen me polish off the burrito bonanza plate. I liked to eat. Sue me.

"No," I admitted. "I just don't want to go home yet."

"Well, good, 'cause that's not where we're going." Tugging on my hand, Jay crossed the street, heading in the opposite direction of where he'd parked his car. "There's a reason why I wanted to come to Daywood, and it wasn't just for the chips and salsa."

"Okay…"

"We have an appointment."

"An appointment?" I echoed.

Mysterious, he just nodded and kept leading me down the sidewalk.

We trekked three blocks before Jay stopped in front of a blue ranch-style house. It had a 'For Rent' sign in the front yard.

"This is the street I grew up on." Nostalgia was evident in Jay's voice as he looked from one end of the road to the other. "We lived here until I was about eight. Until the divorce."

"In this house?" I pointed at the blue one.

"No." He motioned to where the street came to a dead end. "The brown one four doors down." Then he swept his arm toward the house in front of us. "This place is perfect for you—two bedrooms, attached one-car garage, and the backyard is right up against the meadow I've talked about."

I studied the small rental property. It was cute. The possibility that it could be mine was almost too surreal to think about.

A house. A real house. Not in a trailer park.

As I glanced back at Jay, conflicting emotions rose to the surface. I was happy that he'd taken the time to find a nice house for me. But that meant…

"You really want us out, huh?" I asked, dropping my gaze to the ground.

Call me codependent, but when I thought about spending a night without Jay, that old familiar drowning sensation I used to live with every day returned.

"Hey." Jay pressed a finger under my chin and tipped my face up until I had no choice but to look at him. "No, Casey. I don't want you to leave, but you want more than what Brenton has to offer. There's a church that has a preschool program just five blocks from here. And right next to it? There's a diner that's hiring. This is your chance to move up in the world and I'm encouraging you to take it." His hand fell away, and now it was his turn to stare at the concrete beneath our feet. "And I was hoping that maybe… eventually… at some point, you'd want me to move in?" Before I could react, his panicked eyes darted to mine. "You don't have to answer right now. Think about it. I'd pay half of everything. It's only five hundred a month, so that would be totally doable for us—"

I stopped his rambling by placing my fingers over his mouth.

Us.

He'd said *us*.

He wanted to do this with me. With Gus.

A laugh burst from me as I jumped forward. My arms went around Jay's neck. He returned the embrace, hugging me with those strong arms. The arms I'd come to associate with safety and comfort.

I ran my nose along the skin on his neck, loving his

citrusy scent. Loving the way it felt to have his arms wrapped tightly around my waist.

Loving him.

I love him.

Surprisingly, the realization wasn't startling. It was like my mind was finally catching up with what my heart had been saying for days.

"Hello, there." An unfamiliar voice had me detangling myself from Jay.

I followed it to the front stoop of the house. A thin, middle-aged man stood there in khakis and a green polo shirt.

"Casey, this is Bruce, the property manager," Jay introduced us, hooking an arm around my shoulders as he led me up the driveway.

"Hi, Casey. It's nice to meet you." Bruce shook my hand. "Your boyfriend said you and your son are looking for a place."

I looped my arm through Jay's and corrected, "We are. The three of us."

I felt Jay's intense stare boring into the side of my face, and I snuck a quick glance at him. He was looking at me with a mixture of hope and apprehension, like what I said was too good to be true.

"Then let's get the tour started." Bruce clapped his hands once. "As you can see, the yard is a good size and the flowerbed has several different perennials that come up in the spring and summer."

My eyes went to the white hydrangeas. I hadn't even seen the rest of the house yet, and I could already imagine filling vases with the flowers. The driveway was big enough for Gus to ride a tricycle and draw with sidewalk chalk.

And another bonus—we were close to downtown, but far enough from the business district for it to be quiet. With the dead-end street, there was hardly any traffic.

"Let's see inside, shall we?" Bruce opened the door for us, and Jay motioned for me to go first.

As soon as I crossed the threshold, I was sold.

It was cozy, modern, and clean. The floorplan was open concept, making the small space appear bigger. I could picture a comfy couch where I stood in the living room. Gus's toys could go in the corner, and the dining space was large enough for a six-seat table.

Oh my god. This place could really be mine.

"The interior has been completely remodeled," Bruce continued, walking to the kitchen. "New carpets and neutral gray paint throughout. The vinyl flooring and the counters in the kitchen have been updated. The bathroom, too. The roof was redone three years ago. All appliances are included."

"Washer and dryer?" I asked hopefully.

I was accustomed to using the small stacked version that fit into a tight closet. I didn't care if it couldn't wash large loads. As long as I didn't have to go to the laundry mat, I'd be a happy girl.

"Yes, ma'am." He opened a closet in the kitchen next to the stove, revealing the exact model I used to have in my trailer.

Natural light came through the sliding glass door by the dining area, giving the room a brightness with the light walls and white cabinets. There was a window above the sink overlooking the backyard.

Jay and I shuffled over to it, and I got even more excited when I saw the large concrete patio and the expanse of the grass behind it. Plenty of room for a kid to run around.

Beyond that was the meadow Jay had mentioned. It was beautiful, spanning several acres before butting up to a line of trees. This side of the house faced west, and the sunset was stunning as the bright orb peeked over the horizon in the distance.

I glanced at Jay, studying his face while he gazed at the wildflowers.

His expression was serene, shoulders relaxed. He was probably recalling a lot of memories of an innocent time when he had this view.

I'd never seen him appear so at peace.

We could do this every night. Cook dinner. Wash the dishes. Watch Gus play.

Together.

Jay had already done so much for me. If I could repay him in any way, I would.

"I want it," I told Bruce, facing the man.

He seemed taken aback by my quick decision. "You haven't seen the bedrooms yet."

"I'll go take a look." With quick footsteps, I left the kitchen and took a right down the hallway.

"There's a bathroom here. A nice tub and plenty of cabinet space beneath the sink," Bruce pointlessly listed the perks as he chased after me. "And the bedrooms are ten by ten and twelve by twelve. Good sizes with spacious closets."

I turned a full circle in the master bedroom, noting that Jay's giant bed would fit. It was perfect for us, just like he'd said. I glanced at him.

He was standing in the doorway, devastatingly handsome with his black T-shirt, his piercings, and his bedhead hair.

I couldn't stop my smile when I said, "Where do I sign?"

After writing a check for the first month's rent and the damage deposit, the house was officially mine for the next year.

Ours.

We hadn't even gotten three houses away before Jay

surprised me with a bear hug. My feet left the ground as he lifted me up. I swayed there, legs dangling, for what seemed like minutes.

As I hugged him back, my rough-around-the-edges boy-friend kept his face hidden in the place where my neck met my shoulder.

I got the feeling this was his way of saying thank you.

Sifting my fingers through his hair, I said, "I don't want you to wait to move in. If you're ready, I'd like you with us when we pick up the keys tomorrow night."

We probably wouldn't be able to start living there until I worked out the furniture situation. As in, I had none. But I wanted to know Jay would be by my side from here on out.

Taking a deep inhale, he loosened his hold until I slid down. "You mean it?"

His eyes searched mine for any hint of indecision, but my mind was made up.

I nodded, and he let out an elated, triumphant shout. He lunged for me. Instead of going for another hug, he hoisted me up, slinging my body over his shoulder like a sack of potatoes.

I laughed. "What are you doing?"

"The date isn't over yet."

"But it's getting dark." The world stayed upside down as I bounced with Jay's every step.

"This won't take long," he said cryptically.

This guy and his secrets.

I was starting to get dizzy when suddenly he stopped and put me down. Reaching out to steady myself, I squeezed his biceps while glancing around.

"You brought me to a park?" I asked, confused.

"When was the last time you went to a park?" He cocked an eyebrow. I was about to respond with *recently*, when he added, "Without Gus?"

"Oh. Um…" My face scrunched up while I tried to re-member. "I guess sophomore year of high school. After a soft-ball game, my friends and I hung out on the swings and had popsicles to cool off."

"I figured. So, what'll it be?" He backed away, motioning to the playground equipment. "Swings? Slide? How about the merry-go-round? It's not a Ferris wheel, but—" He gave it a spin. "—it's a ride."

I gaped at him like he was nuts, but on the inside I was melting. Out of all the activities he could've chosen, he went with something innocent and fun. I needed innocent and fun.

Maybe Jay needed it, too.

I wasn't the only one who'd missed out on the last couple years of childhood.

The rickety wheel slowed, and I took the opportunity to hop on. I sat down, knees to my chest.

"Ready," I announced, unable to keep the excitement out of my voice.

Jay spun it again. And again. And again.

Soon, my surroundings were nothing but a blur. Laughing so hard I was having trouble staying upright, I had to grip the bars so I didn't fall over.

Metal clanked and squeaked when Jay jumped on. He dropped down in front of me, caging my body in with his long legs.

Cupping both my cheeks, he closed the distance and dropped a kiss to my nose. It was something he did often, and it made my heart flutter every time.

"Teach me a trick, magic man," I requested as the world kept whirling around us.

With a coy smirk, Jay shook his head.

I pouted.

Laughing, he kissed my lips.

A consolation prize. A quick peck.

I playfully snubbed him by turning my head away. "Fine. Don't share your powers with me."

"I'll tell you a secret instead." He toyed with my prism, and my eyes were drawn back to his. "You think I'm the one with the magic? You're wrong. You've got all the power in the world. You make me believe things I've never been brave enough to hope for. You make me happy, Casey. So fucking happy."

Well, crap.

I couldn't even pretend to be mad at him when he said things like that.

This time when his lips met mine, I didn't resist, and I continued collecting his kisses long after we stopped spinning.

CHAPTER 24

Jay

Quiet murmuring woke me. I rolled onto my stomach, loving the fact that I was back in my huge ass bed. After the date last night, Casey got Gus to sleep, then we automatically fell onto my mattress together. I'd opened my arms, she cuddled up to my side, and we went to sleep.

That was our routine now.

Sometime over the past week, we'd made a habit of falling asleep here after fucking in the living room. Although, it wasn't just fucking to me. It never was.

I never knew sex could be so fun. Casey was adventurous, always wanting to explore new positions and locations. She was up for anything. I mean, *anything*. When I'd casually suggested butt stuff, she seemed open to it.

But Casey's daring side wasn't what I loved most about sex. Our emotional connection was intense. When Casey looked into my eyes, it felt like she was peering into my soul. And by some miracle, she liked what she saw.

Patting the other side of the bed, I found it empty.

It was then that I realized Casey's voice wasn't the soothing tone she used with Gus. Her pitch was higher. Worried.

I shot up in the bed, and the first thing I saw in the shadowed room was an empty crib.

Shit.

Something was wrong. I could feel it in my bones.

I stood so fast it made my head spin, and I staggered to the door. It was still dark outside, and light from the kitchen was casting a yellow glow through the apartment.

Casey was multitasking.

Pacing around the table in circles, her phone was cradled between her shoulder and ear while she fed Gus a bottle.

"When did this happen?" she spoke into the phone.

As soon as Gus saw me, his eyes lit up. He reached out in my direction and Casey sent a thankful glance my way when I took him.

Going over to the couch with my little buddy, I continued to listen to her half of the conversation.

"How serious is it?" Silence and nail biting. More pacing. "Can I come see her? Okay. Yeah. I'll be there as soon as I can."

Casey dropped the phone to the table with a soft clatter. She stood completely still, blinking down at it as if she was in shock.

"What's wrong?" I pressed, unable to endure the suspense.

She looked over at me, her face void of any expression. "My mom got into a motorcycle accident last night."

Oh, shit. "Is she okay?"

"They don't know yet. She just got out of surgery and she's in critical condition."

Her tone was flat, and I had no idea how she could mask her emotions so well.

I knew why she did it, though. Nibbling on her thumbnail, she stared at Gus.

She didn't want him to see her upset.

"Casey," I started, ready to babble out some apologies. I wasn't very eloquent when it came to this stuff. I never knew what to say. "I didn't know she had a motorcycle."

Real smooth, Jay. Real fucking smooth.

Casey shook her head. "She doesn't. She was riding with someone and they got hit at an intersection." Her eyes left Gus, darting to my face. "I have to go."

Now this I could help with.

"I got this," I assured her.

Since she was in a hurry, she didn't bother changing out of her pajamas as she gathered her things. Although, to be fair, yoga pants fit almost every occasion. Rushing around the room, she tossed a couple granola bars into her purse and grabbed a bottle of water from the fridge.

"I don't know how long I'll be gone." Glancing at the clock over the stove, she grimaced. It was just after four a.m. "Gus might not go back to sleep."

"No worries. We'll have a good time, won't we, bud?"

Gus nodded, still guzzling his milk.

After slipping on her tennis shoes, Casey came over to kiss Gus's head. "Bye, bubba bubbie goo man. I'll be back soon."

He popped off the nipple long enough to say, "Bye!"

Then he went back to drinking while pinching my shirt collar.

"Thank you." Casey tenderly scraped her fingers over my scruff before turning to leave.

As the door closed behind her, the bad feeling continued to eat away at me. But, unsettling sensation or not, I needed to put on a brave face for Gus.

"What do you want to do, little man?" I set the empty bottle on the coffee table. "Go back to bed? Cartoons? Admire all your jewelry?"

His face lit up. "Dewey."

Of course.

Amused, I let out a chuckle as he scrambled off my lap and toddled to the bedroom.

The princess bucket was filling quickly. I'd been finding creative ways to present him with a new ring every day.

Gus reappeared with the container and unceremoniously dumped the contents onto the living room floor. Silver and sparkly gems scattered, clinking on the hard linoleum floor.

I made a soft place for us to sit by folding a green blanket in half. For extra padding, I got a couple pillows from the bedroom. Pretty soon, I wouldn't have to do this anymore. We'd have a nice living room with a thick carpet.

Spreading out on my stomach, I lay down as Gus started blinging up his right hand. When he was done, he looked at the leftover rings and decided I needed some.

"Thanks, dude." I smiled as he tried to fit them onto my large fingers. Most of them couldn't make it past the first knuckle, but he didn't seem to mind.

We stayed busy for the rest of the morning, eventually eating eggs and toast while watching *Tangled*. In so many words, Gus expressed his desire for the crown.

I promised him I'd buy him one someday.

To show his appreciation, he left a big smacking kiss on my cheek, complete with some drool.

I smiled as I wiped at it, glad to have him as a distraction.

Because no matter how much I tried to chase away my disturbing gut instinct, I couldn't shake it. Something still felt off.

And I just had to hope I was wrong.

CHAPTER 25

Casey

I didn't know what I would feel when I saw my mom bandaged and lying in a hospital bed, but I was surprised that it wasn't sadness or worry that I experienced first.

Forgiveness.

If that was even an emotion at all, I wasn't sure, but that's what I felt more than anything else.

Her mistakes. Our differences. All the bad shit.

It all went away the second I saw her swollen face and the IV in her arm.

Her eyes were closed, so I quietly pulled the chair over to the bed.

I softly touched her scraped-up fingers, and my eyes stung when I smoothed a fingertip over her bright-red nail polish.

I used to know her hands so well, but I couldn't remember the last time I'd held them.

We hugged on occasion, but her hands... a mother and her child are supposed to hold hands when they cross the street or walk through a parking lot. To stay safe. They hold hands in the middle of the night after a bad dream. For comfort.

Somewhere along the way, we stopped clinging to each other.

I didn't know who let go first.

Didn't know if it was her fault or mine.

But in this moment, it didn't matter.

So I gently wrapped my fingers around hers while grappling with regret.

Suddenly, her finger twitched, and I glanced up to see her sleepy eyes blinking open.

"Hey, honey." Her voice was scratchy. She tried to smile, but it just looked like she was in pain.

Not surprising, considering the info the nurse passed on when I got here. Ruptured spleen. Three broken ribs. A hell of a lot of road rash.

"Mom." I was so relieved she was awake. "I came as soon as I heard. I didn't realize I was your emergency contact, but I'm glad they called."

"I'm happy you're here. Where's Gusser-man?" She didn't move her head, but her eyes searched the room.

I smiled at the nickname. She always called him that. He loved it.

"He's with Jay."

"Your boyfriend?"

"Yeah. My boyfriend."

"He good to you? He better be. Or else."

I let out an amused snort at the protective edge in her warning. "Yeah. He's amazing. Great with Gus, too."

"Good."

I didn't know if I should tell her the news about her own boyfriend. Unlike my mom, he hadn't been wearing a helmet when they crashed. He was dead at the scene.

And just like all her other relationships, I knew nothing about him. Had she been dating him long? Was she in love with him?

Upsetting her was the last thing I wanted to do right now, so I decided to focus on her. "Do you need anything? More blankets? Water? The nurse?"

She made a displeased sound. "I'm sure the nurses will be harassing me soon enough. Let's just be alone for a little while. I've missed you."

I swallowed hard. "I miss you, too. When I said I wanted to get together, this wasn't what I had in mind," I joked. "A little dramatic, Mom."

She smiled wide, then winced. "Oh, don't make me laugh. That hurts."

"Sorry."

"So what's going on with you? You okay? You need money?"

I shook my head. She was still trying to fork over her savings, even at a time like this.

"I signed a lease for a house in Daywood last night," I told her, glad for a happy subject to talk about. "It's really nice. I'd love it if you could come over Friday night when I start moving in. You should be out of here by then, right?"

"I sure hope so. If these doctors hold me hostage for more than a few days I might go crazy." Her face got serious. "I want you to know I haven't smoked for a week."

"Wow. That's a record."

"Yeah, it is. I'm serious this time. I'm done with that." Her hand squeezed mine. "I just hope it's not too late for us."

"Mom…" I felt bad that she could think our relationship was beyond repair, but I hadn't given her much reason to believe otherwise with my short-answered texts. "You're my family. You'll always be my family."

"I've failed you so many times. I ruin things. It's what I do."

"Let's not talk about that now."

"I need to. Gotta get this off my chest." She took a shuddering inhale before admitting, "For the past couple years, I've been jealous of you. Watching you take life by the balls and raise your son has been one of the most awesome things I've ever witnessed, but it also made me wish I could've been more like you."

"You think I'm a good mom?" There was a quiver in my voice, emotional from her praise.

"The best I've ever seen."

I will not cry. I won't.

I choked out, "Thank you."

"Your father," my mom began, and I almost jerked back from how foreign the words sounded coming from her. "I never talked about your father because I didn't have anything good to say. If I badmouthed him, I felt like I was badmouthing half of you. I tried to protect you from who he is, but maybe I failed in that, too."

"What do you mean?" I questioned warily.

Now that she was mentioning the stranger I never knew, I was afraid I wouldn't like what she had to say. I'd never even seen a picture of him. He was like a ghost to me. The only thing she'd ever told me about him was that he was gone. Not dead—just not here and never would be.

"He wasn't a good man," she stated. "He was ten years older than me." Pausing, she took a steeling breath. "And he was my mother's boyfriend."

My eyes went wide. Oh, I didn't like where this was going at all. Maybe I didn't want to hear this. Maybe I should tell her to stop.

But she continued, "He started flirting with me when I was fifteen. They'd been together for over a year, and he'd just moved in. Then they started having problems. Arguing a lot. After they fought, he'd take me out for ice cream or to the mall. Wanted to apologize, he'd said. But those outings went from innocent to inappropriate pretty fast. He'd confide in me, airing out their problems. Then he'd compliment me and say I was the one he should be with. Made me feel special."

Ashamed, she looked away.

For a second, I was speechless. She'd been manipulated when she was too young to know better. We could just call it what it was—she was molested. And she blamed herself.

"You know none of that is your fault, right?" My tone left no room for argument. "You were a kid and he took advantage of you."

"Well, my mother didn't see it that way. When she found out I was pregnant, she broke up with him and threatened to charge him with statutory rape if he ever came around me again. I thought he'd fight for me. I was wrong. Mom couldn't stand to look at me anymore, and she kicked me out. I went to live with Grandma Dottie, and that's how we ended up in Brenton."

I knew the last part of her story. Her grandma had taken her in while she was pregnant with me. Grandma Dottie had died when I was a toddler, but she left the trailer to my mom.

A lightbulb went off in my mind. "Is that why you never let me meet any of the men you dated?"

"Partly. I never trusted any of them enough to bring them around you. I thought I was keeping you safe by staying away. Instead, I left you alone and unprotected. A bad man still got to you."

All the nights she spent somewhere else. I'd assumed she didn't like being with me, but that wasn't the case. She was trying to juggle mom life while dating, without letting the two worlds mesh.

"So, you see," Mom went on, "I've been ruining lives since I was fifteen. Some people make the world better. Not me, though. Not me."

Setting aside our personal struggles, I put myself in her shoes for a second. She'd been preyed on and tossed aside. She'd sacrificed her youth for me. Hell, she'd waited until she was almost thirty to experience dating—healthy, adult dating.

I had no idea her guilt ran so deep, but it was something we had in common. I knew firsthand how one misstep could cause a downward spiral of self-loathing.

Gus was still young. Still a baby. I had his whole life ahead, and I was sure I'd make plenty of bad decisions in the years to come. I just hoped when I messed up, he'd give me the same grace I was about to give my mom.

"Did you do the best you could?" I said, repeating the question Jay once asked me.

She shook her head. "Doesn't matter. It wasn't good enough."

"But was it your best?"

Her chin trembled. "At the time, yeah, I guess it was. I never started my day with the goal of screwing up." Tears filled her eyes. "Every time I look at you, I see everything that's right with the world—" She let out a choked sob. "—and everything that's wrong with me. I'm so proud of you. S-so proud."

"Shhh," I soothed, rubbing a part of her hand that wasn't scratched up. "We can move forward."

"Can we?"

"Yes. If we both want our relationship to be good, I believe we can make it happen."

She smiled a little. "Let's make it happen."

"Okay." I smiled back. "Hey, remember my twelfth birthday? When we went to get our nails done together?"

Closing her eyes, she let out a happy hum. "Yeah."

That day was full of some of my best memories. It was the same birthday she'd gotten my prism for me. But before that, my mom had arranged a girls' day for us. First, we went to lunch at Gloria's, then she took me to the city to get manicures and pedicures.

"When we got to the salon," I continued, "and they had

sparkling grape juice and champagne glasses waiting for us, I thought I was the coolest girl in town."

And halfway through getting our toenails painted, a florist had arrived with a delivery—a vase full of flowers with a 'Happy Birthday' balloon tied to it.

She'd gone all out for me.

"I want more times like that," I told her.

"Me, too," she sighed, seeming sleepy.

"I'll leave so you can get some rest. I don't think the nurses wanted me to stay long." I gave her hand one more pat before standing. "I'll come back tomorrow after work, and if you're up to it, I can bring Gus with me."

"Sounds good. Hey, wait a minute," she said weakly, and I sat back down. "Someday Gus is going to ask about his father. Want my advice on what to say?"

"Yeah, I do."

"Be honest with him when he's old enough to hear it. Just once, don't sugarcoat it. But after that, don't say anything else. Don't repeat the bad stuff over and over again."

"Okay," I agreed.

"And if—and that's a big if—you can find just one good thing about that asshole," she croaked, and I laughed. "You tell Gus that, too." She closed her eyes and her words came out mumbled. "You got your dimples from your father. They look way better on you, though."

If that was the one good thing she had to say about my biological father, I'd take it.

"Thanks for that, Mom," I said quietly. "I love you."

I bent down to kiss the top of her head, but she was already out.

CHAPTER 26

Casey

"What's all this stuff?" I could barely get through the door of Jay's apartment because a pile of baby gear was blocking my way.

"Oh." Getting up from the couch, Jay came over to help me get inside.

I did a double take when I saw my kid strapped to his chest in one of those baby carriers.

Gus was happy as could be, conveniently facing Jay, where the shirt collar was front and center. He gave me a toothy grin around his thumb, his chubby legs bouncing a little with every step Jay took.

My mouth hung open while Jay explained, "Some ladies from the trailer park came over to drop off a bunch of stuff. I guess they pooled anything they didn't need. Clothes and blankets." He pointed at a small plastic laundry basket before his finger moved to the garbage bag. "Stuffed animals. Baby food. And an extra car seat, a highchair, and this." He patted the carrier. "This is the best invention ever."

I couldn't believe it. These women didn't have much to give, but they'd banded together for me. "This is really nice of them."

The car seat was better than the one I had. It was the kind that could convert to forward facing when Gus was big enough.

My eyes went to the carrier, and I saw the name brand on the label. Originally, it probably cost over a hundred dollars.

And Jay looked damn good like this.

Ovary explosion.

"How's your mom?" Jay asked, his face pinched with concern.

"Pretty banged up."

"But she's gonna be okay?"

"Yeah. She was awake and talking. We had a really good conversation…" I trailed off because Jay's tight expression didn't let up. "You seem worried."

Going over to the fridge, he got a bottle of water. He shrugged as he took a drink. "I just get an uneasy feeling sometimes. Like when something bad is going to happen, I just know."

"Like you're psychic?" I raised a skeptical eyebrow.

Seeming a bit embarrassed, Jay scratched the back of his head. "Not exactly. I mean, I can't tell the future."

"But you've been feeling that way today?"

"Yeah. Usually when I get like this, it either has to do with me or someone I'm close to. Your mom and I didn't get off to the best start, but she's an extension of you, so maybe that's why."

Reaching for Jay's water, Gus grabbed it, brought it to his lips, and ungracefully shoved it in his mouth to get a drink. Most of the liquid dribbled down his chin, getting both of their chests wet.

Jay and I laughed, and the funny moment diffused the tension in the air.

I tossed them a kitchen towel. "Well, I guess your Spidey sense was right this time."

Grinning, Jay dabbed at his shirt. "Funny. That's what my mom calls it."

We spent the next hour playing. Sometimes it was still strange having three of us. Jay added a whole new dynamic to our little group. His presence seemed to bring out a new side of Gus. A side that was confident and brave. When Jay swung Gus around the room like he was an airplane, the big belly laughs coming out of my baby boy were unlike anything I'd ever heard.

There was so much joy here, and I found myself smiling until my face muscles hurt.

Worn out, Jay's chest heaved as he flew Gus to the pile of blankets on the floor next to me. I went in for a tickle attack, walking my fingers up Gus's rib cage.

"Who does Momma love?"

"Ammaw," he responded through giggles.

Ornery little guy. This was a game we played often. He knew the answer I wanted to hear, but he loved to list off other names before he gave in.

"Yes, I do love Grandma. But who else does Momma love?"

"Dory."

"Doreen's pretty cool, too. Who else?"

"Day."

I choked out an uncomfortable cough. Not touching that one. Intensifying my tickling efforts, I went for the armpits.

"Who does Momma love?"

"Gus!" he finally relented.

"That's right." I gave him a loud kiss on the cheek. "Momma loves Gus."

My stomach growled, and hunger got in the way of our good time. I went to the kitchen to make lunch, and Jay seamlessly took over with Gus while I was busy.

I was stirring a pot of boiling water when my phone rang on the counter a few feet away. The boys were on the couch, both decked out in enough jewelry to make royalty jealous.

Smiling, I glanced over at them, before dumping the macaroni noodles in the pot. Then I picked up my phone and saw the hospital number.

"Hello?" I answered, expecting to hear my mom's voice on the other end.

Instead it was a nurse. An update, then. Good.

As I stirred the pasta, she verified who I was, but what the woman said next didn't make sense.

I stood completely still as she spoke with a somber tone, explaining something about cardiac arrest and how my mother couldn't be resuscitated.

"What?" I said dumbly.

"I'm so sorry. We did everything we could."

My chest felt like it was caving in. "No. There must be a mistake. The patient is Laura Maxwell. She's too young to have a heart attack. I was just there this morning. She was fine. She's fine."

I didn't even realize I was raising my voice until Jay rested his palm on my shoulder. He gestured for me to give him the phone. Numb, I handed it over.

He spoke quietly, asking questions I was too shocked to think of. Finally, hanging his head, he nodded. "Okay. Thank you."

When he looked over at me, I knew it was true. The sympathy in his eyes couldn't be faked.

A tugging on my pants made me glance down. Gus was reaching for me, and I picked him up. He was wonderfully oblivious to what was going on. So innocent, smiling around the thumb in his mouth.

Jay came over to hug us both.

"I'm so sorry, Casey," he whispered by my ear, too quiet for Gus to hear. "The surgery went well, but her health wasn't good. Her heart wasn't strong enough. Your mom's gone."

Gone? It didn't feel like she was gone. If the woman who gave me life no longer existed, wouldn't I know? Shouldn't I sense the loss?

I waited for the tears to come, but my eyes stayed dry. I blinked, wondering why I wasn't crying. Was I in shock?

"What can I do?" Jay asked, sounding as helpless as I felt. "Just tell me what to do."

Nothing. Bring my mom back? Reverse time, so I could make sure that crash never happened?

When Jay stepped away, his lips were pulled into a frown as he studied my face. "Do you want to be alone for a while? I can take Gus to the park—"

I shook my head violently, clinging to his T-shirt. "No. Stay with me. Just stay with me."

The last thing I wanted was to be alone.

Comfort and security fell over me like a warm blanket as Jay engulfed me once more. He always had that effect on me. In his arms, I could handle anything.

"I'm not going anywhere," he promised.

CHAPTER 27

Jay

I fucking hated funerals. The gray suit Jimmy gave me was constricting and hot. Graveyards creeped me out. No one knew how to act, because people dealt with death in their own way. Some tried to lighten the mood by telling Casey a funny story about her mom. Others couldn't stop crying.

It was awkward as fuck.

But the worst part? Watching Casey try to keep it together while everyone else lost their shit.

She was so poised. Completely emotionless. Just like she had been all week.

I kept waiting for her to break down. I had yet to see her shed a tear since we heard the news six days ago. She'd been on a weird sort of autopilot.

She smiled at the right times, played with Gus, went grocery shopping, and showered every day. She'd arranged the funeral service, all while still going to work as usual. My suggestion that she take a few days off had been shot down immediately. The time wouldn't have been paid, and Casey wanted to stay busy.

Then last night, we'd started moving into the new house as planned. Jimmy had borrowed the eighteen-wheeler from Hank's Auto Shop to transport all the furniture Casey ordered from a store in Champaign. He delivered it to us—free of charge—and helped me get everything moved in. This morning he went over to my place to pack up my stuff, including the recliner, crib, and bed.

Of course, Casey had insisted on helping, even though she had to be at the funeral home by noon.

She was full steam ahead, totally functional, adulting like a fucking boss.

To most people, it would've been impressive. But it just made me even more worried for her.

Casey's idea of coping with her mom's death was to run herself into the ground.

And the cleaning. So much cleaning.

Casey hated housework, but every evening when she got done cooking dinner, she went to town on my apartment. She claimed we had to make it spotless before we moved out, but it already was.

I glanced over at her.

She was a beautiful ticking time bomb, standing next to me on the grass in the fitted navy-blue dress she'd borrowed from Mackenna. She was holding a single white rose the funeral director had given her from the bouquet on top of the coffin. Her hair was long and straight, and her makeup was applied flawlessly.

"I see so much of your mom in you," an unfamiliar woman said, blotting her eyes with a tissue before clumsily patting Casey on the head like she was five years old. "I'm so sorry."

The thirty-something brunette walked away, stepping carefully so her stilettoes didn't sink into the softened ground.

It'd rained most of the morning, and storm clouds were rolling back in, darkening the afternoon horizon.

"I don't know most of these people," Casey muttered quietly, running her prism back and forth on the silver chain as the line of sympathizers began to dwindle.

"They all seem to know you, though," I commented.

It was obvious her mom had talked about her all the time. If Casey ever doubted her mother's love, she didn't have to anymore. She was that woman's pride and joy. Funny how much you learned about a person after they died.

About a dozen biker friends of the boyfriend Laura lost came to pay their respects. Old coworkers from her construction days told tales of good memories on the job. Friends from other towns talked about how they'd miss hearing Laura sing on karaoke night at their favorite bar.

Several people asked about Gus, seeming to know him, too. Jimmy and Mackenna had offered to take him to their house while we got through the short ceremony. For once, Casey hadn't hesitated to take them up on it.

Doreen was the last in line.

"Casey." She wrapped her arms around my girl, drawing her in for a long hug. "You'll be okay. You know that, right?"

Blinking rapidly, Casey nodded. She cleared her throat and swallowed hard. It was the first sign of any chink in her armor.

"Good girl." Doreen pulled back. "I'm here for you. Anything you need."

"Thanks." Casey squared her shoulders as she reconstructed her walls.

With a composed expression, she watched Doreen leave the cemetery. Rain started coming down in a light drizzle.

"Want me to get an umbrella from the funeral director?" I asked, remembering they were provided.

Another thing about funerals? They were fucking expensive. Who knew it cost so much to die? At least Laura's savings was enough to pay for it.

"No," Casey answered flatly.

"What do you want to do?"

I was trying not to lose my patience. Somewhere deep

inside, she was going through some hard shit. I wanted to help, but I couldn't if she wouldn't show me some emotion. I just wanted her to talk to me.

"Let's go home." Her eyes swung my way. "I'm looking forward to spending the night at the new house."

"All right, baby." Gripping her chin, I leaned down to place a kiss on her nose.

Lacing our fingers, I led her to my red Corolla. We were both damp once we got there, and I offered Casey my jacket. She thanked me before pulling it around her shoulders.

Since the new car seat from Casey's neighbors was better than the one she had, I'd been given the old one. I liked seeing it in my back seat. Liked knowing it meant I was needed.

Right before I ducked into the car, a prickling sensation made the hairs on the back of my neck stand up. It was the kind of feeling you got when you were being watched.

I looked back at the expanse of headstones, searching for anyone who might've been lingering.

But I saw no one.

Cemeteries. Fucking creepy.

The car ride away from Brenton was silent, but when I flipped on my turn signal to take the road to Tolson to pick up Gus, Casey put her hand on my forearm.

"Not yet," she said. "Let's go to Daywood first. Just you and me for a little while."

Surprised, my eyebrows shot up. I knew Casey like the back of my hand and being away from Gus wasn't something she tolerated well. Jimmy told us to take as long as we needed, but I figured Casey would want to go get Gus right away.

Apparently, I was wrong. But, hey, if she was asking something of me, I was going to do it.

I steered left.

After several minutes of more silence, Casey sighed. "It's been hard for me to put on a happy face for Gus all the time. I don't want him to see me sad."

Fucking finally. She was letting me in.

"You don't have to put on an act with me either," I told her seriously. "You can cry."

Her chin quivered and she turned her head away to look out the window. "If I start, I might not stop."

"That's okay. I don't mind." Seconds ticked by. Okay, so maybe she wasn't ready to open up. "If you'd rather be alone, I can take you home and I'll go get Gus."

"No," she burst out, glancing my way. Then she softened her voice. "Stay with me."

She'd said that so many times in the past week. Like she was afraid I'd disappear. Sometimes she mumbled it in the middle of the night if I tried to get up to pee. She'd tighten her hold on me in her sleep, begging me not to go. So I'd lie back down, test my bladder control, and respond with the same promise every time.

"I'm not going anywhere."

～

"It kills me to see you like this, baby." I shut the garage door as we took off our shoes. "I wish there was something I could do to make it better."

"There is." Casey kicked her strappy black sandals toward the wall.

I perked up. "Anything. Just name it."

Her hands flattened on my stomach and started moving upward. My abs clenched and rippled under her soft touch. Biting her lip, her thumb bumped over every button on the way to my collar.

"Show me a trick, magic man." Her voice was sultry. Seductive.

My dick twitched, responding to her the way it always did—overeager and ready to party. But this wasn't exactly the best time to get it on.

Apprehensive, I narrowed my eyes. "What kind of trick?"

"The kind where you make me forget who I am for a while."

The top button snapped open under her fingers, and she continued down to the next one.

I grabbed her wrist. "Casey… You're grieving. I don't want to take advantage of you while you're in this state. Besides, I don't want you to forget who you are."

"Then remind me that I'm yours. That's all I want to think about right now. Please."

I couldn't say no to her. Not when she was telling me exactly what I could do to lessen her pain. If physical intimacy was a temporary solution, I could supply it in excess.

"Turn around," I ordered huskily.

She immediately complied, letting my jacket slip off her shoulders. Pushing her hair to the side, I found the zipper at the nape of her neck and pulled it down. The silky fabric parted, revealing the smooth, creamy skin on her back.

My fingertips skimmed the length of her spine, and she shivered.

With the gentlest caress, I slid the dress off her shoulders, trailing my fingertips down her arms. It fell away and pooled at her feet.

Even though it was mid-afternoon, there wasn't much light. The rain was coming down in sheets now. Wind blew, thunder rumbled, and lightning flashed.

A storm raged outside, but it couldn't touch us here.

Slowly, Casey faced me and my eyes roamed her from

head to toe. She was a vision of perfection with no bra, black lace panties, and her necklace.

Grazing her sides, I wrapped my hands around her middle and pressed her almost-naked body to my clothed one.

My cock was already rock hard, and she gasped when she felt the bulge in my pants.

I lowered my lips to the skin on her shoulder, inhaling her sweet scent as her fingers went to my hair.

God, I'd missed this. We hadn't had sex all week. That, along with Casey being emotionally distant, had made her feel so far from me. Disconnected.

I didn't like it.

"How do you want it, baby?" I dragged my tongue over her collarbone, and she let out a shaky sigh.

"However you want to give it to me."

Ah, she wanted me to be in control. I could do that. Wasn't sure she'd like it, though. If she was looking for a rough, hard fuck, she wasn't getting it today.

I was gonna go slow.

Usually, there was a sense of urgency when we had sex. We never knew if Gus would wake up.

That wasn't a concern right now.

The next couple hours were ours, and I'd make every second count.

"Take off my clothes," I demanded, spreading my arms.

She didn't waste any time.

The tie was gone in seconds, discarded to the floor with her dress. Button by button, she quickly undid my shirt. Then my zipper was coming down. Each article of clothing came off until I was in nothing but my boxer briefs.

"In a hurry?" I smirked.

"Yes," she breathed out, gripping me by the back of the neck.

The next thing I knew, our lips were locked, and Casey was devouring my mouth.

I picked her up, grabbing handfuls of her ass as her legs wound tightly around my waist. My unrushed footsteps took us down the hall to our bedroom.

Hers and mine.

The drawers were half-filled with her panties and half with my underwear. Our socks. Our T-shirts and pants.

Same with the closet.

Every inch of this room was split between us.

I wasn't kidding when I'd told Casey she was the one with the power. She'd given me everything I ever wanted. She made the impossible my reality.

When I settled us onto my giant mattress, my hardness nestled between her thighs, I stared down at her gorgeous face.

I could look at her all day.

I traced her absent dimples with my thumbs.

Her eyebrows furrowed and she frowned. "What?"

"I'm so fucking happy. It doesn't seem fair that I feel this good when you don't."

"Then make me feel good." Bucking her hips, she rubbed herself against my erection.

Smirking at her impatience, I responded, "Yes, ma'am."

When I scooted down on the bed, Casey tilted her head in question. We hadn't done oral yet, but if she wanted her mind blown, this was the way to do it.

Hooking my fingers in her panties, I dragged them down her legs and tossed them to the floor.

"What are you doing?" She sounded scandalized and she attempted to close her legs.

I pushed them wide again. "Don't get shy on me now."

After everything we'd done, after all the dirty things we'd

talked about doing in the future, after all the ways I'd defiled her body... having my mouth between her thighs was her hard limit?

My face was just inches away from her glistening pussy. It was hard to tear my eyes away from it, but I managed. My questioning gaze collided with her vulnerable one, and I got my answer.

She was already emotionally raw. Exposing herself in a new way was too much right now.

I patted her knee. "Okay, baby. We don't have to—" She gasped when my warm breath fanned over her clit. "—do this," I finished.

I started to push myself up when she stopped me by flattening her hand on the top of my head.

"Wait. Do that again."

"Do what? This?" Getting closer to her center, I formed an 'O' with my lips and lightly blew on her sensitive flesh.

Her back bowed. "Yes. That. More."

Lowering my head, I gave her slit a slow lick.

Holy. Fucking. Shit. Her taste was sweet and musky.

Addicting.

I went back for more, groaning against her flesh as my tongue traced her clit. "Casey?"

"Huh?" She was panting now.

I wanted to tell her I loved her. I loved her more than I'd ever loved anything or anyone.

But proclamations of love seemed inappropriate today. I didn't want the first time I told her how I felt to be associated with the sadness hanging over her head.

So instead, I warned, "You might want to hold onto something."

Then I dove in.

I widened my tongue, covering as much area as possible

before stiffening it. I swirled it around her sensitive bud, enjoying the whimpers coming out of her mouth.

Inserting two fingers, I didn't waste any time driving her to the brink. Tapping upward, I repeatedly hit her G-spot while my mouth sucked on her clit in rhythm with my fingers.

"Ohh." Her back arched.

I sucked harder.

She moaned.

I went faster.

Her fists squeezed the pillow so hard her knuckles turned white.

She started to thrash, trying to move away from me as she dug her heels into the mattress.

"I don't think so, baby." I pinned her in place by clamping my free arm around her middle.

"Jay," she hissed. "So intense. I can't—can't take it."

I lifted my head long enough to say, "You can."

Lashing at her clit with my tongue, I increased my efforts by adding a third finger.

Now she was going crazy.

A guttural groan left her as her pussy gushed onto my hand. Tugging at my strands, she started rocking her hips, fucking my face while gripping my head.

Fuck yes.

The sting on my scalp only turned me on more. My cock was trapped against my stomach and the mattress, and I involuntarily started humping the bed.

I zoned out while I gorged on Casey's pussy.

In this moment, nothing existed outside of this room. I lost myself in her sounds of pleasure, the way she moved, and the look of ecstasy on her face.

Moaning.

Writhing.

Head tilted back. Mouth open. Eyes closed.

I did that to her.

I made her strong and wild. I loved how she responded to my touch, pulling me closer, then pushing me away.

"I—I'm co—com—" Finally, her inner muscles clenched and she let out a series of screams.

By the time I slid inside her, I was shaking with the need for release. I was slicked with sweat—we both were—and our hearts were beating in time with each other when I pressed our chests together.

Outside, the rain had subsided, and the sky cleared long enough for the sun to poke through the clouds.

Bright rays came through the window, illuminating us. Although the prism was in my shadow, it caught the light anyway, and some stubborn glints found a way to shine.

Cupping the side of my face, Casey smiled, and twin dimples appeared.

I kissed them. First her right side, then her left.

I tenderly caressed her cheek. "There's my rainbow."

"My magic man," she responded, combing some messy strands away from my forehead.

Then my mouth found its rightful home on her lips. I surged forward, burying my cock as I spread her thighs wide.

Hooking her ankles behind my back, Casey tilted her hips, allowing me to sink deeper. I felt her tight walls surrender any resistance as she opened herself to me.

With torturously slow grinding thrusts, I showed her what it meant to be loved.

Our bodies moved together in perfect rhythm. Our eyes were locked on each other. Our breaths mingled.

"I've never felt anything as good as you," I said on a ragged sigh, my lips brushing hers with every word.

And it was the truth.

In my past, I'd dabbled in a lot of different drugs. The good shit. The stuff that made you feel invincible.

I used to consider it a perk and a responsibility to test a product before I sold it. Being stoned out of my mind, having hallucinations, and feeling like I could almost touch heaven were all part of my life experiences.

But the highest high didn't compare to the euphoria of being with the love of my life.

CHAPTER 28

Casey

I'd once heard that you don't move on when someone dies. You just move forward.

I didn't know if that was true, but happiness was creeping back in.

Even though it'd only been three days since I laid my mom to rest, I was getting used to the new normal.

I liked living in Daywood. Our neighbors were nice. Two of them had brought baked treats over since we moved in.

And having two bedrooms was a dream. For the first time ever, Gus had his own room. The kitchen had a lot of storage space, and the refrigerator was big enough to stock two weeks of groceries.

Sharing a bed with Jay every night wasn't too bad either.

Maybe the timing of the move was a good thing. Maybe that fire really was a blessing in disguise.

Because being away from the trailer park helped me avoid reality.

Sure, I still went there when I dropped Gus off at Doreen's, but it was easy for me to pretend my mom's windows were dark because she simply wasn't home.

I was in denial. I knew it, and so did Jay, but it was a defense mechanism I was glad to have. Too many life-altering events had happened in the past few weeks, and I just couldn't process it all.

I stopped stirring the spaghetti on the stove to glance back at Gus. He was in his highchair, and he'd gotten more of the baby food on his face than in his mouth.

Laughing, I went over to him with a damp rag. I'd just gotten the banana puree wiped off when Jay walked through the front door. After taking off his shoes, he came straight to the kitchen.

He planted a kiss on Gus's head, then he came over to nuzzle my cheek.

He made a satisfied sound. "Smells good."

I looked at the stovetop where the meat sauce was simmering. The guy didn't have very high standards when it came to food, which was a good thing, since I was a shit cook.

"It's just spaghetti."

"I wasn't talking about the spaghetti." He waggled his eyebrows at me as he made his way over to the sink.

Naughty man.

He turned on the faucet and splashed his face with cold water. "It's hot out there."

It wasn't uncommon for him to come home dirty—I learned that pretty quickly since he started working for Jordan. But tonight he was practically soaked. Dark wet spots were seeping through the blue fabric of his Burwash T-shirt around the armpits and the neckline. I caught a whiff of his sweat mixed with his deodorant.

Sexy.

I trailed a finger down the back of his damp neck, remembering how sweaty we'd gotten the other day.

"You're stickier than usual," I commented playfully.

"That's what happens when you jog six blocks in ninety-degree heat."

Frowning, I craned my neck to glance out the front window at the vacant driveway. "Did your car break down?"

"Nah. It's with Nora." He patted himself dry with a white kitchen towel. "She came by the shop on her way home from school. She wanted to borrow my car tonight to go to the movies with a friend. Figured she could take it and I'll walk by my mom's house tomorrow morning to get it back." He shrugged. "She's sixteen. She needs a car."

He was so soft when it came to his sister. I loved that about him.

"Do I get to meet your family sometime?" I questioned timidly, going back to stirring dinner so I didn't have to see his face on the off chance that he said no.

Jay hadn't mentioned anything about introducing me to his mom or sister, and I felt silly asking. Like I was inviting myself to a party where I wasn't welcome.

But I should've known Jay would be on board. He was completely committed to me, which was one of the reasons I felt so safe with him.

He was my constant. My rock. The one thing I could always count on.

Gripping my waist, he hugged me from behind, and I could see his smile in my peripheral vision. "You want to?"

"Well, yeah." I hiked a shoulder. "They're important to you, and now we live so close to them. Plus..." I swallowed hard, pushing down the grief.

Seriously, it was annoying. No one ever talks about the 'irritation stage' of grief. How the sadness hangs around like a bad ex who won't go away. How it sneaks up on you when you least expect it. How it tries to butt into your conversations and take over a happy moment.

"Plus what?" Jay pressed.

I turned around and lightly touched his stretched-out collar. Gus's handiwork. All of Jay's shirts were getting loose around the neck, thanks to my little boy.

"I don't have anyone left," I answered, keeping my voice even. "It's just Gus and me now."

"Baby," Jay said, his tone thick with regret. "I'm sorry. I didn't even think about setting something up because you're already overwhelmed enough as it is. And you're wrong—it's not just you and Gus. You have me, and my mom is going to love you guys. Seriously, be prepared to be smothered."

A grin lifted my lips. "Yeah?"

"Yep. How about this Sunday?"

I was nodding when Gus decided to demand attention.

"Day! Dewey?"

"Did someone say jewelry?" Flashing his empty hands, Jay went over to the highchair.

Shaking my head, I held in a giggle. He was such a showman. Gus's eyes were comically wide as Jay dramatically wiggled his fingers.

Then he held out two tightly closed fists. "Choose a side, my man."

Gus hit them both with his sticky hands.

"How are you so smart?" Uncurling his fingers, Jay revealed two rings—one on each palm.

And just like that, my irritating sadness fled. There was no room for grief when Jay was here to chase it away.

CHAPTER 29

Jay

"**W**hen was the last time your car had an oil change?" Jordan asked, coming up behind me.

I closed the passenger door to a Dodge Intrepid that was now gleaming inside. "Been a couple months."

"You wanna learn how to do it?"

I grinned, excited. "Yeah."

It was a slow morning at the shop. Other than the car I just finished, we didn't have any appointments on the calendar.

"Drive your car to the pit, and we'll get started." Jordan zipped up his blue coveralls as he walked away, and I jogged out to the parking lot.

I'd never had a dad to teach me these kinds of skills. Innocent stuff, like working with tools and playing catch. I didn't know how to change a flat tire or how to throw a proper pitch.

I couldn't wait to learn everything, so I could pass it on to Gus. Maybe he didn't see me as a dad yet, but in time, he would. I could be that for him, if he wanted.

When I got to my car, I experienced that hair-raising feeling again. The same one from the other day at the cemetery.

Rubbing the back of my neck, I glanced at the houses across the street and the gas station next to the shop. Cars passed by, and there was a woman jogging past the thrift store with her dog at the end of the block.

Nothing seemed unusual, so I shook the paranoia off.

As I hopped into my car, I spied Gus's dragon puppet sitting in the car seat. I smiled at the reminder of how much Casey trusted me. How ingrained in their lives I was.

Yesterday, I'd picked Gus up from Doreen's so Casey could work the dinner shift. She'd said the tips were better in the evening, and I was happy to help. After all, more money for her was better financial stability for all of us.

Inching forward, I drove through the open garage door, watching Jordan's hand signals as he directed me to the right spot. When he told me to stop, I removed the keys from the ignition, got out, and met him around the front of the car.

"Gonna pop your hood," he said, moving toward the driver's side. "We'll check a few things over first."

I heard the metallic click, then I propped the heavy hood up with the rod. I was studying all the unfamiliar auto parts when I heard Jordan clear his throat.

"Jay," he said, his voice strained.

At first, I thought maybe he was hurt. Maybe he threw his back out or something.

But when I rounded the car, I saw him standing there with a solemn expression and a small plastic bag in his hand.

As soon as I saw the white powdery substance, it felt like the wind got knocked out of me.

It'd been a long time since cocaine was in front of me, but I'd recognize it anywhere. There wasn't much of it in the baggie, and I blinked at it, wondering if I was seeing things.

"Where did you get that?" I asked, baffled.

"Found this under your seat," Jordan said, accusatory.

He thought it belonged to me. Of course he would. It was my car. My driver's seat.

But those weren't my drugs.

Confusion flooded my thoughts as I tried to figure out where they came from. When the realization hit me, I was so shocked that I had to remind myself to breathe.

Nora.

Two seconds went by as my mind screamed a dozen denials.

But it had to be her. She borrowed my car the other night, so it was the only devastating conclusion I could come to.

I slowly shook my head. "That isn't mine."

I'd uttered that lame line so many times in my life, but this was the first time I'd ever said it when it was one hundred percent true.

Jordan's eyes were skeptical slits. "Do you know who it belongs to?"

Looking down, I nodded. "I do, but I can't tell you."

I couldn't rat my sister out. Not in this small town where rumors spread like wildfire. She already had a target on her back because of my history. People were watching her, waiting to see if she was a bad seed, too.

And now she was taking the same path I swore I wouldn't let her go down.

"It isn't mine." I made eye contact with Jordan and held it, wanting him to see the transparency in my statement. "I don't touch that stuff anymore. You can drug test me if you want."

He looked so disappointed when he crumpled the bag in his fist. "It doesn't matter whose it is or how it ended up there. I can't have this kind of stuff in my shop. Guilty by association is a risk I can't take. I could lose my business. Everything I've worked for."

"I understand. Believe me, I do. It won't happen again."

"It won't," he agreed. His lips pressed into a thin line

before he blew out a breath. "Because I'm letting you go. I'm sorry, Jay. I really wanted this to work out."

Fired. I was getting fired.

Fear made my heart speed up when a horrifying thought came to mind. "Are you going to report me?"

"Against my better judgment, no, I'm not. I won't be the one to send you back to jail."

Equal parts relieved and upset, I scrubbed a hand down my face. "Thank you."

Without another word, he walked to the bathroom. I heard the toilet flush, then he silently went to his office.

I was still standing in the same spot when he came out with a wad of cash.

He folded the bills and pressed them to my palm. "This is what you earned this week. I wish you the best of luck. Really." His eyes went to my car again, his gaze pinned on Gus's car seat in the back. "Be careful about who you're hanging around with. You've got a little one to look after now."

Oh, God. The blows kept coming.

He was right. My stomach twisted when I thought about how I'd unknowingly put Gus in danger. How I'd driven around with those drugs mere feet away from him.

If I'd gotten pulled over…

I shook my head, ridding myself of the nightmarish scenario.

"Bye, Jordan."

Giving him a nod of respect, I turned to my car. I put the hood down, got behind the wheel, and reversed out of Burwash Auto Repair.

My jaw clenched as a cocktail of unpleasant emotions swirled in my chest. Anger. Fear. Guilt. Devastation.

I stepped on the accelerator when I got out onto the street. The shop got smaller in my rearview mirror, and I wasn't sure if I wanted to punch something or cry. Probably both.

I was so fucking sad. For me. For Nora.

For Casey and Gus. Losing my job wasn't okay. We had rent to pay. Bills. Groceries to buy. How was I supposed to do that when I didn't have a paycheck?

I spent the next ten minutes aimlessly driving around town.

I didn't want to go home yet. Casey had Thursdays off, and she was there with Gus. I couldn't face her right now.

I blamed myself for this.

The sins of my past were still lurking. Maybe they always would be. It might've been Nora who made the mistake this time, but was it my influence?

When I sped past a burger joint near the high school, I hit my brakes when I saw curly blond hair. School was back in session, and it was lunchtime. Students had open campus lunch, and I was going to seize the opportunity to have a talk with my sister.

Slowing to a stop, I honked the horn once.

Nora glanced up from the picnic table. She smiled when she saw me, the brand-new braces on her teeth on full display.

She looked so innocent. So young. The opposite of a cokehead.

But I knew looks could be deceiving.

I gestured for her to come to the car. Gathering her burger and fries, she said something I couldn't hear to her friends.

One girl, a blonde with stick-straight hair, called after her, "Oh my God, Nora. You can't get in cars with random guys."

"He's not a random guy," Nora said, glancing back at the group. "He's my brother."

The girl's face went from suspicious to intrigued as she eyed me. "That's your brother? Can I come, too?"

"No," I interjected, my hard tone final.

"Hey," Nora said happily, shutting the door and fastening her seat belt. "This is a nice surprise."

She wouldn't be saying that in a few minutes.

I didn't respond as I hit the gas.

"Whoa." Nora scrambled to collect her fries when they almost fell off her lap. "Did you forget how to drive while you were in the slammer?"

Normally, her joke would've amused me, but I didn't feel like laughing. Easing up on the accelerator, I coasted down a side street.

Nora shifted anxiously in her seat at my silence. "Are you mad? Is this because I got pulled over? I swear I wasn't speeding—"

"Hold up. You got pulled over? By a cop?" I glanced over to see her nodding guiltily. "In *my car*?"

"It wasn't a big deal." Her voice was pleading. "I was going fifty-seven in a fifty-five. It was sort of ridiculous. He didn't even write me a warning. Why go through the trouble of stopping me?"

I knew the answer to her question. "Because he knows my car and he thought you were me. It was Officer Crocker, wasn't it?"

Nodding, Nora nibbled on a French fry.

That guy had it out for me. He was the one I outran that night years ago. Although he'd never said it, I always got the feeling he was pretty pissed he got outsmarted by a junkie.

"But nothing happened?" I asked, wondering why Nora seemed so calm about everything. Because I was freaking the fuck out. "He didn't search the car?"

"No. He just asked to see my license, then he told me to drive safe."

"You're goddamn lucky, you know that?"

I slowed when I saw the park ahead. The same park Casey and I went to on our date. I pulled up to a shaded area away from any other cars.

When we stopped, I spoke while looking straight ahead at the merry-go-round. "When did you start doing drugs? Be honest with me."

"What?" My sister sounded genuinely offended. "I don't do drugs."

I turned toward her, searching her brown eyes for a hint of dishonesty. "Don't lie."

She sputtered. "I-I'm serious. Why would you think that?"

"So, you weren't using the other night when you were supposed to be at the movies?"

"No. We went to see *Aladdin*. I probably still have the ticket stub in my purse. It's at home, but I can find it after school if you want me to prove it—"

I cut her off with a wave of my hand. She wasn't lying. I could tell. Tears were filling her eyes, and Nora couldn't fake-cry to save her life. The hurt look on her face wasn't one of someone who'd gotten caught—she was insulted.

"I can't believe you think I'd do that," she whispered shakily. "After what happened to you..."

"Who'd you go out with?" I asked. "Who else was in this car?"

"Just Zoey."

"The blonde with you at lunch?"

A quick nod of confirmation. "Why?"

"Because my boss found cocaine in my car," I said, and Nora sucked in a breath. "It's not mine. So, that leaves you or Zoey."

"Oh my God. It wasn't me," she rushed out. "I promise. And I didn't even know Zoey was using."

"I believe you," I rasped.

"It makes sense now," she mused, sniffling as she became more emotional. "Zoey went to the bathroom a few times during the movie. She said she was on her period, but her time of the month was two weeks ago."

Pinching the bridge of my nose, I hung my head. The last thing I wanted to hear about was my sister's friend's menstrual cycles, but Nora was right—the details added up to Zoey being the culprit.

When they got pulled over, she must've panicked and tossed the drugs under the driver's seat. That way, it appeared as though the illegal substances didn't belong to her.

It was a move I would've done back in the day.

Yeah, I'd been a shitty friend.

And so was Zoey.

"I don't want you hanging out with her anymore," I said, firm. "Do you understand me, Nora? She's not the kind of person you want to get tangled up with."

Agreeing, she nodded quickly before a look of horror took over.

"Are you going to get arrested again? I don't w-want you to go back to p-prison." She was crying in earnest now, fat tears rolling down her cheeks.

"I'm not. Jordan's being cool about it."

Relieved, she buried her face in her hands. She'd always been tender-hearted and trusting. I loved that about her, but it made me worry. Someone like her could easily get lured into the wrong crowd.

When Nora glanced up, she nervously chewed her lip. "Are you going to tell Mom?"

"No."

"Thank you." She deflated with a sigh, but her reprieve didn't last long.

"You are," I informed her.

"Shit."

Shit was right. Mom wasn't going to handle the news well. After everything my father and I had put her through, the mention of any addictive substance was a major trigger. Wouldn't be surprising if Nora was grounded until graduation. Maybe that was a good thing.

I gazed out at the swings in the distance. A mother was pushing her two kids higher as they laughed. Gus would love the tall slide. This weekend, I'd planned to see if Casey would let me bring him here.

Just the thought of telling her what happened today made me want to vomit, so I pushed her out of my mind.

I glanced back at Nora. "I need you to understand how serious this is. The consequences I'm facing. What this is going to cost me." I paused, drawing in a breath to try to reel in my temper. "For one, I'm unemployed now. I had a good thing going at Burwash. A job I liked. A decent income. That's gone."

"I'm s-sorry." She flinched at my hard tone.

"Two, I picked my girlfriend's son up from the babysitter yesterday." I was having trouble keeping the anger out of my voice thinking about the what-if. "Do you know what that means?"

The only answer I got was more crying and sniffling.

"I drove around with drugs in my car while I was caring for a small child. What would've happened if I'd gotten pulled over? If they searched the car and found the shit your friend left behind?" Not waiting for her to answer, I spelled it out for her. "They would've arrested me. I would've been locked up for years. Maybe decades. Slap a child endangerment charge on top of a probation violation, and I could've been spending half my life in that shit hole."

I didn't even want to contemplate what could've happened to Gus and Casey, but the terrifying thought shoved its way through anyway. Child Protective Services probably would've gotten involved. Since I was living with them, they might've had to investigate Casey and question if she was fit to be a parent.

Jordan was right—guilty by association was a risk.

I was a risk.

"But that didn't happen, right?" Nora said positively, drying her eyes with the short sleeve of her pink T-shirt. "It's okay."

I let out a growl of frustration. "It's not okay. What am I going to do now?"

"Find a new job," Nora suggested, as though it was an easy solution.

She didn't understand the ways of the world or the struggles I'd faced in the past few months. A guy like me only got so many chances, and I was afraid my luck had run out in this town.

I put the car in reverse, glancing at the half-eaten burger on Nora's lap.

"Eat your food," I said softly, unable to let go of what she looked like when we were kids—underfed, with skinny legs and ribs sticking out.

The ride back to the high school was a solemn one. Positioning the air vent to blow at her face, Nora attempted to clear the red splotches on her cheeks as she took bites of her lunch.

Before I dropped her off at the side entrance by the parking lot, I needed her to promise she'd find better friends.

"I will," she assured me.

"I know it's hard to get away from people, especially when you're in a small town, but it's better to be a loner than to spend your time with someone who doesn't care about you."

"I know."

"And Zoey doesn't care about you. Not if she does what she did the other night."

"I get it. I seriously do. I don't want to end up like—" Suddenly her mouth snapped shut.

"Like what? Like *me*. Say it," I ordered. "Because you're exactly right. Say it, Nora."

"Like you," she finished, almost too quiet to hear.

"Good girl. Get back to class. Don't want to be late."

She got out of the car and shut the door. Before I could pull away, she knocked on the window. I pushed the button to roll it down.

"Will I still see you at dinner on Sunday?" she asked hopefully.

Shaking my head, sadness weighed on me when I replied, "I don't know."

I didn't stick around to see the devastation on my little sister's face.

CHAPTER 30

Jay

As I sped down a familiar country road, the old abandoned farmhouse came into view. Blackened shingles were peeling off the roof, and the white siding was so dirty it was gray in most places. Several windows had been busted out—a casualty of intruders and partiers who knew they wouldn't get caught at a place that'd been long forgotten.

Honestly, I couldn't believe it was still standing.

A pair of siblings had inherited the property years ago. Rumor had it, they couldn't reach an agreement about what to do with the house.

So it sat here, rotting.

The gravel driveway crunched under my tires as I slowly crept to the shaded side of the barn. I rolled the windows all the way down and shut off the car as doubts and insecurities flooded my thoughts.

I'm not good.

I ruin everything I touch.

I'll ruin her.

And Gus. He wasn't my blood, but my heart yearned to claim him. I wanted him to be mine. I wanted to hear him call me dad.

But my worst fear was coming true—I was letting them down.

Closing my eyes, I breathed in the sweet air and listened to the wind rustling the leaves of the trees overhead. Tall cornfields kept me hidden, and I enjoyed the quiet moment.

Out here, I could think.

Back in the day, this was the spot I came to when I wanted to get high.

It was also the same place I saw Casey for the very first time. The night of the illegal fight between her ex and Jimmy was a blur of fuzzy memories.

Except for her.

Her dark hair and sad eyes were crystal clear in my mind.

That night was a pivotal moment in my life. It felt like the road to my future had started in this place.

Maybe it was ending here, too.

My phone started buzzing in the cupholder, and when I picked it up, I saw Jimmy's name on the screen. I didn't feel like talking, but something told me to answer it.

"Hello?"

Jimmy cut right to the chase. "Hey, I was just at Burwash's. It really sucks that things didn't work out for you over there."

Shit. Fuck. Double fuck.

How much did Jimmy know? Maybe Jordan wasn't going to be cool about it like I thought. Less than an hour had gone by, and news had already traveled to someone from another town.

"Yeah." I nervously shifted in my seat as sweat broke out on my forehead. "What'd Jordan say?"

"Not much. Just that as of today, you no longer worked there. I stopped in to borrow a part we needed for a repair. I asked about you, and that's when he told me I'd just missed you and you wouldn't be back. So, what happened? You didn't like it?"

Grateful for Jordan's discretion, I released the breath I'd been holding. "I'd rather not get into the details."

"Understood. Well, whatever it was, I'm sorry. I thought you'd be great at that job."

I rubbed my temple. "Yeah, so did I."

"I wasn't going to bring this up, but now that you might be looking for work, I guess I should mention it." The jingling of keys and a door opening in the background came through the speaker. "Mackenna said something about a stagehand position at a stadium. Some of the bands she writes songs for have concerts there, and they need crew members to build the sets."

"Yeah?" Interested, I sat up straighter.

I had experience constructing the rides at the carnival. This was a job I could do.

"Yeah. But here's the kicker—it's in southern Illinois, near St. Louis."

My heart dropped, and I swallowed hard. "Oh."

"I know," Jimmy went on. "Disappointing that it's too far away."

"Maybe that's not a problem." The words felt like sandpaper in my throat, but I said them anyway. "I could move down there."

"But, you and Casey… It's a three-hour drive."

I ground my teeth, tightening my grip on the steering wheel. I didn't want to get into my relationship, so I let my silence speak for me.

"All right, all right," Jimmy said, getting the hint. "Hey, Mack. Where you at? Mack Mack mo Mack, banana fanna fo— Oh, hey." He lowered his volume to a whisper. "Sorry. I didn't realize Will was sleeping. Can you talk to Jay for a sec? He needs info about the stagehand position."

"Oh, sure." I heard a feminine yawn. Then rustling of blankets and a kiss.

Intense envy struck me right in the chest. They were so happy. So lucky to have each other.

They made having a family seem so easy.

"Hi, Jay," Mackenna said softly. "So, it pays twenty dollars an hour and it's usually evenings and weekends. The schedule is a little staggered, because it all depends on when there're shows. It's not just concerts. Sometimes it's sporting events, too. Want me to text you the number of the manager?"

"Yeah," I told her, not needing to hear more.

It was money. If I took the job, I could send money back to Casey. I could still help her, even if I couldn't be around.

Pain lanced through my chest, and I rubbed at it.

This was going to break her heart. It was already breaking mine, but my options weren't great.

If I stayed, I'd likely have to mooch off Casey for a while. Maybe a long while. She'd have another person to support. I'd be making things harder for her, not better. Eventually, resentment would build. She'd start to think of me as a hinderance.

But if I left, I'd be giving up the best thing that'd ever happened to me.

At least the second choice would be quicker. Like ripping off a Band-Aid.

Seemed like no matter what I chose to do, Casey would get hurt. So would I.

Mackenna and I said goodbye, and a text with the number immediately came through after I hung up.

I wasn't a big believer in signs, but this wasn't just a sign—it was a flashing billboard. What were the odds that I'd get offered a job right after I lost mine? A job that paid well. A job that would take me away from the people who were probably better off without me.

I sat in that spot for a long time, going back and forth over the dead-end options.

Eventually, I came to a decision, and I backed out of the long driveway to head home.

But first, I had one more stop to make.

CHAPTER 31

Casey

It was weird dropping Gus off at Doreen's on an afternoon when I didn't have to work. After his nap, I gave him a good snack, then we went to Brenton.

I tried not to let guilt invade my excitement as I drove back to Daywood. I was doing this for Jay. Okay, it was for me, too.

Having alone time—adult time—was important. I planned to surprise him with a home-cooked dinner. Nothing fancy. Spaghetti was on the menu again. But after that, we'd have a whole hour to ourselves.

I'd make up for my shitty cooking skills by doing that thing he liked in the bedroom.

Well.

There were a lot of things he liked in the bedroom. I had plenty of opportunities to get creative.

In a hurry, I pushed past the speed limit a little because I didn't have a ton of time before Jay got off work.

But when I turned the corner and our house came into view, I let out a string of curse words. Jay's car was parked on the street, which meant my surprise was ruined.

No, not ruined—I just had to come up with a different idea.

It was too early for dinner. We could go straight to sex and work up an appetite.

Fine. Better than fine. In fact, I was totally on board with the change of plans as I raced into the house.

"Jay?" I looked for signs of him, but it was totally quiet.

I walked down the hallway, expecting to find him in the bedroom.

Instead, I found a mess. A couple drawers were partly open. Some socks littered the floor. A pile of T-shirts and jeans sat on the bed.

Was he reorganizing his clothes?

Going to the kitchen, I peeked through the window to the backyard, and my heart pitter-pattered when I saw Jay sitting by the meadow. His dark-blue shirt was stretched over the muscles of his back, and the sun glinted off his hair, bringing out the red tones.

The sliding door squeaked when I opened it, but Jay didn't turn around.

"Hey," I called out, thinking he must be deep in thought.

Still, he stayed facing away. I frowned and slowed my approach as I got close.

Taking the seat next to him, I bumped his shoulder with mine. "Bad day?"

"Yeah, you could say that. Where's Gus?"

"At Doreen's. Surprise." Grinning, I threw my hand out in a ta-dah gesture. "I wanted to ambush you with a sexy date."

"Oh." He looked down, and that was when I noticed the Dollar Store bag in front of him.

I pointed at it. "What's that?"

He pulled out a sparkly crown.

"It's the crown from *Tangled*," he said, rolling it back and forth in his hands. "Well, not the exact model, but it's the closest thing to it that I could find. Gus won't know the difference."

The jewels glittered in the sunlight, and I knew Gus would love it.

"That's really sweet of you." Smiling, I rested my head on his shoulder and breathed in the smell of wildflowers. "So, are you gonna tell me what's wrong?"

"In a second." Setting the gift on the ground, he pivoted in my direction and scooted back a little. "I need to show you something."

"Okay." I swiveled toward him.

We were facing each other now, and Jay held his hand up, palm forward. "Do you see a coin in my hand?"

Another magic trick. I tilted my head to the side, studying his thick fingers.

"No," I replied.

"That's because it's hidden here." Closing his fist, he revealed a quarter that'd been stuck between his middle and ring fingers on the backside. "You keep it here. When you want it to seem like you're making it appear, let it slide through your fingers to your palm. You can do this with rings, too. You try it. Practice it." He placed the coin in my hand.

At first, I was happy. He was finally sharing one of these secrets with me.

But then the pieces of the puzzle started falling into place.

The ransacked clothes. His sullen mood. Teaching me something I wouldn't need to know if he was around.

My eyes narrowed. "What's going on, Jay? Why are you showing me this now?"

At least ten seconds ticked by before he eventually answered, "I've gotta go away for a while."

I dropped the quarter, letting it fall to the grass. "Why? Where are you going? How long will you be gone?"

"I don't know."

I wasn't sure which question he was answering. All of them? The last one?

"Is this goodbye?" I voiced the impossible thought. "Are you—are you breaking up with me?"

More silence stretched between us as Jay gazed at me with a look so filled with pain, I physically felt it in the pit of my stomach.

"Not because I want to," he replied, his tone rough with emotion.

"Wha—but—I don't understand." I was so shocked that I literally couldn't comprehend what Jay was saying.

I trusted him.

I depended on him.

Life without him was unfathomable.

"Let's go inside." Jay stood and held out his hand.

Numb, I grabbed it and he helped me up. He didn't let go as we walked to the house, but as soon as we got through the door, he put distance between us.

Leaning against the counter by the sink, he was staring at the floor when he said, "I got a new job, but it's down by St. Louis."

"What's wrong with the job you have? I thought you liked it."

"I do. I did," he sighed. "I got fired today."

"What?" I gasped. "Why?"

"Jordan found drugs in my car. He's being pretty merciful about it, considering he could fuck up my life if he wanted to. He tossed it, and we're not going to speak of it again."

Speechless, I swayed on my feet. My pulse was pounding so hard I could hear the rush of blood in my ears. The last five minutes couldn't be real.

If I knew two things about this man, it was this: He wouldn't leave me, and he wouldn't have drugs.

Jay glanced up and looked me in the eyes. "It wasn't mine, Casey."

Sagging with relief, I grasped the stove to steady myself. "I believe you."

His expression turned angry. "Why?"

"Why what? Why do I believe you?"

He gave me a curt nod.

"Because," I explained with a shrug. "I just do."

Stalking toward me with measured steps, he asked, "How do you know I'm not lying?"

"Because I know you." Any woman might be intimidated with a big guy like Jay towering over them, but I lifted my chin at his smoldering face. "I know you wouldn't do that."

His hands planted on either side of me, caging me in. "I could if I wanted to. Do you know how easy it would be to dial up one of my old suppliers? I still have their numbers memorized." He tapped his temple. "One phone call, and I could be passed out in a gutter somewhere. I miss it sometimes, you know—being high. I'll always be an addict. Once a junkie, always a junkie."

Now he was just being a brute.

I gave his chest a light shove and he backed away.

Moving forward, I poked his shoulder, punctuating each word as I prodded his flesh. "You're. Not. That. Anymore."

When he realized I wasn't buying into his bullshit, he burst out, "Fuck," before burying his head in his hands.

"Was it Nora?" I asked, putting two and two together.

"One of her friends," he confirmed, sounding defeated.

"See? I knew it wasn't you." I tried to touch his shoulder, but right as I made contact, he spun away.

"Damn it, Casey," he lashed out, using a harsh tone I'd never heard from him before. "I told you to keep your standards high. You remember that? You promised you would." He pointed a finger at me. "You promised."

"Yeah. So?"

"So what the hell are you doing with me?" His chest rose and fell with quick breaths, fists clenched at his sides. Angry lines sat between his furrowed eyebrows. "You deserve better."

It sank in then. No amount of comforting or convincing would change the image he had of himself.

And I was losing him. He was still here, but I could feel him drifting away already.

"What the hell are you doing with me?" he repeated, spreading his arms.

"Loving you," I answered, whisper quiet.

CHAPTER 32

Jay

Loving you.

She loved me. Neither of us had said that word yet, although I'd thought it at least a few dozen times.

I felt my face soften when I saw wetness shimmering in Casey's eyes.

"You shouldn't," I told her. "I'm not good for you."

"Yes, you are."

"Think of your son. Think about your future."

"I am." Her breath hitched. "And I can't imagine our life without you in it."

Her lower lip wobbled, and tears started flowing from her eyes in continuous streams. Her shoulders bounced with sobs she was trying to restrain, but the occasional whimper escaped as she hugged her middle.

And I was completely wrecked.

Through everything that'd happened in the past few weeks, she'd been strong.

She didn't cry when she thought she lost her son at the carnival. She didn't lose her composure when her house burned down. She didn't wallow in grief when her mom died.

The fact that I was seeing her fall apart now, and it was my fault?

Fucking brutal. "Think of your future. Think of Gus. Loving me is wrong for you."

"I can't help it. Sometimes we don't get to choose who we love. You said that. You said we love on accident. Do you think you could—" A sob interrupted her sentence. "—you could love me, too? Love me on purpose," she begged in a shaky whisper.

The sight of her tears triggered stinging in my own eyes. She didn't know how much she meant to me.

She was my everything. My whole world. My heart.

Closing the distance, I wrapped my arms around her. "Casey, I'll love you on accident everyday for the rest of my life."

"You love me?"

"More than anything."

"Then don't go."

"I have to, baby. Gotta go where the money is. You can keep my recliner and the bed. The apartments I looked up are furnished. I'm going to send you half my paycheck."

Casey looked up with red-rimmed eyes. "So, what, we're gonna do the long-distance thing?"

Honestly, I'd considered that option, but I decided against it.

I shook my head. "I'd just be holding you back."

"From what?" She went from sad to pissed, her face screwing up. "Meeting someone else? Is that what you want? You want some other man rolling around with me on your king-sized mattress?"

The mental image was so disgusting and enraging that I had to back away. I grabbed the side of the sink so hard my knuckles cracked.

"No," I said through gritted teeth.

I had to leave before she said more shit like that. Before she convinced me that this was a terrible idea.

Pushing away from the counter, I took long strides down

the hall to the bedroom. I hauled my gray duffle out of the closet and started haphazardly stuffing clothes in as fast as I could.

"I don't want your furniture or your money. I want *you*." Casey stood in the doorway, her eyes following my motions as I packed. "I'm willing to cover the bills until you can get another job around here."

"I refuse to be a burden to you."

"Oh, but it was okay when I accepted your help? When I crashed at your apartment? When I let you buy a crib and toys and food? Was I burden then?"

She was fuming. I'd never seen her this angry.

Good.

I wanted her to yell at me. Hit me. Anything but crying would do.

"Of course not." Zipping the bag, I slung it over my shoulder as I approached the door, but Casey was in the way.

She didn't budge. "Then how is this any different?"

"It just is. Move."

"No."

So fucking stubborn.

Even in my turmoil, I admired her tenacity. In a way, it was refreshing to see her this worked up after she'd spent so much time masking her emotions.

"Move," I repeated. "Or I'll move you."

"I'd like to see you try." Her fingernails creaked against the wood as she tightened her hold on the doorjamb.

My dick perked up.

There was something incredibly hot about seeing her fight so hard to keep me here. And she was making a lot of good points. I was having trouble remembering why I was so dead set on leaving.

"Dammit, Casey."

I dropped the duffle to the floor. My hands went to her waist and my lips landed on hers. Her lean legs wrapped around my middle as I picked her up.

Walking forward, I pressed her back to the wall in the hallway, anchoring her body with mine while my tongue invaded her mouth.

Her fingers stabbed through my hair and my palms moved down to her supple ass.

I rocked my erection against her softness while my hands wandered. To her tits. To her beautiful face. To her dimples.

We were a frantic mess of groping hands, clacking teeth, and ragged breathing.

I dragged my tongue along her jaw, moving down to suck on her neck. Tasting her. Drinking her in and locking the feel of her body away in my memory.

"I love you, Jay," Casey gasped out.

Her words warmed my heart and doused me in cold at the same time.

I knew what loving a bad man could do to someone. I saw what it did to my mother. It filtered down to her children, infecting me like a disease. I was tainted, and I always would be.

Nora wasn't out of the woods yet. She was naïve and impressionable, and peer pressure was a bitch.

Protecting Casey and Gus was more important than my selfish desires.

Dropping my forehead to Casey's, I allowed myself to be completely transparent. "I love you. The kind of love you talked about when Gus was born… the kind that changes you? Turns you into someone new? That's what I feel for you and Gus." I gave her a slow kiss and released my grip on her thighs, letting her feet slide to the floor. "And that's why I have to go."

Before she had a chance to protest, I snatched the bag and hightailed it to the front door. My hand was on the knob when Casey's broken voice stopped me.

"You're not even going to say goodbye to Gus? You're just pulling a permanent disappearing act?"

Oh, she brought out the big guns. My throat tightened, and tears blurred my vision. I glanced back, allowing her to see how much this hurt.

"Don't ask me to do that," I pleaded. "This is hard enough as it is. Give him the crown. Tell him it's from you. Do magic tricks but—" my lungs convulsed with a sob that wanted to get out. "—but let him forget me."

"No," she cried, running forward. Her fingers curled into my shirt at my waist while she pressed her face to my chest. Wetness soaked through the cotton as she wept. "Please don't go. I'm begging you. I need you. Don't make me do this alone. I can't. I can't."

"Yes, you can." I pressed a kiss to the top of her head. "You did it long before I came along. You'll be fine."

"No, I won't." She looked up and tenderly touched my face. "Please stay with me. Stay with me."

Evidence of my agony leaked from my eyes, but I quickly wiped the moisture away. "Not this time, baby."

Tears gathered under her chin, and they fell, splashing onto the prism on her chest. Suddenly, she reached behind her neck and unclasped the chain.

Taking my hand, she closed my fingers around the necklace. "I want you to have this."

"I can't take this from you." I tried to push it back at her, but she wouldn't accept it.

"And I won't let you leave without it. Please?" Her voice wavered. "For when you need a rainbow."

Fuck.

Even when I was breaking her heart, she was thinking of me. She was giving me one of her most important possessions.

And I was a selfish bastard, because I wanted to take it.

My fingers shook as I fastened the chain around my neck. Tucking the prism into my shirt, I reveled in the fact that it was still warm from Casey's body heat.

I cupped her face, rubbing my thumbs over her absent dimples while I kissed her nose.

Then I backed away, turned the doorknob, and left my happiness behind.

CHAPTER 33

Casey

Blindsided was an understatement.

I sat on the couch for at least an hour after Jay left. Aside from my quiet sobbing, the only sound in the room was a ticking clock in the kitchen. I kept thinking he'd come back. He'd realize his mistake. But with each passing second, I lost hope.

I didn't know what to do without Jay. I relied on him, trusted him, loved him… and he was gone. The magic he'd brought to my life was snuffed out, and now I had to deal with all this shit on my own.

Life had really kicked my ass lately.

So much had changed in the past month. A housefire, a death, moving to a new town.

Falling in love and getting my heart broken was now added to the growing list of crap I couldn't handle.

Love was supposed to make you stronger, not weaker. But maybe love was for fools, because I'd never felt more lost than I did now.

I looked around at my house.

It was clean. Jay must've done a quick pick up before I got home, because the basket of toys was neatly placed in the corner and the highchair was wiped off. Dishes had been piled up in the sink earlier. I knew if I looked in the dishwasher, they'd be there.

The beige couch still carried the new furniture smell, but the two blankets folded over the back had a lingering scent from Jay's apartment. One of them was his baby blanket with the blue bunnies on it. The wooden console and TV were also Jay's.

Guess I could keep those, too.

He was in such a hurry to get away from here that he left a lot behind.

Left me behind.

Fresh tears welled in my eyes, and I grabbed another tissue while I wallowed in my devastation. I mopped at my face and blew my nose. The balled-up tissue joined the rest of the pile on the coffee table.

Eventually, it was time to go get Gus. On the twenty-minute drive to Brenton, I tried my best to suck it up. I couldn't let him see me like this.

But the water works wouldn't stop.

I was serious when I'd told Jay if I started crying, I might not be able to shut it off. I seemed to have an endless supply of tears. Every time I blinked, more dripped down my face.

When I pulled into Brenton Estates, I slowly rolled past the empty lot where my trailer used to sit. It was just a piece of flattened land now. A patch of dirt.

Instead of parking by Doreen's trailer, I found myself stopping next to my mom's. The floodgates of grief stayed wide open as I gazed at her yellow siding.

I hadn't mourned my mother yet. I'd taken refuge in a safe bubble Jay created. Now that barrier was gone, and nothing was stopping the sorrow from pummeling me at every angle.

I had no choice but to face it.

And it hurt.

I didn't realize it was possible to feel sadness in my extremities, but my heartache spread outward, affecting every part of my body. My fingers and toes were ice-cold, despite the warm weather. My arms and legs ached. Head foggy. Chest heavy.

A breakdown was coming. The worst of it hadn't hit yet, but I could feel it approaching like a slow-moving storm.

Sniffling, I opened my glove compartment where I kept a stash of tissues. I grabbed a handful and blotted at my face.

Then I dug my phone out of my purse and shot off a text to Doreen.

Me: Running late. I need to go to my mom's house for something.

Doreen: No worries. Take your time. Gus is chowing down on some SpaghettiOs.

Decaying wood groaned under my sneakers as I climbed the stairs of my mom's old porch. The keys shook in my trembling hand, jingling loudly as I unlocked the deadbolt.

Stagnant air assaulted my nose when I walked through thc door. It was musty from being unlived in, and it carried a lingering hint of the menthols Mom smoked.

I used to hate that smell.

Funnily enough, now it brought back pleasant childhood memories.

It reminded me of hugs. Saturday morning cartoons. Lemonade in the summer. Hot chocolate in winter. Listening to my favorite boybands in my room. Learning how to do my makeup and borrowing Mom's clothes when I was big enough.

Following the smell, I walked past the floral loveseat and took a left down the hall. I peeked into my old room. It was empty, just how I'd left it the day I moved out.

Swiveling right, I went to my mom's room.

I pushed the door open. It'd been almost two years since I was in here, but the space was exactly how I remembered it.

Mom's bed was made, and the daisies on her comforter were glowing in the light streaming through the window. An antique vanity sat next to it, littered with makeup brushes, a bottle of her favorite perfume, and a ceramic bowl filled with her jewelry.

Gus loved playing with her necklaces and rings. She used to bring them over sometimes. There was no reason for them to sit here, unused.

One by one, I collected the shiny objects, slipping the rings onto my fingers and wrapping the necklaces around my wrists. I felt closer to my mom this way. As if touching something she wore could connect us somehow.

I remembered doing this when I was a kid.

When I was little, I wanted to be just like her. There was a point in time when I was completely unaware of her faults. In my eyes, she was perfect.

Lifting my hand to wipe away more wetness from my face, I caught my reflection in the mirror.

I winced, taken aback by how bad I looked. Eyes red and swollen. Splotchy cheeks streaked with tears. Nose raw from wiping it so many times.

With the excessive amount of bling I was wearing, I appeared somewhat deranged.

A sob hiccupped out, and I shed the jewelry, carefully tucking each piece into the front pocket of my purse. When it was down to the last ring, I tried to imitate the magic trick Jay taught me.

Seemed simple enough.

Wrong.

I was clumsy, my unpracticed movements obvious. I dropped the ring twice, but I fumbled with it until the trick was somewhat passable.

Maybe I could fool a baby. That was a big *maybe*.

Next, my eyes went to the digital picture frame. It was turned off, the screen dark. I'd gotten it for my mom last Christmas, and I'd loaded it with pictures of Gus's first six months.

Picking it up, I pressed the button on the side. It switched on, and I was surprised when pictures I'd never seen before popped up.

I sank down, sitting on the side of the bed as I watched my life from my mom's perspective.

The first picture was of my mom sitting next to me in the hospital bed after I had Gus. She was holding him while I slept.

The next images were taken during my pregnancy. My huge belly the day before I went into labor. Me, holding up the yellow onesie at Target. A picture of me from the side when I was just starting to show.

Precious moments flashed, going backward in time. A selfie of the two of us making silly faces at the camera when I was fourteen. My twelfth birthday. A Christmas when I was nine.

My chest rose and fell with sobs as I watched our life together, gutting my already-wounded spirit. I couldn't get enough air, and I wondered if I was having another panic attack.

In the last picture, my mom was helping me climb a tree when I was probably four or so. I looked scared but happy as I held onto her hand for support.

A half-laugh, half-sob burst from me as I covered my mouth.

I was more important to her than I knew. I'd spent so much time thinking I didn't matter.

Yes, our relationship was far from ideal. We had our problems.

But I loved her, and she loved me, too.

I held the frame to my chest, wishing I could step inside any of these moments just to be with her one more time. Just to tell her that I loved her, and despite everything we'd been through, I was proud of her.

That couldn't happen, though. The sharp edges of the black frame poked my sternum, reminding me that I was just hugging a piece of plastic.

I'd never get to hug my mom or hold her hand again.

I finally allowed myself to face reality: she was gone, and she wasn't coming back.

Strange noises echoed off the wood-panel walls, and it took me a second to realize they were coming from me. I didn't even recognize the wailing sounds coming from my throat. Big, heaving sobs racked my entire body, but for once, I didn't try to suppress them.

I gave into the grief, whole-heartedly.

Hanging my head, a constant stream of tears dripped from my face, soaking my shirt as my chest convulsed.

Minutes passed as I let myself feel everything.

This breakdown wasn't just about death—this was a culmination of years of pent-up stress and struggle. I cried for my childhood cut short. The challenges of raising my son alone. The strained relationship with my mom and the fact that we wouldn't have a chance to fix it.

And Jay. I didn't want to believe he was gone, too.

But he was.

Through my blurry vision, I looked straight ahead.

The sliding door to the closet was open. All my mom's shirts and dresses were neatly hung. Her shoes were lined up on the floor.

Standing on wobbly legs, I staggered across the room. I slung my arms around the clothes, gathering the heap. I buried my nose in it, inhaling the familiar scents of cigarettes and Chanel.

I rubbed the fabric on my cheek, the same way Gus did to my shirts.

Muffling my endless sobs in cotton and polyester, my knees gave out. I collapsed to the soft brown carpet, still clinging to the clothes.

I had no idea how long I stayed on the floor. All I knew was that by the time my eyes dried, it was nearly dark outside.

I took a cleansing breath as I pushed to my feet.

Mentally pulling myself together, I straightened the hangers and smoothed the wrinkled shirts. Among the blouses and sequin tops, there was a sweatshirt that seemed out of place.

It was a patchwork of pastels. As a young child, I liked to snuggle with my mom when she wore it because it was soft. I used to think it was the most beautiful shirt in the world.

In reality, it was actually quite ugly. Judging by the faded mint green, baby pink, and light purple, it probably dated back to the 1980s.

I wanted to keep it.

As I tugged the shirt off the metal hanger, I ran my finger over the collar and had a happy thought—Gus was going to stretch it all to hell.

The corners of my lips twitched with a small smile when I remembered my little boy.

I wasn't alone; neither was he.

As long as we had each other, my heart could never be completely broken.

~

If Doreen noticed my frazzled state, she didn't mention it, bless her. She'd been all smiles when I came to retrieve my son. She wished us a goodnight and told Gus she'd see him tomorrow morning.

When I steered onto our street in Daywood, my headlights illuminated my driveway.

My empty driveway.

A small part of me had hoped I'd see Jay's car there.

Just wishful thinking.

Coming home to the darkened windows was just another slap of reality. The relationship, the whirlwind romance—it was over just as swiftly as it began.

The sooner I accepted that, the better. All I could do was hope Gus didn't miss him. It was one thing for Jay to break my heart. But Gus? No one got to hurt my son.

Fatigue weighed on me as I lifted him out of his car seat and carried him into the house.

"Day?" He craned his neck, searching the living room.

Well, shit. So much for hoping Gus would carry on with life, blissfully unaware of a certain person's absence.

What was the right thing to say?

Instead of answering him, I decided distraction was the best route for now. I pulled one of my mom's rings from my purse and gave it to him. I was way too exhausted to attempt a trick, but Gus didn't seem to mind my lack of finesse.

"I love you so much, bud. You know that?"

Gus nodded, rubbing his cheek on my collar as his head bobbed up and down.

"It's just you and me now. We'll always have each other, no matter what."

"Day?"

Damn it.

"We're going to be okay," I told him. "We'll be okay."

Maybe if I said it enough times, I'd start to believe it.

CHAPTER 34

Casey

"Hey, Doreen." I kept my voice quiet so I didn't wake Gus. "Sorry to be calling so late."

"It's all right. I wasn't asleep yet. Is everything okay?"

Rubbing my forehead, I sighed. "No. Gus's cold is settling in his chest and I'll have to take him to the doctor tomorrow. I already told Gloria I wouldn't be in."

"Darn. When his nose started running yesterday, I'd hoped it was just the sniffles."

For most kids, that would probably be the case. But every time Gus came down with a virus, it became more than just a little cold.

The cough came on suddenly tonight before bedtime, and given our past experiences, I knew it would only get worse as time went on.

The urgent care clinic was already closed, so I'd contacted the on-call pediatrician. She'd given me two options: wait to be seen until morning or take him to the emergency room.

I really didn't want to spend most of the night in the ER, so I'd broken out the nebulizer machine and hoped for the best.

I glanced at the clock over the stove. Ten p.m.

Pushing the button on the coffee maker, I said, "Well, I'll keep you updated. It's gonna be a long night."

"Try to get some sleep," Doreen encouraged. "You've been running yourself ragged."

That was true. Tragic events aside, in the week since Jay left, I'd busted my ass at work, applied for new jobs at three restaurants in Daywood, and submitted an application to the preschool for Gus.

"Oh, that reminds me." I grabbed a mug from the cabinet. "The preschool has an opening for Gus in January. I wanted to let you know as soon as possible. I'm sure we'll still need you from time to time."

"That's wonderful, and of course I'm always happy to have him." Doreen paused. "How are you, Casey?"

Her question wasn't just one of those things you ask someone in passing to be polite. I could hear the concern in her voice, and I was touched that she cared about my well-being.

"I'm… getting by."

I could've lied. I could've told her I was great. But I didn't have the energy to pretend anymore.

While I was at the church checking out Gus's future classroom, I saw a flier for free counseling. Apparently, they offered therapy for a wide range of issues, including grief and general life struggles.

I was going to take them up on it. I needed to. If not for myself, then for Gus. He deserved to have a happy mom.

It'd been complete radio silence from Jay.

Seven days he'd been gone, and I was proud of myself for not giving in to the urge to call him. If he wanted to talk to me, he knew how to use a phone.

Plus, I wasn't necessarily sad anymore—I was pissed. I was mad at him for waltzing into our lives, giving me a taste of true happiness and security, then taking it all away.

Honestly, I hoped he was miserable.

At some point, he was probably going to send us money. Just

to spite him, I planned to send it back. I didn't need it. Finances were tight now, but once I sold my mom's trailer, I'd be fine.

Absentmindedly, my hand went up to toy with my prism, and for the hundredth time, I realized it wasn't there. Instead, my fingertips grazed the nylon band and the ring Jay had won from the fair.

Turns out, after wearing a necklace for so many years, I couldn't be sane without one. Gus's ring would have to be the replacement until I found something better.

Faint hacking noises from the bedroom put me on high alert.

"I gotta go, Doreen." I didn't stay on the line long enough to hear her say goodbye.

Abandoning my coffee, I dashed down the hall to my bedroom. Co-sleeping was probably a bad habit to get into, but I'd been allowing it a lot these days. Gus and I both seemed to sleep better when we were together.

Besides, I'd be doing some serious hovering tonight. Might as well be comfortable while I was doing it.

Gus was sleeping soundly when I sank to the mattress. Leaning down, I put my ear over his chest. I listened to the air whooshing in and out of his lungs. A little wheezy, but it didn't sound terrible. Then again, I wasn't a doctor.

I gazed at his adorable face.

He'd been a perfect angel lately.

His car-induced fits had improved, so the drive to and from Brenton wasn't bad. He'd been okay with me taking showers and drying my hair. He'd even been cool with me borrowing his ring.

Maybe it was a fluke, but it was almost as if he could sense that I was fragile.

I hated the thought of leaning on my toddler for support, but if he was offering to improve my day, I wouldn't argue.

I curled up next to him, both loving and hating this bed. It was the softest surface I'd ever slept on, but I couldn't look at it without thinking about Jay. Without remembering how he'd touched me. Loved me.

I'd washed the sheets, but I swore I could still smell him, as though he'd embedded himself in the fibers the same way he'd chained himself to my soul.

How long would it take for me to stop feeling like a piece of me was missing?

I spent the next few hours trying to stay awake while thinking about anything but Jay. Like the helicopter mom I was, I checked Gus's temperature and breathing every half hour, trying my best not to disturb his sleep.

Around one a.m. he woke up, and I jerked awake when I realized I'd dozed off.

Blinking, I looked over at Gus, and my heart dropped when I saw the rapid rise and fall of his chest. His cries were weaker than usual because he wasn't getting enough air.

"Can you cough for me?" I patted his chest as I demanded, "Cough. Cough for me. August Michael, *cough*."

He didn't. He was too young to cough on demand, so he just kept struggling to breathe with an unnerving rattle on every inhale.

We couldn't wait until eight in the morning.

Gus needed help now.

"Okay," I said, scooping him up. "Let's go, bud."

Rushing to the door, I grabbed the emergency diaper bag on the way out.

CHAPTER 35

Jay

Clenching my fist, I fought the sinking sensation in my gut.
Yeah, my Spidey sense was back. Although, that wasn't new. I'd been battling an unsettling feeling ever since I left Daywood in the dust.

I thought I knew what regret was. I'd done enough shit in my life to be familiar with it. I also knew what withdrawals felt like, and this was the worst I'd ever experienced.

This was agony.

Leaving Casey and Gus introduced me to a whole new level of anguish and self-disgust.

Something's wrong.

The thought suddenly popped into my head, but I shoved it away.

Rubbing at my abdomen, I kept telling myself my chest was tight because my heart was ripped to shreds and my stomach churned because I felt trapped.

I was in a prison of my own making. The walls were built with ego and fear, and the door was locked by my own self-loathing.

"You using this machine?" The gruff voice came from behind me.

I glanced in the gym mirror to see a thirty-something guy approaching. He was impatiently eyeing the bench press I was currently occupying, and for good reason. I'd just been sitting here for at least ten minutes doing nothing.

Zoning out, lost in thought.

I did that a lot lately.

"I'm done," I grunted out, standing, before moving to the next machine.

"You're a grumpy motherfucker, huh?" the man asked, humor in his tone.

"Guess so."

He took the hint that I wasn't in the mood to chat, and he stopped talking.

I'd seen him around the apartment complex several times. Mostly at this gym, which was one of the nice amenities the place offered.

But I didn't know his name. I didn't know anyone's name around here. I hadn't retained that kind of information. If it wasn't work related, I didn't care. Even the roommate I'd gotten matched with was a stranger. He must've had a significant other he stayed with a lot, because I had yet to run into him around our apartment.

Not that I was there very often either.

When I wasn't building and tearing down sets, I was at the gym, kicking my own ass.

My muscles were sore, my joints stiff. My body was pretty pissed at the treatment it'd been getting, but I deserved to hurt.

I deserved worse.

The only reason I'd been able to make it through this week was because I took a lesson from the Casey handbook of life—I'd pushed myself to the point of severe exhaustion. Until I couldn't think. Until I couldn't feel anything except for overwhelming weariness and physical pain.

I'd been working as much as the stadium would let me.

Which, in my opinion, wasn't enough. Apparently, they had a rule that if you worked six days in a row, you had to take a day off.

Bullshit.

I didn't want to rest.

And to make matters worse, a section of the concert hall was having maintenance done over the next two days, so the whole place was shut down.

Having a lot of time on my hands wasn't a good thing. Even now, as I added weight to the butterfly press, unwelcomed memories floated in.

Casey's dimples. Her laugh. The way it felt to have Gus tug on my collar.

For some reason, my mind was more active at night.

It was eleven p.m. but I couldn't stand the thought of lying in bed right now. My insomnia was worse than ever. Even on the rare occasion that I did fall asleep, my dreams were haunted by tear-filled blue eyes, rings, and Ferris wheels.

After my pectorals were thoroughly pissed, I got up and went to the free weights.

My biceps trembled in protest as I counted out reps with the forty-pound dumbbells. My muscles burned, the cords in my neck strained, and the veins in my arms popped out.

I kept going until I couldn't lift them again.

A shout left me when I almost dropped one of them on my toes. Breathing hard, I set the weights back on the rack.

God, I was such a douche. I'd become one of those dudes who moaned and groaned in the gym. That was a new low for me.

Just as I turned away, glittering light caught my attention in the full-length mirror. Casey's prism. I hadn't taken it off since she gave it to me.

I touched the glass, remembering all the times I'd seen her pretty fingers play with it.

As I stared at the rainbows on my chest, the foreboding feeling I'd been denying intensified.

Alarm bells went off every time I thought of Casey and Gus. No matter how much I tried to shake the bad feeling I'd been carrying around all day, it wouldn't go away.

Something's not right.

Panic clawed its way up my windpipe as I sat down on a nearby bench. I closed my eyes, and I let my thoughts wander. I ended up at the meadow. Casey was there.

She was everywhere.

The mental energy it took to block her out was unreal, and I just couldn't do it anymore. Somewhere along the way, she'd become my safe place.

And, for the first time in a week, I allowed myself to consider the possibility that I was wrong. That maybe—just maybe—Casey and Gus weren't better off without me.

Could anyone else protect them better? Love them more?

Well, maybe. Probably. Eventually, someone would realize they were the jackpot every man dreamed of.

But was I willing to let Casey settle for me? That was the real question.

The answer: yeah, I was.

I couldn't go on like this. Couldn't go on without her.

Call me selfish, but if her settling meant being with me… I'd just have to spend the rest of my life trying like hell to make it up to her.

I'd already made enough mistakes in my life—falling in love with Casey wasn't one of them but leaving her was.

And now that I was letting the weight of my decision crash down on me, it was like flying free and drowning at the same time.

I missed them—my family—and I didn't belong here, so far away from them.

My stomach twisted again.

I wasn't sure if my bad feeling had to do with Casey or Gus or both. All I knew was that I needed to get to them as soon as possible.

Last time I ignored my gut, Casey's mom died. The time before that, her house burned down. I just had to hope I was wrong now.

"Fuck this," I burst out, getting to my feet.

The big dude took out one of his earbuds. "You say something?"

I just shook my head as I jogged out to the stairwell. Taking three steps at a time, I climbed to my fourth-floor apartment.

CHAPTER 36

Jay

I t didn't take long to pack my shit. I'd been living out of my duffle, just shoving the dirty clothes into a garbage bag with the plan of going to the laundry facilities at the apartment complex once I ran out of clean underwear.

The only other thing to take was the new comforter I'd bought for the full-size mattress my bedroom came furnished with. It'd been on clearance and funny thing—it was blue with white clouds on it. I'd been sleeping with it flipped over so I didn't have to look at the sky. After all, it reminded me of Casey.

But I smiled as I carried it through the parking lot along with my other bags. I couldn't wait to give it to her. It wasn't exactly the same as the one she'd lost in the fire, but I knew she'd love it.

I'd just gotten everything dumped into my trunk when I felt that prickling sensation again. My scalp tingled and goose bumps skittered over my arms.

This time, when I glanced around, I saw movement out of the corner of my eye.

Looking to my left, I squinted at a shadowy figure emerging from behind the dumpster.

My pulse skyrocketed.

When someone approaches you in a dark parking lot in the middle of the night, the outcome usually isn't good.

As the man got closer, I sized him up, noting he was probably a couple inches taller than me. I was bulkier, though. His lean frame didn't quite fill out the black T-shirt, but then again, his stealthy, silent steps told me he had agility on his side. Sometimes the wiry ones could really hold their own.

I considered myself a lover, not a fighter, but I'd had my fair share of scuffles. I could take him if I had to.

When he stepped into the light of the lamppost, I immediately recognized the black-framed glasses and brown hair peppered with premature grays.

"Ethan," I huffed, relieved, pressing a palm to my still-racing heart. "Shit, man. What the hell are you doing here?"

"Been following you for a couple weeks." His reply was casual, like stalking someone was totally normal. And I guess for him, it was.

I barked out a laugh. "Do you know how creepy that is?"

He canted his head to the side and gave a half-shrug. "Yeah."

Ethan Smith—and I highly doubted that was his real name—was a private investigator. Freelance. As far as I knew, he worked mostly in the adoption world. His clients were usually kids who'd come of age, and they were looking for their biological parents.

He'd come to me at the prison because the man in the cell next to mine had a son he didn't know about. The kid was looking for his father, but Ethan didn't want to reconnect the two if this guy was violent or dangerous.

So, Ethan asked me to watch my neighbor. To listen. To discreetly ask around about him.

Since I didn't have anything better to do, I'd agreed. After a few weeks of observation, Ethan came back, and I had answers. The inmate was doing time for auto theft, which Ethan seemed to already know, but his behavior was good. No fights.

Stayed out of trouble. Even bought books from the commissary for another inmate who was trying to learn to read.

I never knew what the outcome was for the guy, because he was released a month later.

Ethan disappeared after that, and I hadn't thought of him since.

"It was you at the cemetery," I concluded. "And outside of Burwash's. You were watching me."

"Yeah. I saw you get fired. Pretty brutal."

I blew out a breath. "The drugs weren't mine—"

"I know that." He cut me off with a flick of his hand. "So, remember when I told you I'd pay you back for that favor someday? That's what I'm here to do."

"Okay…" Confused, I waited for him to continue.

"You hate this job." He hitched a thumb over his shoulder, pointing in the direction of the stadium a few blocks away.

The large dome building was visible in the distance.

I shrugged. "Yeah, I guess I do."

"Because you're away from Casey Maxwell and her son?"

Feeling protective, I narrowed my eyes. "How much do you know about them?"

Lifting his eyebrows, he gave me a 'really?' look. "I know a lot of things I shouldn't."

I nodded. I knew what that was like. People used to come to me for more than just drugs. Sometimes they wanted information. I had a knack for finding out people's business. I was good at observing and asking the right people the right questions.

Hell, that was how I found Casey in the first place. What started as a favor for Mackenna ended up changing the course of my life.

"So what?" I leaned against my car. "You offering me a job?"

"Yes."

"Like, you need an assistant?"

"No. I'm giving you my business. All of it. It's good money."

"I don't understand," I said warily.

Sighing, he dipped his head. "I have to go away for a while. I can't leave my clients hanging."

"Shit. You're going to jail? What for?"

As much as I appreciated the guy's offer to pass down his entire business to me, I was skeptical. I wasn't sure if his investigating methods were legal, and considering he was on his way to the big house, I could assume they weren't.

Shaking his head, he chuckled. "No, not that kind of going away. I have a project that's—" Pausing, he seemed to struggle for the right words. "—different. Long-term. I need to disappear."

"You didn't go falling in love, did you?" I joked.

His gaze fell to the asphalt. "That's classified information."

Oh, yeah. He totally fell in love. Probably with one of his clients.

He shrugged off his backpack. "I've got everything in here. Can we have a meeting in your car? We're going to want privacy for this. There are three surveillance cameras in this area."

I glanced around, wondering how he could tell such a thing, when I spied a dark lens over the back entrance of the apartment complex. Huh. Didn't notice that thing before.

Once we were both in the car, Ethan didn't waste any time getting down to the details. He unzipped his backpack to reveal a sleek silver laptop.

"This has all my clients' records in it. I've already reprogrammed the password—it's your birthday. You'll want to change it as soon as possible." Next, he dug around in the bottom of the bag. "A digital camera. A surveillance camera. A wire. Contact info for an FBI agent I'm cool with."

Eyeing the equipment, I rubbed my jaw. "This is really high-tech stuff."

"Yep. So, most of my clients are around the Midwest. Some travel is required. Since your probation won't let you out of state until next year, you'll be limited in the cases you can take."

I raised my eyebrows at him. He even knew about my probation terms. I wasn't sure if I should be impressed or put off.

"It's all on the up and up," he went on. "Most of the time, anyway. I admit I've hacked a few systems illegally. You don't have to do that, though. I mostly track down public records and adoption agencies. A lot of interviewing. Some watching. It's five hundred dollars up front from the client, and you'll get five hundred more when the job is fulfilled. You'll find the contract in my documents. I have an open case in Springfield, Illinois, right now. Foster kid aged out, and he's trying to find any blood relative in the area."

Ethan slapped a wad of cash onto the middle console, and I picked it up, counting out five one-hundred-dollar bills.

He'd literally answered every question I could've possibly asked, and he seemed so confident I was going to say yes.

"How do you know I'm going to accept?" I asked.

He blinked at me. "Aren't you?"

Well. Yeah. I'd never considered this kind of job, but I had to admit it was appealing.

Man, Ethan was a weird dude. Too smart for his own good. A little arrogant. Mysterious. He had a tiny gap between his two top front teeth, and it made him look younger. It was a contrast with the gray hairs at his temple. Judging by his wrinkle-free complexion, he couldn't have been much older than mid-twenties.

"It's noble work, reuniting people," he continued, as if I needed convincing. "The outcome isn't always what they hope for, but at least they can get closure. If you take four jobs a month, it's a decent income for part-time work. You can live wherever you want. Some might even say this job is somewhat… magical." He smirked.

"Why me?"

"Your reputation precedes you, my friend. Your name has popped up more than once when I was solving a case—I just happened to only utilize your skills once. Plus, I see a bit of a kindred spirit in you."

I was flattered. And also grateful that people knew me for something more than just drugs.

"All right." I rubbed my hands together, excitement flooding my veins. "Let's do this."

Over the next hour, Ethan gave me a crash course on all the tricks of the trade. How to hack certain systems—if I chose to go that route. How to trace people with their cell phone location. How to spy on someone without getting noticed.

I felt like I was learning magic all over again.

"So this is it?" I glanced at the backpack between us.

"That's it."

"Am I ever gonna see you again?"

"Probably not," he answered honestly before sliding a business card my way. A number was scrawled on the back. "You can call me here if you have questions. You're the only one who has this particular number, so I'll know it's you."

Seriously, what a weird dude.

He'd just grabbed ahold of the door handle when I asked, "Are you gonna be okay?"

Looking over his shoulder, he gave me a half smile. "I hope so."

CHAPTER 37

Jay

I didn't want to scare Casey by dropping in unannounced, but I didn't want to wake her by calling either. The sunrise was almost here. As I parked in the driveway of our little blue house, a light gray glow illuminated the horizon.

Pretty soon, Casey would be making her way out to the kitchen. She'd turn on the coffee maker and get a Pop-Tart for Gus.

I could've waited. If I was a patient man, I would've.

But I still had the key.

Convenient.

I was quiet as I let myself in the front door.

Toys were all over the living room, and dirty dishes were piled high in the sink. Remnants of a spaghetti dinner were still on the table.

My lips quirked up. My messy girl.

Creeping down the hallway, I kept my footsteps silent as I peeked into the dim bedroom. Anticipation made my heart pound so hard I could feel my pulse in my head.

But the bed was empty. The blankets were wrinkled and tossed back.

The unnerving gut instinct flared up again.

I pivoted in the other direction, peering into Gus's room. Same thing. An empty mattress and no sign of the people I loved.

What happened? Where were they?

Running out to my car, I grabbed Ethan's backpack—my backpack now—and sprinted back into the house. I sat on the couch, set the laptop on the coffee table, and got it hooked up to Casey's WiFi. Then I took advantage of Ethan's tracing program.

I typed in Casey's cell phone number, then I waited for it to show me a location.

"Shit," I whispered.

They were at the hospital.

～

Déjà vu hit me when I saw Casey walk out into the emergency room lobby with Gus on her hip. He was halfway asleep, and they both looked as rough as I felt.

Casey's hair was in a messy ponytail. She wore flower print leggings and an oversized T-shirt. Gus was still in his dinosaur pjs, and it was obvious they'd left home in a hurry.

Last time this exact scene played out, Casey looked at me like I was her hero.

That wasn't the case now.

She took a couple steps before her eyes collided with mine. Three seconds went by as we stared at each other, and I could've sworn I saw her face light up for a tiny moment.

Then anger took over.

Her lips thinned, her jaw clenched, and she glared before resuming her walk to the exit. She sauntered right past me, her head held high as she left the building.

Fuck.

I ran after her. "Casey."

She didn't stop. If anything, her legs worked faster.

"Casey, please," I begged, making it to her side.

"What are you doing here, Jay?"

"I had a bad feeling. What's wrong with Gus? Is he okay? Is he hurt?"

A fierce scowl, blazing with the fire of a thousand suns, was aimed my way. "You don't get to know that. You gave up the right to our personal business the second you walked out of our lives."

Ouch. True, but ouch. "I'm sorry. So damn sorry."

"You can't just come back every time you sense something's wrong. Because if that's the case, then you'd be popping up all the time. It's not fair to Gus. It's not fair to me, either."

"I know. If I could take the last week back, I would."

"Oh, really?"

"Yes, really. I have a lot to tell you, if you'll just listen." We stopped by her car.

"How did you know we were here?" she demanded, spearing me with her angry stare.

"It's a long story, but I sort of got a new job. I'm officially self-employed and I'd love to talk about that later. But please, for the love of God, tell me Gus is okay."

"Day," Gus said weakly, reaching for me as his head lolled on Casey's shoulder.

"Yeah, Buddy. I'm here."

Swift, unexpected tears filled my eyes as Casey transferred her squirming son to my arms. I didn't even try to blink them away. They spilled down my cheeks, running into my four-day scruff.

My eyelids fluttered shut as I cradled Gus against me, and another tear broke free.

I'd missed him so much.

Swaying, I rocked us both, and he let out a happy sigh when he grasped my shirt collar. I pressed my nose to his head, breathing in the powdery scent of his hair.

Not a peep from Casey. I almost couldn't believe she was allowing this, but I wasn't about to question it.

This was peace. I'd forgotten what it felt like to be completely content, and I didn't want to let it go.

I don't know how long I held onto Gus, but when I finally opened my eyes, I noticed two things: he was asleep, and Casey was watching us while she sat on the hood of her car.

There was an endless well of pain in her eyes, and I hated myself for being the one to cause it.

"He's been asking for you, you know." Casey hugged her knees as she drove the knife deeper into my chest. "He's cried about wanting you."

"What'd you tell him?" I wasn't sure I wanted to know the answer.

"Nothing. I changed the subject. He's too young to understand why someone would be here one minute and gone the next." She swallowed hard, like the next words were hard for her to say. "And that's why you have to leave. Don't come back, Jay. Next time you have a bad feeling, just… ignore it."

"That's not the only reason I'm here—"

"Yes, he's okay," she cut me off, explaining, "Asthma. This happens almost every time he comes down with a respiratory virus. They gave him a steroid shot and a breathing treatment. On top of that, he has an ear infection. We need to get going." Pursing her lips, she hopped down to the pavement and reached for Gus. "I have to go by the pharmacy to pick up his antibiotics."

My fingertips lingered on Gus's chubby bare feet as he left my arms. "Can I meet you at home?"

Casey cut me a sharp look when I called it home, but I wasn't backing down. Not this time. Not ever.

Casey had every reason to be wary. In fact, I welcomed her anger and her skepticism.

I'd obliterated her trust, and if she needed me to prove myself all over again, I would. I'd beg. I'd do anything she asked me to, if she'd just let me back in.

"We need to talk," I said, standing behind her as she buckled Gus in his seat. "Well, I don't know if you have much to say, but I do. I'd really appreciate it if you'd hear me out."

Blowing out a breath, she nodded, moving to open the driver's side door. "Okay. I'll see you soon."

"Wait." I touched her shoulder before she could duck inside and she turned, apprehensively chewing the inside of her cheek. I held out an empty hand. "This belongs to you."

Her lips twitched, and I couldn't tell if it was the beginning of a smile or a frown.

Waiting for her to respond, I let her stare at my palm and wonder what kind of illusion I had up my sleeve.

"What belongs to me?" she finally gave in, impatiently lifting her eyebrows.

No tricks this time. Only honesty.

Picking up her hand, I pressed it over my heart. "This."

CHAPTER 38

Casey

The coffee maker sputtered, and the wonderful aroma of the fresh brew made it to my nose. As if I needed the caffeine. I really, really didn't. I was jittery as hell.

I guess someone else smelled it, too, because I heard the shuffle of footsteps behind me. Not baby feet. Big feet, belonging to a muscly redhead.

"It was awfully presumptuous of you to fall asleep in my bed," I said without turning around.

Jay grunted. "I didn't mean to fall asleep. And it's *my* bed."

Oh, the gall of this man.

When I got home, I found him face-down on the mattress. Since the bed was occupied, Gus and I took a long nap on the couch this morning. Then we went about our day, having lunch, watching movies, and doing his nebulizer treatments.

All the while, Jay slept like the dead, and I had the whole day to work myself up over him being here.

I got Gus to bed about an hour ago, and all I'd done since then was think. Overthink, actually. Every possible outcome had run through my mind, from Jay saying he wanted to get back together, to him taking his damn bed and never returning.

"Is it?" I glanced over my shoulder at him. "If I remember correctly, you gave it to me."

He opened his mouth to respond, but then his eyes went wide when they saw the clock.

"It's nine? At night?" Peering out at the dark backyard, he was utterly confused as he raked a hand through his wild hair.

It would've been adorable if I wasn't so upset.

"You slept for fourteen hours," I told him. "Have you not been sleeping?"

"Not really." He grimaced.

I softened, because that was when I noticed how bad he looked.

He was still sexy as ever, but his coloring wasn't great. His skin was paler than usual, there were dark circles under his eyes, and I remembered earlier when he held his hand out to me. There were red scabs on his palms, like blisters had formed and broken open.

"What's wrong with your hands?"

He glanced down at his injuries. "Oh. I've been in the gym a lot. That, along with the stadium work… I guess my hands took a beating."

"What else have you been up to?" My tone was casual, but inside I was practically shaking.

Not that I'd made a lot of personal progress, but this conversation had the ability to wreck me all over again. I was terrified of what he might say next.

"Missing you," Jay rasped, moving toward me.

My insides leapt with happiness while my rational side warned me to keep my distance.

I stepped away. If he touched me, I'd melt. Or cry.

Or I'd beg him to stay again, which was cringe worthy. I couldn't believe I'd been so pathetic. I'd literally tried to stop him from leaving, thinking I could keep him here by physical force.

How humiliating.

"Let's go talk on the couch." I poured cups of coffee for us both, dousing it with the caramel creamer Jay liked so much. Handing a mug to him, I gulped at the hot liquid as I went to take a seat.

"So." Setting my cup on a coaster, I leveled Jay with an emotionless stare when he sat down. "Talk."

He put his coffee next to mine, and remorse swam in his eyes when he looked at me.

"I made a mistake." He reached out, then stopped. "A huge fucking mistake."

His hand hovered over mine, like he was unsure if that was going too far. The hairs on my arm stood on end, as if they were trying to reach him.

He settled for grazing my knee instead.

Chills rippled over my body at the contact. I could feel the scrape of his calluses through my leggings, and it took everything I had to not react.

"Which mistake are you referring to? You'll have to be more specific." Keeping my distant demeanor, I stayed still.

"Taking that job. Moving out. Leaving." He shook his head. "Take your pick."

Swallowing thickly, I didn't respond for several seconds.

My voice cracked—giving away my emotional state—when I finally said, "I thought we were partners. A team."

"We were. We are."

"No. You don't leave your teammate. That literally makes it *not a team*."

His lips quirked up at my snarky tone, then his face got serious again. "You have no idea how terrified I was."

I gave him a hard look. "You think I don't know about fear?"

"I don't want to mess him up, Casey." Jay's tone was tortured as he looked down the hall toward Gus's room.

I barked out a humorless laugh, and his head snapped my way at the unexpected sound.

"Welcome to parenthood, Jay. That's what being a parent is. Seriously, it's ninety percent hoping like hell you don't screw up your kid. Despite what you might think, you're no different from anyone else. Your past doesn't make you worse than the rest of us. We're all scared out of our minds. The only difference between us—" I waved a finger back and forth before jabbing it toward him. "—is that you can walk away anytime you want."

"No, I can't," Jay exclaimed passionately. "Don't you get it? I can't. I stayed away from you for a week and I'm falling apart. I feel like I'm dying. Even if I think—I *know*—you'd find someone better someday, I don't want that. I want you to be with *me*."

"What if you change your mind again?" I challenged. "What if something else happens, and you decide I'm not worth sticking it out for?"

Jay's nostrils flared and his lips thinned. "I *never* said you weren't worth it."

"Actions speak louder than words. You got spooked and you bolted."

Suddenly, Jay was off the couch. His knees hit the floor, and then he was in front of me, wrapping his arms around my waist and burying his head in my lap.

Shocked, my hands froze mid-air as he began rambling, "I thought I was doing the right thing for once." His words were muffled against my thighs. "I've always wanted what's best for you, and I know I'm not it. But I'm okay with that now. If you'll take me back, I'll spend the rest of my life striving to be better, and maybe—maybe someday I'll be good enough."

My eyes misted.

Compassion for Jay overflowed. This was all so new to him.

I'd had nine months to mentally prepare for Gus. I'd been doing this parenting gig for a while now, and I still had freak-out moments. Jay jumped headfirst into the father-figure role. It was a lot for someone to take on in such a short amount of time.

"You are good enough." My fingers found their way into his hair. "You always have been."

"I need you. I need my family." He tightened his hold, drawing me closer and nuzzling my stomach. "I'm sorry, Casey. Please, let me come back. There's only one path to happiness for me, and you and your son are it."

"I don't like the thought of us taking a step backward in our relationship," I admitted, continuing to play with his messy strands. "But I'd rather have that than not have you at all. It's okay if you're not ready for us to be this serious. If you don't want to live together—"

Lifting his head, there was a determined look on his face when he said, "I'm here to stay. Go ahead and try to kick me out. I dare you."

It was so stubborn, so demanding, that it strangely reminded me of Gus. Seemed I had two very strong-willed men on my hands.

I was totally okay with that. Nothing could've made me happier.

A laugh broke free. "Get up and kiss me already."

"Thank fuck." He lunged forward, knocking me back on the couch as his body covered mine. With his mouth going to my neck first, Jay inhaled deeply and rubbed his scruff on my skin, like he was trying to mark himself with my scent. "I was ready to do some serious groveling."

"On your knees?" My mind went somewhere else. Somewhere perverted.

"Uh huh." He licked up to my ear before giving the lobe a gentle bite.

"You still can if you want to… just sayin'…" I gasped when his hand suddenly cupped me between my thighs.

"You want me to worship this pussy, baby?"

God, I loved it when he talked dirty.

I made an incoherent sound of confirmation as I spread my legs.

Growling, Jay grinded his erection on my pulsing center. "Missed you so damn much. Can't wait to be inside you."

His lips melded with mine, then his arms scooped under my back as he lifted me off the couch. My legs automatically went around his waist. We continued to kiss down the hallway, but when we got to the bedroom, my excitement was deterred when I saw that a half an hour had passed since I peeked in on Gus.

Before Jay could dump me on the mattress, I wiggled out of his grasp, planting my feet on the floor. "I hate to ruin the mood, but I'll be checking Gus's breathing every thirty minutes tonight."

"Will you teach me what to look for?" Jay asked hesitantly, like he expected the answer to be no. "I happen to be very well rested. I can help."

Nodding, I took his hand, leading him to the crib. Very quietly, I explained the signs of an asthma attack and had Jay listen to Gus's chest. My heart warmed when he said he wanted to know how to work the nebulizer. I promised to teach him when Gus woke up, which would probably be soon, since he didn't sleep well when he was sick.

Until then, we had some making up to do.

And apparently, Jay's idea of making up was licking my clit until I came.

I was still trying to catch my breath when he crawled up my body.

"I have something else that belongs to you." He reached

into his shirt—because he was still fully clothed—and pulled out my necklace before undoing the clasp.

When he moved to put it on me, he smiled when he saw the new necklace I'd been wearing.

His eyes went to mine. "You have my ring on."

Embarrassed, I glanced away. "Yeah."

"You really do love me," he teased playfully.

"Yes, I do," I said, serious.

"I love you, too." Gripping my chin, he forced my gaze back to his. "My ring looks good on you, baby."

Untying the nylon, he slipped the ring off and added it to the chain with the prism. Then he clasped it around my neck. I liked the way it felt with the extra weight.

"Thanks for letting me borrow your prism," Jay said, "but I don't need it as long as I have you."

He gave me a gentle kiss. I could taste myself on his lips, and there was something so erotic about it.

I glanced at the clock. "We have twelve minutes. Think you can get me off again?"

"With my cock," he confirmed, shedding his shirt and un-buckling his pants.

"Hurry," I demanded impatiently.

I'd never seen anyone get undressed so fast, and I giggled when he paused his mission to give my knee a love bite.

When he finally filled me, all humor fled as he kissed my nose. "I'm sorry I'm so selfish when it comes to you. I just need you too much."

"I don't think needing me means you're selfish. It means you choose love."

"I'll always choose you, Casey. On accident. On purpose. Everyday."

CHAPTER 39

Jay

"**T**his is the last one, bud. Then you're home free."
I strapped the little turtle mask on Gus's face and
pushed the button to turn on the nebulizer.

The loud hum started up, and the wispy fog floated
around his face as he breathed in and out. He settled comfortably on my lap to watch *Frozen*, totally used to the routine.

We'd been doing this for two weeks, and I was normally
the one to administer his medicine now.

For some reason, he gave Casey hell over his breathing
treatments. He cried, kicked, and tried to take the mask off.
She couldn't believe he just sat here for me, but she was glad at
least one of us could get him to cooperate.

I loved the special bond he and I shared.

When the albuterol ran out, I shut off the machine, carefully removed the mask, and kissed Gus's soft blond hair.

"Everybody loves a Gus," I sang deeply, way offkey. "He's
a crazy, silly Gus. Everybody loves a Gus. He's a crazy, silly
Gus."

Yeah, I couldn't carry a tune to save my life. Gus didn't
seem to mind, though.

I heard a snicker from somewhere behind me, and I
glanced over my shoulder to find Casey leaning against the
wall in the hallway.

"What do you think?" I asked cockily. "Should I try out for a talent show?"

Rolling her lips inward, she tried not to smile. "Don't quit your day job."

I huffed out a laugh. "Ouch."

Now that Gus was free from the confines of the nebulizer, he scrambled to the floor and went to dump out his basket of toys. Seventh time he'd done that this afternoon. Man, kids were messy.

"Speaking of day jobs." Casey sauntered over, and my eyes followed the tantalizing sway of her hips. She sat on my lap, looping her arms around my neck. "I just got a call from Conway Café. I got the job."

"That's great." I rubbed her thigh, noting her smile didn't quite reach her eyes. "Why don't you seem excited about it?"

"They said I have to work a couple Saturdays a month. There's a rotating schedule with the servers to keep it fair. Doreen has been going away most weekends to visit Shelby."

It was cute that she was fishing for a babysitting offer. Didn't she know it wasn't necessary to ask?

I hoped someday she wouldn't consider it babysitting when I watched Gus. It'd just be something called parenting.

Good thing my new job had flexible hours. I'd already solved the case Ethan gave me. The boy from Springfield had a cousin living outside Chicago. A family man, financially stable with no criminal record. I didn't reunite the two—that part was up to them. My job was done as soon as I found the relative my client was searching for.

Since then, I'd snagged two more cases, and Ethan had gone MIA. In the first week, I'd called him way too many times to ask questions, all of which he patiently answered. Then all of the sudden, his phone was disconnected.

Guess I was on my own now.

"Baby, you don't have to beat around the bush," I told Casey. "Here, I'll save you the trouble of asking me if I'll watch Gus." I cleared my throat. "Casey, I need a boys' night out every once in a while. Gus is the perfect partner in crime, so I'll require the occasional evening to go stir up some trouble."

"Oh, yeah?" An adorable wrinkle appeared on her nose when she narrowed her eyes. "What kind of trouble are we talking about?"

"The kind where we go to the self-serve frozen yogurt place and fill a cup with a dollop of every single flavor." I gave her a wicked grin.

Casey made an amused sound. "You rebel. You're so hot when you live on the edge."

"Ogurt?" Gus perked up at the word and came over to persistently pat my knee. "Ogurt."

The Yogurt Shop was just a five-block walk away. We'd taken a stroll there two evenings in the past week. Apparently, we were going for a third.

I looked at Casey. "What do you say? I'll even wear the baby carrier."

She grinned.

"I'm not saying no to that." Pulling Gus onto my lap with her, she tickled his tummy. "Who does Momma love?"

"Day." He wiggled and laughed.

"Yes, I do love Jay. Who else?"

"Ammaw."

Casey's smile fell a little. "Yeah. I love Grandma, too. Who else?"

"Gus."

"That's right, bubba goo. Let's get your shoes on."

As he slid down, I gripped Casey's hips, anchoring her to me for a few seconds longer.

"Come 'ere." Cupping her face, I brought her lips to mine. "I know it's hard for you when he says that. You okay?"

"The reminder is sad," she admitted. "But I'm not looking forward to the day when he stops naming her. When he forgets her. You know?"

I loved it that she was more open with me now. Since my return, she'd been a lot better about letting her feelings out.

A few days ago, she took the leap to go to counseling at the church. She'd come home puffy-eyed, but happier. Lighter. That night she told me she wanted to go back, make it a regular thing.

I was so proud of her.

My girl knew how to take life by the balls.

I rubbed my thumb over her cheek. "I know she can't be replaced, but my mom loves him to pieces already. She'd be thrilled to be a stand-in grandma."

"I really like her." Casey's dimples came out to play as she smiled.

Last Sunday, we spent the whole day at my mom's apartment. While hunting for 'treasures' in Nora's room, Gus found her makeup. Correction: he bathed himself in her makeup. Which resulted in some hilarious pictures. Mom made pot roast, and every time she saw me with my new girlfriend, she was practically bursting with joy. And when she watched me with Gus, there were happy tears in her eyes.

"She likes you, too," I told Casey. "She's got this idea in her head that you're good for me."

"That's because I am," she replied confidently.

While she grabbed her purse, Gus dragged the carrier over, an impatient frown on his face. I hooked it up before setting him inside.

Then we were out the door.

The September air was a perfect seventy-two degrees, and

the trees were turning bright colors. Resting her head against my shoulder, Casey let out a content sigh.

"I love you, Jay."

"Love Day," Gus's little voice piped up.

My jaw dropped and warmth spread through my chest.

Not only was that the first time he'd said he loved me, it was also the first time he put two words together.

Excited, Casey looked from Gus to me. "That's his first sentence!"

I smiled wide. I got to witness a first. And it was for me. Gus loved me.

"I love you, too, buddy." I cleared my throat, trying to dislodge the lump in my esophagus. "I love you both."

Kicking, Gus grunted because the carrier was sagging, and he was too far away from my collar for his liking.

I reached up to tighten the strap, and when I did, my tattoo peeked out from under my sleeve.

I thought back to that night so many years ago when I made that wish.

When I was lost and broken and living life all wrong.

I couldn't bring myself to regret any of it. Not anymore. Slowly, I was forgiving myself for my past. Because if it wasn't for that, I wouldn't be with the family I have now.

Hand in hand, we walked down the street I grew up on. We were making memories, building a life together.

Loving each other.

And that was real magic.

EPILOGUE

Jay
Two Years Later

"**D**ad?"

"Yeah, buddy?"

I heard the pitter-patter of feet behind me in the kitchen. Gus's hand slipped into mine, and he started tugging me toward the back door.

"Can we go outside and play with my rock bee-clection?"

For the record, "bee-clection" translated to collection. Gus had a whole slew of words he added "bee" onto the front of, just because he could.

Bee-scape equaled escape.

Bee-tacked—attacked.

Bee-stroyed—destroyed.

Bee-sgusting—disgusting.

It made his imaginative story telling ten times more entertaining. He also really liked the word 'because.'

Because he could.

"Sure," I replied. "Just let me grab my coffee."

I didn't usually drink coffee this late in the day, but I was dragging ass.

Gus still woke up on occasion, and since Casey had to work today, last night's midnight party was all mine. No idea how this kid could have so much energy on so little sleep, but he'd been unstoppable all day.

Following Gus out to the patio, I dropped onto one of the plastic chairs while he went to the flowerpot that held all his rocks.

He still had his rings—his interests had just expanded to other shiny objects. Rock hunting had become one of his favorite hobbies. There was something special about finding a glittery object down by a riverbed or at a park.

Casey and I had gotten him a rock polishing kit for his third birthday, and ever since then he'd been obsessed.

In a lot of ways, he reminded me of myself. Once he got focused on something, he was a hundred percent all in.

And as he'd gotten older, his hair had darkened just a bit. Sometimes in certain lights, it appeared reddish, and people said he looked just like me.

I never corrected them to say he wasn't biologically mine. He was as much my son as anyone ever could be. If, by chance, we happened to resemble each other, then hey, I'd just take that as one hell of a compliment. After all, he was a handsome dude.

It didn't take long for Gus to make the transition from Day to Dad. In fact, it happened right after I proposed to Casey. Two months after my return, I got down on one knee by the meadow. My hands shook while I opened the jewelry box, revealing the teardrop-shaped opal surrounded by tiny diamonds.

Of course Casey said yes, and we were married the following spring. Also next to the meadow.

We had so many memories here.

The past two years had been the best of my life. It'd been pretty great for Casey, too. A year ago, she started cosmetology school, and now she worked at a salon in Daywood. She loved her new job.

And I loved mine. Being a private investigator was the

best. There couldn't have been a more perfect profession for me. I didn't love having to travel away from home for certain cases, but Ethan had been right—it was noble work. Fulfilling.

Grinning, I watched Gus line up his rocks on the concrete according to size.

He was wearing a purple princess dress we'd found at a garage sale last week. Totally worth the one dollar to see the smile on his face when I bought it for him. Underneath it, he had on a baseball T-shirt that said 'Daddy's Little Slugger.' He had a closet full of those kinds of clothes now, because I loved claiming him as mine.

"How's your poop water?" Gus asked nonchalantly.

"My what?"

"Poop water." He eyed my mug.

"You mean coffee?"

He gave me a pointed look, lifting his eyebrows. "Poop. Water."

I laughed. "It's pretty great."

Just then, he plopped down onto his butt, but the momentum made him fall backward.

His dress flew up and his legs kicked. "Ahh, don't look at my pickles!"

Pickles was a mashup of penis and testicles. The stuff this kid said. Never a dull moment with Gus.

I laughed so hard I almost spit out my coffee. "What happened to your underwear?"

"I took it off."

"Why?"

"My pickles doesn't like them." While he was lying on his back, he took the opportunity to study the clouds in the blue sky. "Dad, that one looks like a castle. Can I wish for a castle?"

"You can wish for whatever you want."

Sitting up, he looked at me. "You make a wish, too."

I scratched at my jaw as I thought about it, and I smiled when I realized something. "I already have everything I want."

"Know what I want now?"

"What?"

"A popsicle."

"Well, I can make that happen." I slipped inside the house for a second, depositing my cup in the sink before going over to the freezer.

I pulled out two red popsicles—the kind inside the long plastic sleeve—and cut off the tops. Leaving the sliding door open, I let the September breeze flow into the house while handing Gus his treat. "Wish granted, good sir."

"Thanks, Dad." He gave me a cheesy smile.

My mouth wasn't the biggest fan of going from a hot beverage to ice, but as I returned to my seat, I sucked on mine anyway.

Gus took a huge bite and immediately regretted it.

"Ahhh." He threw his head back, refusing to spit any of it out as he chewed. "It's so cold."

"You're gonna get a brain freeze," I warned, chuckling as he spun around in circles.

The satiny dress billowed out around him.

Suddenly he stopped and dizzily walked over to me before climbing onto my lap. "Can I sit with you and you can feed it to me? Because—because my hands are too cold." He dropped the popsicle, trusting me to catch it.

Now I had one in each hand, and my fingertips were going numb. Gus tugged on my collar and rubbed it against his cheek. I fed him another bite, and he repeated the ridiculous misery from before.

"Guuuh. This is the evil popsicle because—" Crunch, crunch. "—because—" Crunch. "—because, see?" Opening his mouth, he pointed at his cherry-coated tongue. "Because."

Figuring I should join him in the pain, I took a large piece into my mouth.

"You're right." My face screwed up. "It's really cold."

"Here, I'll help. I'll breathe my breath into your mouth." Grasping my cheeks with both hands, he puffed air at me. "Is that warm?"

I laughed. "Not really."

He laughed, too, like he was the funniest person alive. And to me, he was.

"What's all this giggling about out here?"

The sweet voice made a bolt of pleasure zing up my spine.

I looked over to see Casey leaning through the open doorway, wearing the white salon T-shirt and skinny jeans. Her hair was shorter than it used to be, falling a few inches below her shoulders. Deep dimples framed her mouth as a grin stretched over her gorgeous face.

"We're just being silly guys," Gus replied, still cracking up.

"What would my silly guys like for dinner?"

"Bee-sghetti!"

Casey gave us a nod. "I can manage spaghetti."

Yeah, my wife still wasn't the best cook, but damn if she didn't try. Too many times I'd found her in the kitchen, surrounded by a dozen dirty bowls and a messy counter as she fretted over a flat cake or a burnt casserole.

I slid Gus off my lap. "Let's go help your mom."

"'Kay." He propped his half-eaten popsicle against the concrete step, then he disappeared inside.

I did the same with mine, since I figured we'd probably end up eating dinner out here anyway. But before I went through the door, I turned back.

My eyes went to the meadow, and I breathed in the autumn air.

Life couldn't get more perfect.

～

Casey

Nerves made my hands clammy. I anxiously twisted the sheets as I waited for Jay to join me in bed. Tonight was different than any other night we'd ever been together.

Because tonight I was going to ask Jay for something.

Something I hadn't been sure I'd ever want again.

Something, it turns out, I *did* want—badly.

I heard the faucet shut off in the bathroom. The hallway lit up as Jay opened the door, then everything went dark when he flipped the switch.

Moonlight glinted off his abs as he approached. Tugging the blankets back, he let out a sexy growl when he saw I wasn't wearing any clothes.

Prowling up my body, he grazed my ankle, kissed the inside of my calf, and bit my knee.

"Baby," he whispered.

His breath was minty, and when his lips fused with mine, I almost forgot what I wanted to talk to him about.

I felt his hard cock nudge my lower belly.

Oh, damn.

He'd already taken off his boxer briefs. He wasn't playing around.

Pushing my thighs apart, he settled between them. His hand went to my slit, and he hissed when he found how wet I was.

"Fuck yes." His lips closed around one of my nipples and he sucked hard.

My legs automatically spread wider, and his tip prodded my entrance.

"Wait," I panted. "I need to talk to you."

He let out an impatient sound. "Can it wait until after? I need to get into this pussy."

Gasping, I tipped my head back and my core started throbbing. He knew just what to say to get his way.

But this topic couldn't wait.

"I stopped taking my birth control yesterday." The words burst from me in a rushed whisper. "I want a baby."

Jay froze, the head of his cock partly submerged in my entrance. "You do?"

I nodded, my cheek rubbing against his. Rolling halfway off me, he put distance between us so he could see my face.

"A few weeks ago, when I went shopping for Mackenna's baby shower," I began, unsure of how to explain the longing ache I felt.

She and Jimmy were expecting again. A girl this time. I couldn't have been happier for them, but seeing her round stomach, feeling the baby kick against my hand… I wanted that for myself.

"The baby shower…" Jay pressed, wanting me to continue.

I sighed. "I stood in the baby clothes section at Target for like twenty minutes, just looking at all the little outfits." Tears sprung to my eyes when I remembered standing among the ecstatic expectant mothers. "I kept seeing all these pregnant women, and they were so excited. I didn't get to feel that. Not in the same way. Yes, I was happy about having Gus, but I was also terrified. I was too young. Too alone."

When I thought back to when Gus was just born, the difficult times hadn't faded away. I could still recall the crying and the lack of sleep.

But the quiet moments were in the forefront of my mind. The way it felt to have his tiny soft body sleeping on my chest. The newborn smell. The little sounds he made when he was happy. His first smile.

Jay stayed silent, so I continued, "All those people who told me I'd miss the days when Gus was an infant… well, they were right. I do. I miss it so much. I didn't get to enjoy him like I wish I could've. I was so overwhelmed, but it would be different now. We'd be raising a baby together, and it's not like I don't know what I'm doing. I've done it before. And Gus is almost three and a half. By the time we have a baby, he'll be at least four, and I'd like them to be somewhat close in age. Your mom helps a lot. We're financially stable—"

"Are you trying to convince me?" Jay cut in. His face was too covered in shadows for me to read his expression.

"Yeah. I guess I am."

His white teeth flashed with a grin. "You don't have to talk me into it, baby. I've wanted this for a long time."

"You have? But you never said anything."

"That's because I didn't know if you wanted more kids yet. You're still young, Casey." He paused, caressing one of my dimples. "The truth is, I already have everything I want, but the thought of you having my child, seeing you pregnant, getting to experience that *with* you—it's more than I could ever hope for." He chuckled. "I was just thinking today, nothing could make me happier than I am now. But this. This would make me happier."

"We'll have to get a bigger place," I mused, but before Jay could get too disappointed about moving, I added, "But I was talking with the Chapmans, and guess what? They're putting their house on the market."

The Chapmans lived only two doors down. It was a two-story house, with four bedrooms and a two-car garage. The kind of house I never dreamed I'd be able to have. But with our combined incomes and how much we'd put away in savings, it was totally doable.

Even better, we'd be on the same street and Jay could still have his meadow.

Wrapping his arms around me, he buried his face by my neck. "What'd I do to deserve you?"

"Everything," I whispered. "You saved me. You protected me. You chose me."

"I always will."

Jay's lips found mine in the dark, and love flowed into me until I felt like my heart might explode.

We were going to add to our family. A vision of a little girl with red pigtails and blue eyes popped into my mind. Gus would be such a good big brother.

Positioning his cock at my entrance, Jay surged forward, and I lost the ability to think about anything but how good it felt. I whimpered as the ridge of his head stroked my insides.

Once Jay was fully seated, I placed my hand on his jaw.

"Show me a trick, magic man." The way I waggled my eyebrows indicated I didn't mean with a deck of cards.

He smirked. "Oh, I'll show you several."

And then he made good on his promise.

THE END

Want more Good Guys? I've got a whole series about them. In fact, you can find the first three standalones in The Good Guys Box Set. Keep reading for an excerpt from Jimmy and Mackenna's story, DROPOUT!

DROPOUT EXCERPT

Jimmy

After Grandma left for her date, I had the house to myself. I threw all my soiled clothes into the washer, then gave Sweet Pea one last glare as he climbed on top of his cage, happily rattling a toy as if he had nothing to be ashamed of. In fact, he seemed pretty damn proud of himself.

"Crazy-ass bird," I muttered, then went to the kitchen to search for food in nothing but my underwear.

I opened the freezer and grinned.

"Hell yeah," I whispered as I took out the pre-made hamburger patties.

One look in the fridge and pantry told me that Grandma had stocked up on all my favorite foods. The woman was a saint. A foul-mouthed saint.

Dropping three burgers into the pan, I switched on the ancient radio on the counter and turned the volume all the way up.

As the burgers sizzled, I got out the buns and set them on a plate. Next, I doused them in mustard and ketchup, then went to flip the burgers over. Something popped in the pan, spraying my chest with hot grease.

"Ow, fuck!" I hissed, stepping back from the stove. I wiped at my reddened skin with a damp dish towel, once again cursing the bird that was responsible for my lack of clothing. If I'd had a shirt on, this wouldn't have happened.

I spotted Grandma's apron hanging on a hook by the kitchen doorway. I looked down at my unprotected torso, then back at the frilly fabric.

So, that's what those things are for.

After mulling it over, I knew the best option was for me to wear it. Anything was better than having first-degree burns on my nipples. After tying it on I went back to my lunch, singing along to the radio.

Once the meat was thoroughly cooked, I turned off the heat and slid the pan off the back burner. I was about to pick up the spatula when I heard a squeak behind me.

Thinking it was that damn bird again, I started to turn around, ready to tell him not to take a dump on my food.

Imagine my surprise when I ended up face to face with a girl. A gorgeous-as-fuck girl.

For about three awesome seconds we made eye contact, and my gaze dropped to her full pink lips. Her black tank top hugged her body, and the color almost matched her long dark hair. Her skin was pale—creamy. This time of year, a lot of people spent time outside in the sun. Her fair complexion told me that she either didn't have the ability to tan, or she didn't spend a lot of time outside. Either way the look suited her, the contrast stunning.

I noticed her eyes were focused on my chest, specifically the nipple that was peeking out from behind the apron—the girly apron that was barely covering my body.

Then she started rambling on about my underwear.

I didn't have time to process what was happening because a flash of bright color flew through the room. Startled, I stumbled back, knocking my plate off the counter.

Sweet Pea flew overhead and dropped a watery bird turd on my shoulder with an audible splat.

He let out a squawk as he hit the kitchen window, then

knocked over an old coffee tin full of pennies my grandma always kept next to the sink. Coins scattered everywhere.

I took a step forward, attempting to catch the frantic bird, but he flew out of my reach, leaving just as fast as he came.

My foot slipped on one of the buns and I reached out to grab on to something to keep me from falling on my ass.

Unfortunately, the object closest to me was the flour container. I managed to stay upright, but the flour wasn't so lucky. An explosion of white powder filled the room as it hit the floor, covering the orange and white checkered linoleum along with the pennies.

I heard a feminine gasp and awareness hit me like a freight train.

I was practically naked. I was wearing an apron. I almost fell over while being practically naked in that apron. I had parrot shit running down my arm.

And a beautiful stranger was staring at me, with her perfect mouth hanging open in shock.

This wasn't my finest moment.

I switched off the music and the silence that followed was deafening.

"Who are you?" I barked, the question coming out harsher than I intended as I grabbed some paper towels and wiped at the mess on my skin.

"Mackenna. Beverly's neighbor," she replied, her eyes narrowing. "Who are you?"

"Jimmy." When I got a blank stare, I felt the need to elaborate. "Beverly's grandson."

"Oh." She blushed, looking away. "I thought her grandkids were younger."

"Nope. All grown up," I said, spreading my arms, causing her to glance back at me. I was reminded again of how exposed I was when she averted her eyes to the ceiling and bit her lip. She was obviously uncomfortable, and I couldn't help having a little fun with the situation—anything to distract myself from the embarrassment I was feeling. "And you must be the kid who moved in next door."

"Excuse me?" she asked, her eyes cutting back to me.

"The one who knits Grandma's blankets. I take it that's you?"

"Yes, except I'm not a child, obviously." Now it was her turn to spread her arms, and her breasts strained against the material of the tight shirt.

I bit back a groan as my eyes trailed over the rest of her body. "Obviously."

There was nothing childish about her. She was above average height for a girl, probably about 5'7". Toned thighs led to soft hips. Those curves gave way to the dips in her narrow waist. And those tits. My guess was a solid c-cup. Fucking perfect.

Somewhere in the recesses of my mind, my inner gentleman was screaming at me to stop leering and estimating her bra size.

But I couldn't look away.

Her nipples were hard, which probably meant she was either cold or turned on. And it wasn't chilly in here. Grandma set her thermostat at a balmy 75 degrees, often keeping the windows cracked even though she had the air conditioning on.

Knowing this girl could be feeling the same instant attraction I was made my dick twitch. Suddenly I was very grateful for the apron, because it was hiding the stiffy I was sporting.

ACKNOWLEDGEMENTS

To the hubs and kids—You guys are the best. Thanks for being my biggest cheerleaders.

To my personal assistants—Somehow I ended up with three of you! Haha. But each of you are a huge help to me. Amber, Nikki, and Jen, I couldn't ask for a better team.

To my betas—Melissa, Amy, Renee, Jessica, Amber, Miranda—thanks for being the first to read MAGIC MAN. Your insight and suggestions made this book better.

To the others who help get my books ready for readers' eyes—Tanya, your graphic design talent is special and I'm so glad we make a great team. Julie, you're the best proofreader. You find all my mistakes. And, Stacey, you make the inside so pretty.

And to my readers, THANK YOU for loving my books. All of you mean so much to me.

OTHER BOOKS

GOOD GUYS SERIES:

Trucker

A Trucker Christmas (Short Story)

Dancer

Dropout

Outcast

Magic Man

The Good Guys Box Set

THE NIGHT TIME TELEVISION SERIES:

Untamable

Untrainable

Unattainable

STANDALONE NOVELLAS:

His Mimosa

ABOUT THE AUTHOR

Jamie Schlosser writes steamy new adult romance and romantic comedy. When she isn't creating perfect book boyfriends, she's a stay-at-home mom to her two wonderful kids. She believes reading is a great escape, otters are the best animal, and nothing is more satisfying than a happily-ever-after ending. You can find out more about Jamie and her books by visiting these links:

Facebook: www.facebook.com/authorjamieschlosser

Amazon: amzn.to/2mzCQkQ

Twitter: twitter.com/SchlosserJamie

Bookbub: www.bookbub.com/authors/jamie-schlosser

Newsletter: eepurl.com/cANmI9

Also, do you like being the first to get sneak peeks on upcoming books? Do you like exclusive giveaways? Most importantly, do you like otters?

If you answered yes to any of these questions, you should consider joining Jamie Schlosser's Significant Otters! www.facebook.com/groups/1738944743038479

Made in the USA
Coppell, TX
22 February 2020